Extra Special

Stella Etc.

Karen McCombie's Scrumptious Books

Sadie ROCKS!

Happiness, and All That Stuff
Deep Joy, or Something Like It
It's All Good (In Your Dreams)
Smile! It's Meant to be Fun

ALLY'S WORLD

Collect all 16 fabulous titles!

Stella Etc.

7 sunshiney, seasidey, unmissable books

And her novels

Marshmallow Magic and the Wild Rose Rouge
An Urgent Message of Wowness
The Seventeen Secrets of the Karma Club
The Raspberry Rules

Karen McCombie

Extra Special
Stella Etc.

SCHOLASTIC

Scholastic Children's Books
An imprint of Scholastic Ltd
Euston House, 24 Eversholt Street
London, NW1 1DB, UK
Registered office: Westfield Road, Southam, Warwickshire, CV47 0RA
SCHOLASTIC and associated logos are trademarks and/or registered
trademarks of Scholastic Inc.

First published in two volumes as *Frankie, Peaches and Me* and
Sweet-Talking TJ by Scholastic Children's Books, 2005
This edition published in the UK by Scholastic Children's Books, 2010

ISBN 978 1407 11614 3

Printed in the UK by CPI Bookmarque, Croydon, Surrey.
Papers used by Scholastic Children's Books are made from wood grown in
sustainable forests.

1 3 5 7 9 10 8 6 4 2

www.scholastic.co.uk/zone

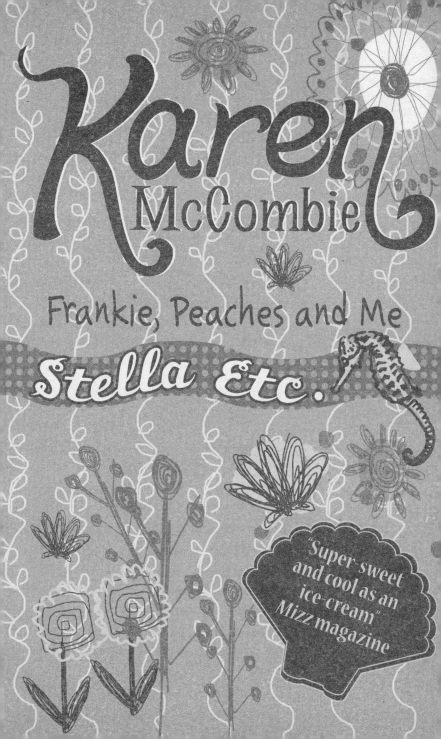

Karen McCombie

Frankie, Peaches and Me

Stella Etc.

Contents

From:	*stella*
To:	Frankie
Subject:	Helloooooooooo!
Attachments:	"Frankie, Peaches & Me"

Hi Frankie!

Sorry I missed your call – we were all out for a walk down at the beach (got a ton of sand in my ears from play-fighting with Jake and Jamie – still can't hear properly).

So on the message you left you said you had a dream about me last night: you dreamt I'd never moved away from London? Well, I guess there are mornings when I wake up and listen to the sound of the sea and the gulls and think, "Er, where am I again?"

But you coming to visit right after we moved here, that was great. OK, so it wasn't great *all* the time, specially not when we were arguing. But when you're marooned 50 metres in the air for half an hour, I guess you've got to pass the time somehow! I know we talked a lot and made up and everything, but anyway, I thought I'd scribble stuff down (see attachment); just stuff about what exactly happened that first week –

you know, the move here, and about Peaches, and Sugar Bay and you and . . . and the rest.

Oops, got to go – I might have half a beach in my ear but I can *definitely* hear somebody somewhere screaming (wish Jamie would grow out of this annoying biting thing). E-mail me back soon, and in the meantime, give your mum a big cuddle from me, send hugs to Neisha and Lauren and everyone, and . . . well, maybe you could say "hi" to Seb next time you see him (if that's not too weird, I mean). . .
Miss you ☹, but m8s 4eva ☺!

stella

PS Peaches says no hard feelings. (He *actually* said "Prrrp!", but I'm pretty sure that's what he meant!)

Chapter 1

Just your non-normal, un-average Saturday morning. . .

"Tinkle, tinkle, lickle star. . .!" Jake crooned in my ear, wafting a toy dumper truck in time to his song, and occasionally thunking it against the side of my head.

My little brother (one of a matching set) was completely oblivious to what was going on, but *I* wasn't. It was Saturday, it was 11.05 a.m., and it was the start of my brand new life. Worse luck.

Meanwhile, in a galaxy far, far away (OK, North London), my friends were probably doing the usual Saturday morning stuff.

Eleni would still be in bed, having a lie-in. (Though how she can sleep while her brother parps his weekend trumpet practice, I just don't know.)

Neisha would be in bed as well, but wide awake, watching telly and getting herself and her duvet covered in toast crumbs.

Lauren would be watching telly too, only in her living room, with her sister, fighting over the remote control (in a battle of boy bands v cartoons).

Parminder would be at the supermarket, helping her mum do the shopping, daydreaming about cute stuff in TopShop while cruising the frozen food aisle.

Frankie . . . well, round about this time in the morning, Frankie would be thinking about texting everyone to see who was up for a trek to the West End or a mooch around Camden Market in the afternoon. Of course, her Saturday morning would be a bit different just this once, 'cause she'd be clearing up from the party last night. My leaving party – and already it felt like for ever ago. . .

"So, Stella . . . what do you think?" Dad grinned at me hopefully, like a little kid who's showing you his model of the Tower of London made out of toilet-roll tubes.

I knew Dad wanted me to say something about the house (um, preferably something *nice* about the house), but all I could think of was what a deeply *non*-normal, *un*-average Saturday morning I was having. I mean, I'd got up at six in a practically empty-of-furniture house, watched some removal men cart away our beds to a waiting lorry, waved goodbye to the place I'd lived in and loved for the 13 years and two months I'd been on the planet, and sat for four hours in our car getting a numb bum and listening to a CD called *Really Annoying Nursery Rhymes That Will Drive You Insane* on a loop.

And now I was here, walking across the crunchy gravel of the driveway with a wriggly toddler in my arms, trying not to cry (I really don't think that was the reaction Dad – or Mum – would have wanted).

"Andy!" Mum shouted, as she lifted another wriggly toddler out of the car. "The removal lorry is here – but I think it's got stuck trying to get round the bend in the lane. Can you go and give the guys a hand?"

I don't know what Dad was meant to do – get a giant hacksaw and cut bits off the side of the lorry so it could get around the corner without scraping the ice-cream-coloured shades of paint off the terrace of tiny cottages next door to us, maybe? Or waft a magic potion at the lorry and make it shrink like something out of *Alice in Wonderland*?

Speaking of fairy tales, I felt like I'd found

myself stuck in the middle of one now, and I *don't* mean that in a good way. Apart from spying a sprawling council estate on the way into the town, the main part of Portbay – the place I was now supposed to think of as "home" – seemed like a higgledy-piggledy, claustrophobic jumble of tiny lanes and centuries-old cottages that tumbled downhill towards the sea. And here was *our* centuries-old cottage, like the house in *Hansel and Gretel*, minus the sweets, but looking suspiciously like a witch might be peeking out of one of the upstairs gabled windows at us.

"It's just perfect, isn't it?" Mum sighed, as she let Jamie slither his wriggling way out of her arms and on to the ground.

Perfect? Perfect for a *Houses from Hell* documentary on the telly. Or the set of a murder mystery, maybe.

"Mmm," I mumbled in reply, wondering if Mum had gone completely mad. The whole building was tatty and crumbly, and I kind of suspected it was only standing upright thanks to the creeping dark-green ivy that was clinging and clawing its way all over it.

"Maybe it's just as well you couldn't come that weekend when we first viewed the place – it's more of a surprise for you now!" Mum smiled, reaching over and taking Jake out of my arms before he blinded me with the scoop of his dumper truck.

"Mmm," I mumbled again, glad that it was so sunny. It meant that I could shield my eyes as I pretended to survey the house, and hide the fact that tears were threatening again.

As far as your average parents went, Mum and Dad were great – they were groovier and trendier than any of my mates' mums and dads. They were interested in fashion and music and stuff, which my mates' parents definitely weren't. They were easy to talk to – when they weren't too busy with work or the boys, which was a *lot* of the time. But no matter how cool Mum and Dad were, when it came down to it, they were adults, and I was 13; there were two of them and just one of me, and so when they decided to move from London to Portbay, I really, *really* didn't have a choice. Course I told them I didn't want to go, and cried in front of them at the hideous idea of leaving Kentish Town and Frankie and all my other friends, but it didn't do any good. They just smiled, and hugged me and told me they understood – which translated as, "Sorry, but it's still going to happen, Stella!" After that, I just went quiet on the whole subject of the move, ignoring it as much as possible, pretending I had projects to finish and tests to study for and hiding out at Frankie's whenever Mum and Dad came down to Portbay to house-hunt.

"Are you going to call Frankie and let her know you got here OK?" Mum asked, noticing that I was fishing in the pocket of my denim skirt for my mobile.

"Mmm," I mumbled, forcing a lookalike smile on my face and turning away.

Frankie always teased me that my silver flip-topped phone looked like one of the phasers out of *Star Trek*. I wished it was – then instead of just talking to her, I could ask her to beam me back to London at the speed of light. Or quicker, if possible.

But my heart sank as Frankie's please-leave-a-message kicked in. And it sank even more with full-on, heart-squeezing, gut-wrenching home-sickness when I listened to it.

"Hi guys! I'm having way too much fun to answer the phone right now, so say what you've gotta say and I'll get back to you! Byeeeee!"

I wished I was back in London having fun with Frankie, instead of being marooned in this freaky little town. I wished I was at her flat now, helping her hoover up crisp crumbs instead of watching Mum rushing to stop Jamie from eating the gravel in our new driveway.

But at least I had one thing, I suddenly remembered, patting the cord bag on my shoulder, where I'd stashed the photo from last night.

The photo of that amazing moment when –

KEEERRRRRRR-UNCH!

"Omigod!" Mum gasped, glancing around in the direction of the lane with dread.

Well, *that* was a good impression to make on our new neighbours – gouging a chunk out of their wall with our furniture lorry before we'd even moved in. Hey, I might *not* be the only person wishing my family had stayed in London. . .

Chapter 2

Oh, we don't like to be beside the seaside. . .

I was holding Jamie upside-down by the ankles –
so that the make-up he'd nicked from my bag
would fall out of his pockets – when I heard Mum
say something on the phone downstairs.

Well, it was more a case of her saying nothing.
And that told me *plenty*.

"Me next! Me next!" Jake suddenly demanded
over the top of Jamie's giggles.

"Shh!" I tried to hush my brothers, ignoring the
fact that Jake had what looked suspiciously like
a pair of my knickers fastened to his head with a
used section of parcel tape (he must have ripped it
off one of the cardboard boxes). Honestly, trying
to unpack with these two around was as easy as
nailing jelly to a tree. And when it came to getting
them to shut up, I had *no* chance.

"Well, the neighbours probably secretly hate us,
but they acted very sweet when we offered to pay
for the damage. Oh, our place? Well, it's messy

and nothing works, and we're in total chaos, but it's fine."

(*That* was the chunk of Mum's conversation I'd tuned into when I first spotted Jamie shoving my mascara and strawberry lipgloss into his dungaree pockets.)

"Hey, you know what Andy's like, Vanessa – he can't *wait* to get started on the place. He's already eyeing up the sledgehammer, and the removal lorry's still in the driveway!"

(Auntie Vanessa hadn't wasted much time – we'd only left London six hours ago and here she was on the phone, pummelling Mum for an update on the Big Move.)

"The boys?"

(Auntie V must have been asking about Jake and Jamie.)

"They're having a great time – they've been thundering up and down the stairs, and getting in everyone's way!"

(And mostly wrecking what little of my room I'd managed to get halfway organized – which Mum and Dad thought was fine, since it distracted Jamie from biting the removal men and Jake from escaping our clutches and shouting "Boo!" at all the cars coming along the narrow lane next to the house.)

"Stella? Oh, you know what she's like – not saying much. . ."

And that's when I *really* started to pay attention – that moment when Mum tapered off and Auntie V must have been talking in her ear instead. I started listening to the silence so hard that I almost forgot that I was holding a wriggling, giggling small boy by the legs (two year olds are surprisingly heavy, by the way).

"Ah, Stella, my little star. . ." I bet Auntie V would've been saying. Or make that *sighing*. That's my Aunt Vanessa's catchphrase when it comes to me, just like she calls out, "Oh, no! Here come the Muppets!" whenever Jamie and Jake come charging anywhere near her. But the difference is, when she's calling Jake "Gonzo" and my more bite-happy brother "Animal", she's doing it with a big grin of affection on her face. When she smiles at me ruefully and sighs her "Ah, Stella, my little star. . ." sigh, I know she's saying it with a big dollop of irony. How come? Well, 'cause of my name, of course. Stella means "star", and the trouble is, I'm anything *but*. I mean, I know Auntie V's really *fond* of me and everything, but I always get the feeling that she's just a *tiny* bit disappointed with me, a bit like a lioness who's discovered that her cub is a broccoli-nibbling vegetarian. . .

So where did Mum and Dad get the inspiration for that name? Well, not from one star; from a few billion, to be precise. The night they took me home from hospital, while I was snoozing and dreaming newborn dreams, they gazed wistfully out of the window, and were amazed to see a sky full of twinkling, sparkling planets. I know the sky is *always* full of them, but when you live in a big city like London, most nights you're more likely to see just some swirly orange glow of the street-lights reflected in clouds than the Big Dipper. And so either Mum or Dad (they argue about which one it actually was) gawped skyward, got inspired, landed me with the name "Stella" and it stuck.

Auntie V loved it. I mean LOVED it. But then Auntie V is generally star-struck anyway. Dad told me that when they were growing up, Auntie V's one burning desire in life was to perform in West End musicals like *Les Miserables* and *Chicago* and stuff. He said she had all the drive and ambition (as well as the figure and looks) to do it. The only thing that held her back was the fact that – stunning and determined as she was – she had all the co-ordination of a walrus on dry land when it came to dancing and a singing voice like a duck with its head in a bucket. So she ditched her big plans and did the next best thing instead, becoming an *agent* for people who worked in musicals like *Les Miserables* and *Chicago* and stuff. And then when her first niece was born (me) and ended up with this particular name (Stella), Auntie V decided it was all fate, and that I would grow up and fulfil her every dream and ambition and be the star that she never was.

Er. . .

Unfortunately for Auntie V, I turned out to be the shyest person I know. I mean, *inside* my head, I'm this chatty person with plenty to say and smart, killer lines that would have everyone cracking up – if they could only hear them. At my old school, I always left the gags and the chatting to Frankie and Lauren and Neisha or whoever. They never minded me being the quiet one of our crowd. (Hey, maybe I was so quiet they wouldn't even notice I'd gone. . .?)

"The good thing is that it's the holidays, so she's got the whole summer to settle in," I heard Mum say. Peeking through the banisters I could see that she was now stepping over some boxes and picking her way into the living room. "Well, of *course* I know it's going to be hard for her, Vanessa. I *know* it's tough to be 13 and have to start over."

Hmm, sounded like Auntie V was sticking up for her shy little Stella the "star" . . . which wasn't a big surprise, considering. I mean, when Mum and Dad announced that they were selling up and moving us all to Portbore (sorry, Port*bay*), Auntie V had laughed out loud. "Yeah, *right*! Like you two would *really* give up your home, your careers, your friends, etc., just like that!" she'd grinned, thinking my parents were only fooling around with this talk of new starts and bracing sea air. She'd *stopped* laughing when they pulled out the estate agents' details for this half-derelict pile of bricks and woodworm that was supposed to be a "cottage of real character". And she went positively *white* after that, frowning so hard her forehead looked all corrugated, before choking out, "Is someone *paying* you to move into this cattle shed?"

It's fair to say that Auntie V prefers sarky to subtle. She always says what's on her mind – unlike me, who always thinks what I never say. So even though there were times when Auntie V could be so sarcastic it made me *wince*, I just loved the fact she came out with stuff to do with the move that *I* never would in a zillion years. Like wondering aloud why anyone sane would want to leave one of the biggest, most bustling cities in Europe for one of the most decrepit, dullsville old towns on the south coast.

("The kids will love growing up by the seaside!" Dad had argued. Um . . . you want a bet, Dad?)

She'd demanded to know why anyone would want to move away from tons of multiplex cinemas that showed everything from the newest Disney film to the biggest Bollywood epic, and settle in a town that probably didn't even have a *video* shop.

("The simpler life will be better for us." Speak for yourself, Dad.)

"And what about all the culture your kids are going to miss out on?" Auntie V had pointed out, reminding my parents that only last week in Camden, our family had got dirty looks in a Moroccan restaurant, 'cause Jamie and Jake had had a food fight with couscous. From now on, the most exotic place we'd be asked to leave would be the fish and chip shop on the seafront.

("We'll bond more as a family," Mum had tried to explain to Auntie V – who snorted as loudly as *I'd* have liked to.)

But all of Auntie V's sarcastic jokes about us swapping a cool, split-level flat in Kentish Town for a broken-down house round the corner from the back of beyond fell on totally deaf ears. So last week, I'd started to take down the posters from my lilac-painted walls, and now I was going to have to put those same posters back up on walls that didn't have any paint on them at all. Or *plaster*, for that matter.

And, worse than swapping walls for rubble, I'd been forced to swap the best bunch of friends a girl could have (that's *you*, Frankie, Lauren, Eleni, Neisha, Parminder) for . . . *no one*. No one at all. And even someone as upfront and confident as Auntie V would find that tough. But when you're *me*, it's just about the scariest thing *ever*. . .

"Kissy kissy boy!"

For a second, I didn't know what Jake was on about: what with Mum disappearing into the living room and out of earwigging range, I'd only just noticed that Jamie – happy as he was to be dangling upside-down – was now going a horrible shade of plum, thanks to all the blood rushing to his head.

I whirled my little brother the right way round, and got down on my knees, holding his shoulders in case he had an attack of the wobbles. But as soon as he grinned and said "*Again!*" I knew that he was all right.

And that's when I saw – out of the corner of my eye – what Jake was up to. . .

"Give that to me, Jake!" I ordered, feeling my blood run ice-cube cold as I spotted the photo he was clutching between his sticky fingers.

Stupid, stupid, *stupid*.

When either of my brothers gets hold of something they shouldn't, there's no way of negotiating with them. All you can do is ignore them till they get bored and dump whatever it is; bribe them; or use brute force (i.e. hold them upside-down till their ill-gotten gains tumble out of their pockets).

"Stella kissy kissy boy!" Jake giggled, holding the photo away from me in one hand while pulling a trailing section of parcel tape away from the eyelid it had just stuck itself to.

"*I'll* do that for you, Jake," I offered, letting go of Jamie (who immediately fell over in a dizzy, sniggering pile), and reaching across to help disentangle the parcel tape from Jake's face.

Actually, it was more a case of "Boy kissy kissy Stella" – and only kissy kissy on the cheek – but that wasn't important right now. What *was* important was that this was my chance: I knew that if I pretended not to notice that Jake was

18

holding on to the one, the *only* photo I had of Seb (it looked like Jake must have been raiding my bag alongside Jamie), then I *might* manage to snatch it back off him before he ate it or gave it to one of the removal men.

"Sticky," mumbled Jake, pointing to the tape holding my knickers on his head.

"I know, Jake," I muttered sympathetically, realizing that this was going to work. One swift flick of the tape, and he'd be so gruesomely fascinated by the fact that half his eyelashes were attached to the gluey brown tape that I'd be able to retrieve Seb, or all I had of him.

Hey, bad timing! Love S xxx he'd scrawled on the back of the Polaroid, taken at my leaving party last night.

Bad timing?! The understatement of the *century*, I think. . . I'd only been in love with Seb for a year, and he practically tells me he feels the same when I'm due to move out of London in a few hours' time!

"There . . . gently does it," I murmured softly, as I slowly loosened the tape with one hand and reached across for the photo with the other.

Then again. . .

Did you know that two and a bit year olds

19

have lightning reflexes? Before I got any further with Jake, I felt Jamie's fat little finger squish something on my chin and bottom lip – by the sweet smell of it, it was half of the pot of strawberry lipgloss he must have retrieved from the landing floor. I'd just tried to gently push his hand away before his finger reached my nostril when a jolt of pain shot up my arm.

"*Jamie!*" I heard Dad call loudly from the front doorway downstairs. "How many times do I have to tell you?! Biting is very, *very* bad!"

"Sowwy, Stewwa!" Jamie lisped appealingly at me, as he stroked my hair like I was a cat.

"RaaaaRRRGGGHHH!" Jake roared meantime, hurtling himself feet-first, face-to-the-floorboards down the stairs towards Dad and the TV set he was carrying into the house.

The knickers still taped to Jake's head flopped in time to him thumping his way at top speed down each step. And the Polaroid? Well, all I could see of it was a crumpled white edge peeking from Jake's tiny clenched fist.

"Bye, Seb. . ." I whispered in my mind, as the baby-toothed dent in my arm throbbed madly.

Bye, the whole of my old life.

And hello . . . *what* exactly?

Chapter 3

The pong, the party and the squished Polaroid

A message from Frankie – *yesss!*

Soz – gran visited, couldn't call back earlier, I read on the tiny screen of my mobile. *So what's new house like? F x.*

The predictive text doodah on my phone didn't know what to make of the reply I was typing in. But *Bleurghhhhh!* was the only – made-up – word that fitted the way I felt about my "home" just now.

Why bleurghhhhh? Frankie texted back. *Tell me l8r – going out now and mobie needs charging. Talk 2moz!*

Seven o'clock on Saturday night, and Frankie was off out, meeting up with Neisha and everyone, while I was here, all alone in my room. My room which smelled of cardboard, damp, Dettol and kiddie sick (*bleurghhhhh!*) – not the sort of combination of whiffs that Christian Dior or some other fancy scent company would exactly be rushing to capture for their latest perfume.

The cardboard smell was 'cause of the cardboard boxes all my worldly possessions were crammed into (hadn't quite worked up the enthusiasm to empty them *all* yet). The damp was 'cause . . . well . . . we'd moved into a mildewed shack of a house ("But think of all the history in this place, Stella! All the charm!" Mum had cooed when I pointed out the historic, charming black mould on the bathroom wall). The Dettol smell was the aftermath of Jamie eating half a jar of raspberry jam and a small bar of soap and then choosing *my* room to vomit up the red, foamy mess after a tiring chase by my concerned mum and dad. Who at this point – after clearing up the gunk on my threadbare carpet and then the pizza boxes from our tea – had decided to go out for an evening stroll and explore the delights of Portbore.

My parents had been *well* chuffed when I offered to babysit, specially after Jamie's spectacular barfathon. But the way *I* saw it, the boys were safely asleep now (only violently erupting volcanoes could wake them once they zonked into their synchronized night-time comas). And anyway, from what I'd seen of it so far, exploring the delights of Portbore would only take about seven minutes.

But for the moment – apart from the pong – I

was quite enjoying those precious seven minutes of peace and not having to smile and pretend to my parents that I was OK-ish and not completely gutted about moving here.

Wonder whose house Frankie's going round to tonight? I thought miserably, as I struggled to open the welded-shut window in my room, desperate to get some clean, fresh air in the place. *Will they be talking about the party? Will they be talking about me and Seb. . .?*

"He's coming, y'know!" Frankie had grinned at me in class yesterday afternoon, on the last day of term, on my last day in London. (Sniff. . .)

"He is *not*!" I'd spluttered, trying to convince myself that Frankie was winding me up. But I knew that no matter *how* loud and lairy my best friend was, she wouldn't be so cruel as to tease me about Seb coming to my leaving party. Would she?

Course she wouldn't. And so later, at Frankie's house, surrounded by my gang of girls, a whole bunch of people from our year that Frankie had invited along, and surfaces *groaning* under the weight of the party food Frankie's mum had made for us, I just about fainted when I saw Seb walk in. He was smiling his usual, gorgeous, lopsided smile, but – wow – he was smiling at *me*. . .

23

"I can't believe he's here!" I'd whispered to Frankie, as I watched Seb amble off to the kitchen with his mate to get something to drink.

"Call it a leaving present from me!" Frankie had laughed.

She'd been chatting to him earlier on in the week, in the lunchtime scrum at the kebab shop on the High Street. Seb was cool that way – he might be in the year above us at school, but he wasn't the type of guy to look down on you like you were way down on the food chain just because you were younger. He always said stuff like, "Hi, how you doing?" to me and my mates. Pity I was too crippled with shyness and longing to say anything in reply apart from "Eee!" (loosely translates as a very, *very* shy "hi!"). Luckily, Frankie doesn't have that problem. Frankie can talk to anyone – parents, teachers, gorgeous boys like Seb – like they're all old friends of hers. And so on Tuesday, over a finger-scorchingly hot shish kebab, Frankie had invited Seb to the party she was holding for me.

And *boy*, would I be for ever grateful to Kismet Kebabs and my best friend for that. . .

"You know something?" Seb grinned at me in that adorable lopsided way of his, when he finally came over, later on in the night.

I didn't – i.e. didn't *dare* – say anything in reply, and hoped a smile would be enough to get him to carry on. It was, lucky for me.

"I always thought you were kind of cute, Stella."

Miraculously, I didn't fall in a crumpled pile at his feet, and even managed to mumble an awkward, "Oh. . ." It wasn't much, but I hoped Seb realized that it meant, "I think the same way about you!" Course it *might* have helped if I'd looked him in the eye and not the kneecaps when I said it. . .

And then Frankie – who'd made this mad, magical moment happen in the first place – managed to ruin it totally by pointing her dad's ancient Polaroid camera in our direction and blinding me and Seb with the flash. I was just trying to blink away the white, fuzzy-edged splodges swirling in front of my eyes when two things happened; first, I heard Seb's mate yell at him to hurry up 'cause he wanted to leave, and then – *wow*, *wow* and WOW times a million – I felt Seb *kiss* me on the cheek. (*Blam!* went another flash.)

Less than 24 hours later, with only a few splinters piercing the skin of my fingers from wrestling open my bedroom window, I could *still*

25

feel the hair on the back of my neck tingle at the memory of that kiss. (But then, how could I forget it, when it was my first ever – from a boy, I mean, and not a parent, little brother or elderly relative?)

And as I sat perched on the window of my shambles of a bedroom – staring out at the tangle of weeds and rubble that was supposed to be our back garden, across jumbled cottage rooftops towards the sea where the gulls cawed and screeched – all I wanted was to be able to go back one, single, *solitary* day and re-live it all again. But not as shy Stella; oh, no. I'd love to be a different Stella altogether, Stella the star, who smiled confidently at Seb and said, "Well, I've always thought you were kind of cute too!" And then *everything* could have been different. Maybe he'd have gone on to declare his undying love for me and we'd have spent the summer zapping off e-mail love letters and planning trips to visit each other.

But, oops . . . I wasn't that Stella. *I* was the sort of Stella who ends up sitting in a smelly room all alone on a Saturday night with splinters in her fingers and without even a *photo* of Seb for company. Good grief, Frankie had gone to all the trouble of getting him to sign the Polaroid last night without me knowing, and now I couldn't find even a crumpled, torn *corner* of it anywhere in this mess of a house.

Urgh. I was in serious danger of being blue. Time to do something. Maybe I should write a list; here was a pen, here was a scrap of cardboard torn off the side of one of my boxes. . .

Things I'm going to like about Portbay:
- calling it Portbore
- seeing the *You Are Now Leaving Portbay!* sign when we're going back to London on visits

Things I'm going to miss about Kentish Town (in no particular order):
- our flat
- my room
- groovy Camden Market just down the road
- the no. 134 bus that takes you all the way into the West End for Saturday shopping trips
- Clive, our mad neighbour, who likes flinging his windows open and singing Frank Sinatra songs at the top of his (very high) voice
- Hampstead Heath being practically on the

27

doorstep
- drooling over Seb in the corridors at school
- all my noisy, funny gang
- Frankie (of course)
- and not forgetting Aunt Esme. . .

Oops – maybe the list was a bad idea. It was making me homesick, not happier.

"Stella, my sweetheart, when things are getting you down, what've you got to do?"

"Do something nice!" I'd smile at Aunt Esme, who was also known as Aunt Mummy for a while when I was first learning to talk. (Mum was a bit hurt by that, but considering Aunt Esme was my childminder and I saw more of her during the week than Mum it was no big surprise, really.)

"That's right, my sweetheart – do something nice!" she'd beam proudly at me, as if she was a teacher and I was her Stella-the-star pupil.

Aunt Esme (not my real aunt, but Frankie's real mum), is *big* on catchphrases. She's also a very big lady, which is lovely when you're a little kid and getting a squashy hug from her. (Or a tearful 13 year old getting a hug when you're leaving London for ever. . .)

"You know, the quiet ones are often the wise

ones!" she'd sometimes whisper to me when I was younger, as I sat silently but happily at her kitchen table, drawing wobbly flowers and blobby cats. "Not like my Francesca, God bless her!"

And then she'd smile benevolently at Frankie, who'd be doing something manic like running around the room at top speed and top volume, pretending to be a fire engine.

Well, I might be living on another planet as from today (Planet Portbore), but all of a sudden I could practically *hear* Aunt Esme's words booming into my ears right now.

Yep, it was time I tried to do something nice.

And so I unpacked my big red plastic box of art stuff and flipped open the lid, staring at the mouthwatering shades of coloured chalk pencils in there (they're kind of expensive, but my favourite thing to draw with). I Blu-tacked up the caricature I'd done of Neisha and Lauren for the school art show last term (I got a credit for it, but Lauren went a bit huffy and said I'd made her look like a Vulcan. I don't think she *gets* that caricatures aren't *meant* to be pretty). I Blu-tacked up my favourite pictures of me and Frankie: a strip of cheesy photo-booth snaps with both of us – OK, Frankie – fooling around. I set out all my leaving presents on the top of my chest of drawers, and held up the necklace Lauren had given me, sniffed the Body Shop gift set from Parminder, smiled at Eleni's home-made compilation CD ("It's all our favourite singles from the last year!") and smiled even more at the hip-hop CD from Neisha (she'd never managed it yet, but she was *still* trying to convert me to all the music *she* liked!). And then there were the posh Rotring art pens from Frankie ("So you can do caricatures of all your NEW friends when you forget about us!!" she'd joked in her card.)

But even though it all got me smiling, none of it really cheered me up, not deep down. And none of it could distract me from the terrible *pong* in here. . .

Except the smells in my smelly room weren't the same any more, I suddenly noticed. The breeze from outside had wafted in, replacing the cardboard, damp, Dettol and puke pongs with . . . what exactly? There was the sea (sort of salty), something a bit whiffy, like cabbage (seaweed, I sussed out) and something much nicer. Was it flowery, like honeysuckle, or jasmine? No – it was more like . . . like peaches and cream, weirdly enough. Where was *that* coming from? Dumbly, I glanced outside the window, though I didn't know what I was supposed to be looking for. A great big pudding lorry passing by, maybe? But all I could see – apart from our weedy, so-called garden and the rooftops and the swirling gulls – was one fat, scruffy ginger cat, wobbling its way precariously along the top of the garden fence, like a high-wire walker at the circus (who's eaten too many burgers for lunch lately).

"Hee hee hee!"

Please no!

"Hee hee hee!"

Surely there was some mistake; *surely* I hadn't missed a toddler-waking volcano in the last few minutes. The only thing that didn't freeze at the sound of that giggle was my heart, which collapsed down to my stomach with total *dread*. In my family, in the last couple of years at least, I'd learned that a "Hee hee hee!" like that meant only one thing: trouble. No, make that *TROUBLE*.

I spun my head around quick enough to give me whiplash and instantly saw Jamie practising his biting skills on one of my chalk pencils, while snapping another in half as he doodled a toddler's impression of the devil (probably) on my bedroom wall.

Good grief, were my little brothers determined to make this miserable house move just that *bit* more unbearable for me?

There was only one thing that could keep me sane at the moment – the thought that in seven days' time, Frankie would be coming for the weekend (yes, yes, YES!). That's if my family didn't drive me so mad beforehand that I'd be on the verge of stowing myself on the first train back to Kentish Town.

But maybe I'd reached boiling point already. As I watched Jamie pull the cobalt-blue chalk pencil out of his mouth and snap *that* in half too, I felt something snap inside of *me*.

"G-g-g-g-g-get out of my room, n-n-n-n-*NOW*, J-J-J-Jamie!!"

Ah, I *wondered* when my stupid stammer would show up.

Now *there* was something I wouldn't have minded leaving far, far behind in London. . .

Chapter 4

The psycho seagull and other weirdos

"Hey, Lou-Lou!"

Over the top of the huge cardboard box we were both delving into this morning, Mum shot me a knowing look. Dad normally always called her "Louise", and saved "Lou-Lou" for the times he needed to suck up to her *big*-time, like when he'd broken something, or spent daft amounts of cash on a flash new DVD player or whatever.

"Listen, is it OK if I leave you girls to do the unpacking for a little while?" Dad smiled, sticking his blond-haired head around the paint-peeling kitchen doorway. "I thought I should try and get the computer up and running. . ."

Dad. If it hadn't been for his heart attack, we wouldn't be here. Not in the *kitchen*, I mean, in Portbore. And not that he actually *had* a heart attack – but Dad didn't know that at the time, not when he was stuck in a packed tube train on the way home from work a few months ago and

33

managed to terrify everyone in the carriage, as well as himself, by collapsing with chest pains.

It turned out that it was just a panic attack (phew). But after getting told by the hospital that his heart was in tip-top shape, Dad *still* didn't look very well *or* very happy. Mum didn't look too great either, and I kept coming across them having these intense, whispered conversations that (hey, funnily enough) stopped dead when I walked into the room.

A week later, they let me in on their little secret – we were moving.

"Your dad's job's been very stressful for years now," Mum had tried to explain at the time. "He – well, *we* – feel like we need a complete change. Somewhere with a slower pace of life. More relaxed."

I think I should remind Mum about what she said back then. She didn't look particularly relaxed as she stopped unravelling plates from old newspapers and glanced up darkly at Dad just now. You'd think he'd just told her that he was off to read the *Beano* or watch *Hollyoaks* or some other total skive like that.

"Andy, it's not very easy to look after the boys *and* do the unpacking by myself!" Mum grumbled, keeping one eye on Jamie and Jake, who were taking turns putting a cardboard box on each other's heads and hitting it.

"But *I'm* helping you, Mum!" I chipped in. "And anyway, we *should* be on-line in case . . . in case Auntie V or someone from Dad's old work needs to get in touch!"

Ha! Auntie V might use e-mail in her office, but she'd never sent *us* one. Her style was to yak on the phone, or round the dining table in our old flat, for hours at a time. And why would anyone from Dad's old work e-mail a) on a Sunday, and b) at all? What would they say? "Andy Stansfield – you are stark, raving mad for giving up a highly paid job as an accountant for a posh magazine company, and dragging your entire family down to a faded seaside resort where you've got no work and a just pile of mouldy bricks to live in!"

"Fine! Fix up the computer, then!" Mum sighed, pushing her layered, dark-brown hair back from her face.

"Oh . . . OK!" Dad shrugged and smiled, then disappeared before guilt got the better of him and he found himself roped into deciding which cupboard to stack the tins in, or distracting the twins long enough to stop them from giving each other concussion.

Of course, the *real* reason I wanted Dad to get the computer set up was so that I could e-mail Frankie and all the rest of my friends. I adore e-mail. No, I don't just adore it, I *adoooorrrrre* it. Texting is OK for stuff like: *Hi, how r u?*, but there's no room for waffling, is there? E-mail is when I get the chance to be as funny and fluent as my friends are out loud.

Out loud is something I have a problem with, if you haven't picked up on that already.

While we're (sort of) on the subject, here are two facts:

1) You're more likely to stammer when you're feeling very shy (or very wound-up).

2) The letter "S" is one of the hardest letters to say when you're prone to stammering.

So it's just my luck to be a) horribly shy, and b) called Stella Stansfield. Imagine how difficult *that* is to say when you're nervous and meeting people for the first time, like when you've moved to a new town, for example. . .

"But Stella, you're lucky that your stammer isn't *too* bad," Auntie V suggested to me once, over the dining-room table. "It's not as though you have it all the time. It's not like that young singer boy Gary what's-his-name."

No, I wasn't as bad as *Gareth* Gates used to be (Auntie V met him at an after-show party for some musical a couple of years or so ago). And I certainly wasn't as bad as people I'd seen in documentaries, who struggled with every sentence, every minute of the day. My stammer only crept up on me now and again, but I guess the *fear* of it creeping up was what made me keep words locked up in my head instead of coming out of my mouth a lot of the time.

"RAAAAARGHHHH!"

"AAAAAARGHHHH!"

Still, the constant noise booming from both my brothers *more* than made up for the lack of noise on *my* part. Today's "RAAAAARGHH!" came from Jamie, who'd just found an old, wooden dust-brush in the crumbling kitchen fireplace and was now thudding it off the top of the cardboard box containing Jake's head. The echoey-sounding "AAAAAARGHHHH!" was Jake trying to let Jamie know that their game had gone too far.

"Stella," my mum looked at me wearily. "Could you be the most fantastic daughter in the world and stop your brothers from killing each other before I parcel-tape them both to the legs of the kitchen table? *Please?*"

I did more than just stop Jake and Jamie from killing each other: I hustled the twins out of the back door and into the garden.

"What will we play?" I tried asking them, knowing that football was out, since there was no such thing as a flat piece of grass or earth out here. Course, we could always play *Hunt* the Football. . . I could turn around and chuck the ball over my shoulder into the overgrown jungle of weed-beds and mutant shrubs, and then we could pass a pleasant week or two trying to find it amongst all that matted foliage.

"CHASE!" yelled Jake, and immediately hurled himself into the greenery, with a roaring Jamie in hot pursuit.

In two seconds flat, all I could see of them was their heads (one fair, one strawberry-blond) bobbing about as they roared and ran. If either of them went down on all fours, I'd end up playing Hunt the *Twin*.

"Prrrrp!"

Hmm. That small sound I heard above (or in spite of) the racket Jamie and Jake were making . . . what was it?

"Prrrrp!"

Maybe we had crickets in our garden (hey, we

could have had a family of sabre-toothed tigers living in that tangle and never know it).

"Prrrrp!"

But it wasn't coming from anywhere in the garden exactly; the "prrrrp" seemed to be prrrrping from an ugly, broken-down brick shed thing over by the right-hand wall. I took two steps closer to it, stumbling over a broken flowerpot and a dented plastic watering can camouflaged in the knee-high spiky grass.

The brick shed had a weather-tattered wooden door and one small window, consisting of three panes of solid dust (that I supposed had *glass* lurking behind it) and one empty space framed by dangerous-looking shards twinkling in the sunlight.

And inside . . . inside I could see something.

Something moving.

A flurry of orange fur slinking around.

My brain flipped from PANIC! (i.e. unidentified-moving-object-that-MIGHT-be-a-sabre-toothed-tiger) to AHA! (i.e. maybe-*probably*-it's-that-fat-cat-I-saw-last-night) to PANIC! again, at the sound of my little brothers' matching screams. . .

"Isn't shingles some kind of horrible skin disease?"

I whispered to Mum, as I squinted at the name stamped in the corner of all the serviettes.

We were sitting in the window seat of a seafront café – me, Mum and my muppety brothers.

"*Yes*, but I think this place is called the Shingle café not the *Shingles* café and it's probably named after the shingle on the beach, don't you, Stella?"

Mum raised her eyebrows, knowing I was deliberately looking on the black side. (Unlike her, gazing at everything in this town through rose-tinted specs.)

Shingle/Shingles, Portbay/Portbore; whatever . . . anyway I'm *sure* the other customers in the café moved their chairs away from us when we walked in, and I wouldn't have blamed them for thinking Jamie was contagious with something gross like shingles. After all, how could they know that the red rash all over his face and arms was 'cause of him running head-first into a nettle patch, and that his bloodshot eyes were only like that 'cause of the sand that Jake had kicked into them on the beach ten minutes ago?

"Ooh! Lovely! Thank you!" Mum suddenly smiled, as the most sullen waitress in the world wordlessly thunked plates of beans and fish fingers down in front of the twins.

I didn't dare to stare, but I couldn't help noticing that the tall, skinny girl currently splattering us with bean juice had the same colour hair as the sabre-toothed tiger/ginger cat in our shed this morning. Unfortunately for her, her red hair clashed badly with her bright pink face. Maybe she'd just had a row with her boss. Or maybe she just hated customers. Or maybe she had the first signs of shingles. . .

Anyway, with a name like a skin condition and a waitress as "welcoming" as that, it was a mystery why there were so many mugs (like us) hanging out in the Shingles café. Maybe the old people I could see were lucky enough to be just visiting (we'd passed a car park stuffed with tour buses), and maybe all the teenagers were here because it was the only café in town and there was nothing much *else* to do in Portbore on the first weekend of the summer holidays (it wouldn't surprise me).

The reason *we* were having our lunch in this dump with a dodgy name was because Mum had given up any attempt at unpacking after my brothers had managed to puncture themselves in our lethal garden. Leaving Dad alone in peace to play on – er, *set up* – the computer, Mum had announced that me, her and the boys were going to the beach, where hopefully Jamie and Jake would tear around in the sand and keep out of danger for once in their tiny lives.

"Isn't the prom beautiful?" Mum beamed, gazing out of the window.

She'd just pushed the regular cutlery away from Jake's inquisitive fingers and given him (and Jamie) a yellow plastic Mothercare set that she always took with her when we went out to eat with my brothers. (I think she was wary of letting Jake near any sharp objects after he speared his leg on the rusty old garden fork this morning.)

"It's OK," I shrugged in reply to Mum's comment, wondering what was so beautiful about a pavement and some painted blue railings. Anyway, I could hardly see the prom – or the sea or the beach beyond it – for coaches of day-tripping OAPs trundling by.

"It was so pretty last night, the way all the lights strung along here flickered on just as it started to get dark!"

Yeah, and it was so pretty the way Jamie was smearing tomato sauce all over his face with his hands while Mum wasn't looking. I took the last two serviettes out of their metal holder and tried to daub the worst of the red gunk off him.

"NO!!" Jamie yelled, shoving me away. (Gee, *thanks*.)

"Last night, me and your dad were talking about how peaceful it is here," said Mum cheerfully, as she turned round and took over wiping-duty from me. "It's not exactly like strolling down Kentish Town High Street on a Saturday night, is it?"

I knew what Mum was getting at. Round the tube station in Kentish Town, these down-and-out guys hung out, drinking tins of lager. The local paper liked to bang on about drug-dealing going on in the area. And even though our neighbour, Clive, never did anything nuts apart from warbling Frank Sinatra hits out his window, I think Mum always had her Weirdo Alert on when it came to him. (Poor bloke.)

Well, fair enough – so I didn't know if there were down-and-outs or any drug-dealing problems in Portbore (probably not), but there's one thing for sure: big cities aren't the only place you get weirdos. In the hour we'd spent mucking about on the beach, I'd seen three total weirdos already: some batty old dear sitting on a bench, feeding candyfloss to a ginger *cat*, for goodness' sake (a furry relative of the puss hanging out in our garden, maybe?); a young lad hopping around on the sand like he had itching powder in his boxer shorts (he *was* being dive-bombed by a psycho seagull, though); and some mad-looking Goth girl kicking her way grumpily through the sand in Doc Marten boots, a black leather jacket and – wait for it – a pink *tutu*.

Help – I'd moved to Portbore, the seaside resort for loonies of all ages (and species). . .

"Oh, I forgot to tell you!" Mum suddenly said, while holding Jake's legs down to stop him from kicking Jamie. "Me and your dad saw a poster last night – there's a funfair coming to town on Friday. You could take Frankie when she comes at the weekend – it'll be brilliant!"

OK, so funfairs are fun. But they're hardly "brilliant" – not when you've been to Chessington World of Adventures (eight times, as me and Frankie have clocked up). And a big wheel is a laugh to go on, but it's not exactly the London Eye (me and Frankie have been on that twice, once with Auntie Esme for Frankie's birthday, and once with school).

"Mmm. . ." I mumbled non-committally to Mum, hoping she didn't think I was being all awkward and negative again.

But she hadn't even noticed my "Mmm..." because Jamie had got Jake back for kicking him by scoring a direct hit with a major squirt from the ketchup bottle.

"Jamie – *NO!* Stella, can you please go and grab some more paper napkins? Oh! Jamie – now *DON'T* bite your brother...!"

Before the inevitable screams and wails broke out, I got up and sped off towards the counter to grab a handful of "Shingles"-printed serviettes from the teetering pile stacked there. It *should* have been one of those nothingy, ten-second chores, but somehow the search-for-the-serviette turned into a not-so-mini trauma for me.

"Um..."

I'd just nipped past a couple of tables of gossiping OAPs when I nearly tripped over a pair of long legs stretched out between two chairs. I kind of hoped that "um..." would do: that the owner of the long legs (one of four prissily perfect girls around my age) would see that she was barring my way and reel her legs in to let me by. Instead, the legs stayed put, giving their owner – and her buddies – plenty of time to look me up, down and back again. Call me paranoid, but you could tell they didn't like what they saw. So I had

on a white T-shirt, a denim mini, stripy socks
and a pair of trainers – so what? I mean, next to
my super-trendy friends back in Kentish Town,
I probably looked *frumpy*. But here in dullsville
Portbore, I must have looked like Kate Moss
trying too hard, all because . . . because of what?
My stripy pastel socks? *That's* what the four of
them were scowling at. Hey, I only bought them
because I'd seen them in *Mizz* last month and
thought they were kind of cute. . .

"'S-s-s-s-scuse me. . ."

Here we go. Here came my stammer, all
because of some stupid tomato sauce, a stupid
serviette, and some stupid, *stupid*, stripy socks.

I didn't stick around long enough to listen to
whether or not the girls were sniggering at me
tripping over my words (like some people at my
old school had, before Frankie stepped in and
made sure they didn't giggle *again*). I just saw
that the legs had withdrawn and that my path to
the counter was clear – so I hurried over, grabbed
a few serviettes, then swivelled round and headed
back by a different route. All I wanted was to
skirt past a few tables of happy pensioners and
get safely back to Mum and the twins and the
uninspiring view of the prom that Mum had been

wittering on about.

Uh-oh.

It wasn't that easy. On my *new* route, I had to pass a table of boys a couple of years older than me – about 15, I reckoned from a split-second shy glance – and *then* I heard it.

"Check the hair!" one of them said.

"Yeah, pure afro!" said one of the others.

My hair . . . you can describe it in a lot of ways: "practically blonde!" (that's Frankie, who thinks anything less than black or dark brown is practically blonde), to "curly-wurly" (Jake), to "ringlety" (Auntie V), to "like an angel's!" (Aunt Esme). But the thing is, if you're going to get technical about my practically blonde (i.e. light brown), curly-wurly, ringlety, "angelic" hair, it *is* – technically speaking – afro. How come that lad had managed to make a simple fact sound like an insult?

"Hey, and check the boobs!" I heard another of the boys cackle, before a bluster of other cacklers joined in.

This was *too* much. I felt like the Number One Freak in a Victorian freak show.

Blushing, *mortified*, I couldn't get back to Mum, Jake and Jamie fast enough. And then – I couldn't believe it – Mum started giggling too.

"Oh, dear – I think you might need to change that top when we get home!" she laughed, pointing at my chest.

I gazed down at my white T-shirt, and clocked the tomato-sauce handprints pressed *straight* on to my boobs.

"Thanks, Jamie!" I grumbled darkly, as my little brother happily giggled to himself, squirting tomato sauce down his shorts.

"I need some air," I told Mum, as I headed for the door, not even bothering to sit down (and get covered with *more* ketchup in embarrassing places).

What I *really* needed, I realized – once I was outside in the fresh, coach-exhaust-scented air – was my friends. So how come no one (except Frankie, yesterday, briefly) had answered any of my phone calls or texts this weekend. . .?

Chapter 5

Four quarters of me

"Oh, Stella! Don't do *that*!" Mum sighed, as she walked back into the bathroom with the boys' clean pyjamas.

"What?" I asked innocently. "Don't you think they look cute?"

Jake and Jamie seemed to like the soapy devil horns I'd shaped their soft baby hair into – they couldn't stop snickering at the sight of each other.

"And couldn't you have stopped them from emptying half the bath-water on to the floor? Look at the state of this carpet!"

I think Mum realized how dumb that sounded almost straight away. For a start, trying to get Jamie and Jake to stop doing something naughty was as hard as juggling custard. And as for the faded, stained old rag of a carpet in this mouldy, damp room, it could probably do with a good wash anyway. Actually, it could probably do with being ripped up and shoved in the skip that was being

49

delivered in the morning. (Dad was supposed to be starting on the house renovations tomorrow, but the only thing I'd heard him threaten to throw in the skip so far was the computer he'd been trying to get working for the last eight hours. . .)

"Right – this little monster's mine," said Mum, rinsing the suds out of the devil horns of the nearest dripping, giggling small boy (who happened to be Jamie, while I got the noisy, roaring one – Jake – who at least didn't bite) and scooping him up.

"Did you manage to get hold of Frankie yet?"

"No," I told Mum, as I did the same to Jake and then clamped my knees like a vice around his ankles to keep him semi-still while I wrapped a big fluffy towel around him. "Aunt Esme said she was out with the girls again."

Aunt Esme had also been a bit surprised, like me, that Frankie hadn't returned the two messages and three texts I'd sent her today.

"Well, you two'll have plenty of catching up to do next weekend anyway, and I'm *sure* Frankie'll have lots of messages from Lauren and everyone!" Mum smiled brightly, as if she could tell I wasn't too happy with the big fat wall of silence from most of my friends since Friday night.

I was *trying* not to let that get me down. After

all, it had only been two days, which might have seemed like a week past *for ever* for me, stuck down here at the edge of the world, but probably felt like about ten *minutes* to Frankie and the others. And I really *was* looking forward to Frankie coming; I couldn't wait to pour my heart out to her about stuff like missing Seb and the embarrassment of what had happened in the café this lunchtime. I tell you, those lads wouldn't dare make *any* kind of comment to Frankie, not if they wanted to live. One ferocious glance from her and they'd be *whimpering*.

"You're not still bugged by what those boys said at the café today, are you?" Mum suddenly quizzed me, reading my mind again. (Wish she'd been able to read my mind better the last few months when I'd been silently yelling, "Don't make me move away!!")

"A bit," I shrugged, rubbing the now soapless, wet-look horns – and a whole shower of wet sand – out of Jake's hair with the towel.

"But when people don't know you, Stella, they'll always pick up on what's unusual about you at first. They don't necessarily *mean* anything by it."

I knew that. My favourite thing to draw was caricatures, wasn't it? And with caricatures, you have to fix on just a few features and exaggerate them. But hypocritical as it might sound, I didn't want anyone "fixing" on what made *me* different. And I wasn't just talking about my hair or my stripy socks or the tomato-sauce handprints across my boobs. What worried me was that here in Portbore, I could tell that our whole *family* was going to seem unusual. Mainly 'cause we look like we aren't even *related* to each other. It's like we all drew straws and just ended up together by accident. I mean, the twins don't even look like *twins*, for goodness' sake. Actually, if I was drawing caricatures of my family, *here's* what I'd pick out. . .

DAD: Tall, short blond hair, blue eyes. (Looks Norwegian, but is actually from Norfolk.)

MUM: Layered dark-brown hair that regularly flops across her face, olive skin, big brown eyes. (Looks Spanish, but is from Hackney, East London.)

JAKE: Short, dumpy, fluffily spiky fair hair, grey eyes. (Looks like Grandpa Stansfield's mini-me.)

JAMIE: Tall for his age, skinny, ultra-pale skin, strawberry-blond wavy hair. (Just like the photos we've seen of Mum's mum – Nana Jones.)

Then there's me. The four quarters that make

up Stella Stansfield (i.e. the genes from all my grandparents) somehow add up to something different from the rest of my family. I ended up with light-brown fizzy ringlets, hazel eyes, and a smattering of freckles right across my nose (like a brush loaded with coffee-coloured paint got flicked my way at point-blank range). No one can figure out where the freckles came from (none of my grandparents are guilty of freckles), but the hair is easy. That's 'cause one quarter of me is from Norfolk, one quarter of me is from Yorkshire, one quarter of me is cockney – and one quarter is from Barbados.

"How come *you* don't look more like your dad?" I asked Mum, though I knew the answer already – I'd asked the question before.

"Sometimes genes can skip a generation," Mum shrugged. "I mean, my skin's darker than yours, which must have come from my father. But you don't see your lovely hair as a problem, do you, Stella?"

I shook my head. I *liked* my curls, apart from the amount of time I had to spend conditioning them, and having stupid, ignorant dorks in cafés sniggering at them, of course.

"I wish I could see a picture of my grandad. . ."

I sighed. I'd said that before, plenty of times, too. I also wished I could've met Nana Jones in person, but I didn't happen to get born till years after she died.

"I know, Stella. But like I've said already, I only ever saw one photo of my father when I was a little girl, and I don't know what happened to it."

How weird: the idea that Nana Jones and this boy fell in love with each other when she was only four years older than I am now – but she didn't dare tell her parents, just 'cause he was black. And how weird that I knew so little about him. In fact, apart from that stuff, I only knew four things about my grandad: 1) he was kind, 2) he was handsome, 3) his name was Eddie, and 4) he'd come from Barbados to live in Britain with his parents when he was just a little boy. Not much to know about a grandparent, is it?

"Remember, it *was* a very long time ago, Stella, and people's attitudes were very different back then," said Mum, doing that unsettling thing again, as if she could read my mind. "They were ignorant about colour, and they were ignorant about things like expecting babies when you weren't married."

And all that long time ago, my grandad left London broken-hearted because Nana Jones split up with him, scared of what her parents thought.

And here's the saddest thing about the whole mega-sad thing: he never knew that he was going to be a dad . . . and one day a grandad, to me and the Muppets.

"How did Nana Jones meet Grandad Eddie again?" I quizzed Mum, trying to piece the story together in my head.

"He was working in Hackney for the summer, and don't ask me what his job was, 'cause I don't remember my mother ever mentioning it."

"Where do you think he could be now?" I asked her, leaning over and grabbing Jake before he managed to clamber back into the noisily draining bath.

"Well, if he's still alive, he could be anywhere in the world, couldn't he? I mean, he could have retired back to Barbados, or even be living two miles from here!" said Mum, as she tried to stop Jamie from ramming both feet down one leg of his Fimbles pyjamas. "There's just no way of ever knowing, Stella – specially since it all happened nearly forty years ago now, and we don't even know his last name."

My mum's amazingly practical. I don't mean that in a horrible way; she just has this talent for not freaking about stuff that you can't do anything about. And she's also got a talent for sorting stuff that you *can* do something about, which is, I guess, why she made Dad move here before he had any more panic attacks and frightened *more* passengers on the tube. . .

"Jake – *leave* the soap!" Mum suddenly ordered, reaching over and prising a bar of Simple out from between his stubby white teeth. "You saw what happened to Jamie last night. Do you want to end up being sick too?"

"YES!" trumpeted Jake.

I hadn't even noticed what he'd been up to. For a second there, my thoughts had drifted back to my old school, where everyone was white, black, Asian, Jewish, Turkish and Greek-Cypriot; where loads of pupils came from Croatia and Afghanistan and Korea and Somalia and a load of other countries you might struggle to place on a map of the world. Back there, it hadn't mattered one bit that my family didn't quite match, or that one quarter of me was from a grandad I'd never seen. All that my friends cared about was the fact that my parents worked on magazines (at least, Mum did till she had the twins) and they reckoned that was very, *very* cool indeed.

But now . . . well, now I guess I was a bit worried that in Portbore, we'd just be the Weird

Family From London. Er, exactly *how* were we supposed to feel at home here. . .?

The teeth-marks were still throbbing on my arm as I headed to my bedroom. (That was the *last* time I offered to read my brothers a bedtime story – I didn't care if Jamie was only acting out the part of *The Hungry Caterpillar*.)

I needed to speak to Frankie; after the freaky day I'd had I needed to feel like me, and not some fizzy-haired alien who'd landed by the seaside.

And then there it was again . . . a waft of peaches and cream, floating above the smells of baby talc and foam bath lingering up my nostrils. I meant to hurry over to my window and look outside again – to figure out where the waft was wafting from – when I stopped dead.

Things might still be in a muddle in my room (like the rest of the house), but I *definitely* would have remembered unpacking a huge, fat, tatty, ginger cat. The one currently snoring its scruffy head off on my bed did *not* belong to me.

"Um . . . hello? Puss-puss, do you want to go back where you belong?" I said, shooing it warily from a safe distance. (I didn't like the look of those battle-scarred ears – it could probably beat me in a fight.)

The cat, probably sensing that I was zero threat to it, snored on – one lethal-looking yellow fang protruding from its dreamily quivering mouth.

"Did you come in through the window, puss?" I asked it, taking a tentative step closer and wondering how I was going to persuade it to go back *out* the window.

The cat, blanking me again, gave a reverberating sigh and stretched itself into a relaxed arc, that practically took up half the width of my bed. (*Was* it a direct descendant of a south coast sabre-toothed tiger?)

And then I saw something *else* I hadn't seen in my room last time I'd looked.

Gently, gently, I took a corner of the brightly coloured leaflet poking out from under the cat's furry white belly and *pulled*.

All the Fun of the Fair! In Portbay from Friday!

Before I got a chance to figure out how the fairground flyer had got here, I got the strangest shivery feeling I was being watched – from one menacing, green, feline eye.

"Frankie?" I whispered into my mobile, as her message service clicked in. "You'd better get here quick. *Everything* about this town is freaking me out. . .!"

Chapter 6

Fairy cakes and sardines

"Good grief, Stella: you've made me look like a meerkat. Crossed with a heron. Wearing very expensive shoes!"

That was the first and last time I'd done a caricature of Auntie V – she'd popped around to our old flat after work one day, and settled herself down at the dining table for one of her regular catch-ups with my parents. She always looks pretty stunning, my Auntie V, 'cause like my dad, she's tall ("these could have been dancer's legs, Stella, darling!") and blonde ("I'd have made a better Roxy in *Chicago* than that Renée Zellweger!"). *Unlike* my dad, Auntie V is totally into exploiting her fake Nordic look, and never dresses in anything but shades of white, cream and fawn, with deep red lipstick and piles of ethnic jewellery ("for a bit of drama, darling!"). Anyway, that particular time, I'd drawn her all elongated and glamorous, from the top of her sharp blonde bob to her pointy camel-coloured ankle boots. I'd been really pleased with it. Auntie V seemed as pleased as if I'd spilt Ribena over her white angora jersey.

"You're obviously very good at drawing, Stella, darling. But why don't you try another style? Why don't you draw something pretty for a change, like flowers or fruit, etc., etc.?"

And now, sitting on a bench on the prom, with my pad in front of me and a chalk pencil in one hand, I suddenly remembered what Auntie V had said that day, however long ago. And the reason I didn't draw flowers, fruit, etc., etc. (Auntie V talked very fast – I think she liked to say "etc." just to save time) was because I was rotten at drawing them. Just like I was rotten at drawing beaches, as I was finding out.

"Stupid sea, stupid sky, stupid caravans. . ." I grumbled to myself, staring off at the ugly jumble of metal boxes perched up on the headland, and then back down at the just-as-ugly boxy blobs I'd scribbled on to the paper. The only thing I liked about my picture was the seagull standing on the prom railing, watching every reluctant stroke of my pencil, and probably hoping I might have half a doughnut or something that I'd like to share with it. I'd drawn the bird with a big crooked beak, crossed eyes and finned feet as big as clown's shoes. But somehow, my cute caricature of the gull didn't fit too well with the atmospheric landscape I wasn't managing to capture. At all.

I felt like grabbing my darkest red chalk pencil from the box and swirling mad, bad, ugly doodles over the whole thing. But then I *was* in a Gold Star Grouch this morning; *everything* was hacking me off. OK, so I'd had my first good night's sleep since I got here – the snoring of the cat-I-was-too-scared-to-move had been kind of soothing (it reminded me of the sound of cars swooshing by at all hours in Kentish Town). But then I got woken up at 7.30 a.m. this morning by the ear-splitting, metallic KERR-*LAAANNNGG* of a skip being delivered in our driveway. (The cat, by the way, was nowhere to be seen – back to wherever it had come from, I supposed. But I still had the flyer for the funfair, wherever *that* had come from.)

Anyway, first there was the KERR-*LAAANNNGG*, and then two seconds later, I had a couple of over-excited small boys bouncing up and down on my bed (with me still in it), yelling "Skip! SKIP! SKIPPP!!!" at the tops of their voices. Dad was *also* very excited by the arrival of the skip (but at least he didn't show it by jumping on my bed); in fact, he was *so* excited that he'd decided he was having a day off from struggling with the computer. Which meant yet again, no e-mails for me.

"Look, it's Monday, so the library will be open. Why don't you see if it's got any computers you could check your e-mails on? Or you could go into town and see if there's an internet café somewhere!" Mum had suggested, when she saw the black cloud of gloom hovering over my head at breakfast. "You could take your pad out with you and do some drawing. It's a beautiful day!"

I had a hunch that Portbore was so behind the times that they'd only just got Channel 5 on the telly, never mind anything as radical as an internet connection (maybe *that* was why Dad couldn't get the computer to work). And I wasn't really in the mood to dig out my chalk pencils. But faced with a choice of watching Dad play at Chucking-Things-in-the-Skip, helping Mum unpack saucepans, or acting as unpaid zookeeper to the Muppets, I decided I might as well take up Mum's offer and escape.

So far, I hadn't bothered to go and look for non-existent computers, but I was seriously considering a new way to pass the time – turning this rubbish drawing of mine into an origami boat and sailing it out to sea. . .

"Oooh, *that's* lovely, dear!"

There was a light thunk on the bench beside me and the sweet smell of toffee as a very old lady settled herself down to inspect my artwork. Despite the baking sun, she was wearing a lime green raincoat and had a pink meringue of a hat on her head.

"It's not really," I shrugged.

"Oh, but it is, dear. Toffee?"

She flipped open a catch on her cream patent-leather handbag and pulled out a rustling bag of sweets. I wasn't sure what to do – in London, you don't tend to get chatting to strangers and you certainly don't go taking Werther's Originals off them. But this lady was hardly a child-snatching psycho – she was about a hundred and twelve, and if she tried anything funny I could just pull her meringue down over her face and scarper.

"Um, thanks. . ." I said warily, helping myself to one of her sweets.

"Good enough for the window of the gallery on the prom. Do you know it?" she asked, unwrapping a toffee for herself.

"Er, no," I mumbled, self-consciously flipping my ropey picture over and finding myself with a blank white sheet (*big* improvement).

The bag of toffee went back in her tiny bag, and instead she pulled out a fairy cake, complete with a pleated paper cup and a cherry on top. She gave it a quick blow, sending a few specks of fluff fluttering into the breeze.

"It's his favourite." She nodded at the gull, which – right on cue – swooped down to her feet, waiting patiently for its treat. "Just here on holiday, are you?"

"No – just moved. To Foxglove Cottage, up on Dingle Lane."

God, I *hated* my new address – it sounded so *cutesy*. (Apart from that, what the heck was a foxglove supposed to look like anyway? And what was a dingle when it was at home?) You know, I hated my new address so much that I hadn't *dared* tell Neisha what it was yet; she was so into Eminem and hardcore hip-hop that I thought she'd laugh in my face for living somewhere that sounded like it was just next door to the Teletubbies.

"Ah, yes. It used to be lovely, that cottage."

"My dad's doing it up," I told her. (Ha! I was looking forward to *that* – the closest my dad had ever got to DIY in the past was ringing people up under the DIY section in the *Yellow Pages*.)

"And where have you moved from, dear?"

"London. North London. Kentish Town."

As I watched the old lady lean forward and feed crumbs of fairy cake to this pterodactyl of a bird, I gently began tap-tapping my pencil on the edge of the blank sheet of paper. And then I started drawing.

"London? Ooh, I went up there once for a day trip," the old lady chattered. "Meant to go to Buckingham Palace to have a look at the Queen, but I got terribly muddled with those tube trains and ended up at a place called Walthamstow Dog Track. Do you know it?"

"Well, yes," I frowned at the top of her bobbing, pink-hatted head, wondering how she'd managed to get *that* lost. "That's where they hold greyhound races. I went with my dad once. Did you get to Buckingham Palace in the end?" I talked and scribbled at the same time, the caricature coming to me a *hundred* times easier than the landscape had five minutes ago.

"Oh, no. Someone showed me how the betting worked, and I stayed and won £5 on a greyhound called Boozy Bessie. Had a lovely afternoon!

Ah . . . it must seem quite quiet around here after London, dear."

"I guess so," I agreed with her, quickly scooping two more chalk pencils – one pink and one lime green – from the box by my side.

"Of course, Portbay wasn't *always* quiet. Not back in the old days, when there was all the piracy and smuggling going on."

"Pirates?" I squeaked in surprise. What *was* this place we'd moved to? *Wait* till I told Mum – bloodthirsty pirates and smugglers were pretty heavy-going compared to a few down-and-outs sharing a can of lager and chatting outside the tube station. . .

"And then there's the house in Sugar Bay. It's got a bit of a history to it, that rambling old place," the equally rambling old lady breezed on, as if pirates and smugglers were run-of-the-mill stuff. "Had a walk over there yet, to Sugar Bay?"

"No – where's that?"

"Well, you were nearly drawing it a minute ago!" she smiled, brushing the last of the cake crumbs from her fingers. "It's a beautiful little cove just on the other side of that cliff. Nothing there now but the old house, and those tin cans, of course."

She was pointing up at the caravans teetering

on the headland. Now that it had finished its snack lunch, the seagull hopped up to join the old lady on the bench, and seemed to be staring disapprovingly at the holiday homes too. Maybe it would fly over and poo on them later.

I wanted to ask more, to find out all about the pirates and the smugglers and the old house and what its story was (and how exactly she'd found out that the gull liked fairy cakes best), but the old lady's attention was suddenly grabbed by something else.

"Would you look at him?" she laughed, nodding her wobbly net-swathed hat towards the beach just below us. "You'd think nobody had ever bothered telling him he was a cat!"

Something went ping! in my head as I recognized the fat ginger cat sunbathing on the sand, eyes closed, four furry feet in the air, big belly on show.

"It was in my room last night!" I exclaimed.

"Peaches was? Oh, he gets around. A real wanderer. Settles himself with whoever he fancies for a while, then he's off. He even lived with me once upon a time. Liked custard cream biscuits and sardines, as I remember."

"Peaches?"

I had to make sure I'd heard her properly – that scruffy, battle-scarred, overweight cat *was* called "Peaches", right?

"Yes, Peaches – because of his colouring, I suppose."

Peaches. If I'd have *had* to guess at a name for him, I'd have come up with stuff like Big Ron or Bruiser or Tank or something. Then again, there had been that weird sweet scent in my room all last night. . .

At that second, another ping! went off in my head, as I realized that the old lady I'd been talking to was the same mad one I'd spotted yesterday sharing candyfloss with a cat. And that cat probably *was* Peaches. Wow – it had to be quite a trek on cat-sized legs, getting to the seafront from my house, way up on the slope overlooking town.

"Now what's this you've been up to? Hmm?"

The old lady smiled at me and leant over for a peek at my pad. I was pretty pleased with the sketch, specially since I'd done it so quickly, and flipped it round so she could see it better.

"Oh!" she exclaimed, her pale eyebrows raised. "It's one of those cartoony things. What do you call them again?"

"Caricatures," I told her, scanning her face

to see what she reckoned of it. I'd thought I'd made it quite sweet – like a cross between an old lady and a Neopolitan ice-cream sundae. I'd even drawn a cherry on the top of her hat.

"That's *very* clever," she nodded slowly. "But I've always thought those caricature things are a bit cruel, haven't you? You want to have a go at drawing something pretty. You should have a wander round to Sugar Bay, paint a picture of the old hou—"

I'd never been so glad to hear my phone ring; for one thing, it meant I didn't have to listen to this batty old dear tell me my drawing wasn't very good (just like Auntie V, though you'd never catch *her* in a lime green raincoat and pink meringue hat). And anyway, it could be Frankie – getting back to me at last.

"'Scuse me – I'd better go," I blustered, hurriedly gathering up my art stuff with one hand, and checking out the number calling on the screen of my phone.

Pah . . . only Mum.

"Bye, dear!" the old lady smiled and waved, as I wandered off at high speed.

"Hello, Mum – what's up?" I asked, hoping she was calling me to say that Frankie had phoned the cottage or that Dad had fixed up the computer *after* all and there were *dozens* of messages waiting for me from my friends back in London.

Wrong.

"Hi, Stella – just a quickie. Can you pick up some more milk on the way home? Jake's just poured the last of the litre into my underwear drawer."

And so I wandered back to Foxglove Cottage with a heavy heart (still no word from Frankie), a heavy shopping bag (filled with a carton of milk, a packet of custard creams and a tin of sardines), and a funny, furry ginger shadow following me up every windy lane. . .

Chapter 7

Trapped in Nutsville

It turned out that while Mum was pouring the contents of her knicker drawer (pants, bras, semi-skimmed milk) into the washing machine, Jamie and Jake were playing quietly together. Playing at pulling down every poster in my room, one by one.

Oh, how I missed my old bedroom, on the second floor of our flat. How I missed the stairgate that stopped the twins from coming in and wrecking my room. How I missed the days when they were tiny babies and couldn't reach doorknobs.

Once I got home, surveyed the damage, had a silent scream to myself and planned ways to kill my brothers, I realized I had to come up with a cunning plan.

And I was staring at it right now, lying flat on my back on the bed. I only hoped those drawing pins were strong enough to keep my posters fixed on to the ceiling. . .

OK, so one problem sorted. Now to try and sort another.

Help – am trapped in Nutsville, I keyed into my mobile, not bothering to sit up. *Please rescue me. Or just talk 2 me! Where r u? luv stella.*

There had never *ever* been a time when me and Frankie had gone for three days without talking, even if it was just by text. We once went for *two* days without talking, when I was on holiday in Greece and something went funny with the mobile reception 'cause of an earthquake. See? It took an earthquake that was 4.5 on the Richter scale to keep us apart. So how come she'd turned silent on me now?

"We'll stay in touch ALL the time, Stella, OK?! Mates for ever, remember!" she'd told me late on Friday night, when Dad came to pick me up from the party. She'd grabbed my arm so tight it practically left a *bruise*. And even though it was dark outside on her doorstep, I was *sure* she had tears in her eyes. Wow – I'd known Frankie since I was three months old (and she was a more mature eight months old), and I'd never *once* seen her cry. You know how couples in movies sometimes say they're each other's other half? Well, it was sort of like that with me and Frankie – I was *her* shy, quiet, bumbling side, and she was *my* fearless, loud, non-crying side. But suddenly everything felt totally muddled. I mean, there she was nearly blubbing on Friday, yet it was Monday night now and if I didn't know her better I'd think she was avoid—

My mobile trilled to life in my hand, jarring my muddled thoughts and nearly making me *lunge* out of my skin.

At last!

"Frankie?" I grinned, sitting bolt upright on the bed as soon as I clocked her number on the illuminated panel of my phone.

"Hi, Stella!"

She sounded fuzzy and far away, further than London, as distant as the dark side of the moon. (She was probably just on the top deck of the 134 bus – you know what mobiles are like.)

"Where've you been? I thought you said you'd get back to me on Sunday! What's been happening?" I laughed, feeling a bit dippy with happiness at hearing her voice.

"Hey, y'know how it is. I was out with the girls and then seeing my gran and stuff and then I ran out of money on my mobie."

"Did you e-mail? 'Cause Dad hasn't set up

73

the computer here yet so I couldn't pick up any messages," I wittered on, accepting her explanation, even if it *did* have a whiff of lameness about it (hadn't she seen her gran on Saturday?).

"Nah – I didn't get round to it."

I felt a twinge in my stomach that *could* have been indigestion, but since I hadn't eaten anything for a while I kind of suspected it was a twinge of *hurt*.

"Oh. Oh, OK," I shrugged, getting up and walking over to the window, where I pressed my head against the cool glass. Out in the garden, I saw the tail end of my ginger shadow disappear through the one broken pane of the outhouse window. "So . . . how's Neish and everyone?"

"Y'know, same old stuff. How's the new place? Still bleurghhhhh?"

For the last few days I'd been *dying* to tell her all about Portbore and the sheer, drop-dead boringness of it all, but suddenly I didn't feel much like doing that. Maybe it was the way she'd skirted over my question about the other girls just then. I mean, didn't she understand that I still really, *really* needed to feel part of our gang, even if I was just a long-distance member?

"It's all right." I shrugged again. "I'll tell you all

about it when you're here at the weekend."

Uh-oh – there was a sudden, hulking great silence when I mentioned the visit. So it only lasted a split-second, but it was definitely *there*.

"Frankie? You *are* still coming, aren't you?"

"Course!" Frankie laughed. "Got my train ticket already, haven't I?"

Urgh . . . I was being paranoid, I was being *so* paranoid. I'd only been here a few days and already Portbore was turning me as mad as half of its inhabitants.

"Friday was brilliant, wasn't it?" I smiled, trying to let go of the paranoia.

"Yeah, it was."

"So . . . seen Seb around?"

"Nah."

OK, I'd switched back to being paranoid. What was it with Frankie? How come she was managing to sound so bored? What was with all these nothingy answers, when normally we'd be teasing and joking and chattering away for hours?

"Listen, my mobie's about to pack up – I forgot to charge it," said Frankie. "I'll give you a phone once I'm on the train on Friday, yeah? It's just that my cousin's coming to stay for a few days, so I'll probably be too busy to get in touch till then."

Her cousin Tania? But Tania came for visits all the time, and Frankie wasn't that wild about her, since she was only seven and just wanted to talk about her Bratz dolls all day.

"So speak Friday – OK?" Frankie repeated in a voice that sounded more flat than friendly.

"O-O-O-OK."

It was only once we'd said our very quick byes that I realized something weird about today. When I'd been speaking to that old lady on the beach this morning, I hadn't stammered *once*. But for the first time in my life, I'd stammered talking to Frankie. What was I saying about everything being muddled?

All at once, I wanted to escape, to get out of my stuffy bedroom and be out in the afternoon sunshine in our bee-buzzing, butterfly-bobbing jungle of a garden, where I could breathe in gulpfuls of H_2O and get my head straight. But I didn't want to go back down the stairs, and have Mum and Dad ask me if I was all right, or the twins hurtle themselves at me for a game or a bite or something.

A distant glimmer of ginger through the outhouse window put the idea in my head. I could be out there in the garden, quick as a flash of ginger fur, if I just followed in Peaches' pawprints. . .

Two minutes and some scrambling later and I was knee-deep in wispy grass and elongated dandelions. Staring up at the route I'd just taken from my first-floor bedroom window (out on to the roof of the kitchen, down on to the old wooden coal shed), I couldn't believe what I'd just done. It felt like my blood was swooshing round at high speed, all diluted with adrenaline. It's just that *I* was the girl who was completely rubbish at PE; I mean, seriously, even just last week I got freaked out when Mrs Kitson our PE teacher expected us to jump off the *trampette*. (You should have heard how much teasing I got off Neisha and everyone over *that*. . .)

And all the adrenaline made me bound over a patch of nettles next. Then with one hefty shove of my shoulder against the door, I plunged into the dim, dusty world of the outhouse.

"Puss? I mean, Peaches?" I whispered, waiting for my eyes to adjust after the brightness outside.

"Prrrp!"

And there he was, curled up like an over-stuffed fuzzy cushion on an old desk by the window. At least, he looked like an overstuffed fuzzy cushion compared to the deflated raggedy one he was sprawled on.

The desk and the chair: that was the only furniture I could see in here. The rest of the space was taken up with rusty old gardening tools and a wall full of shelves cluttered with . . . well, *clutter*.

"What's this place, then?" I asked the cat, glancing nervously around for the owners of the many cobwebs I'd just spotted.

"Prrrp!"

With no tarantulas in sight, and feeling a bit daring, I reached out and put a hand on Peaches' tatty fur. His luminous green eyes blinked up lazily at me, as if he was daring me to tell him he needed to use conditioner. (Had someone tried that already? Was *that* why he smelt so good?)

"Hey, I bought you sardines and custard creams! I know you like them!"

Another blink. Very gently, I tried stroking Peaches – I didn't want to shock him and risk that one yellowed fang inserting itself into my hand.

"Prrrrrrrrrrrr. . ."

Phew. He liked it. Or maybe he was just excited about the idea of sardines and custard creams.

"Y'know, this place is grottier than the cottage – just about!" I mumbled to myself and Peaches, as I pulled out a wobbly-looking wooden chair and sat down to survey the cobwebby junk-fest in front of me.

Meanwhile, Peaches made it plain that he didn't care what I was doing, as long as I carried on with the stroking thing. He stretched his short thick legs out into a luxurious stretch, giving me a closer glimpse of the thing he was sitting on. (Boy, that cat liked sitting on things.) It wasn't a saggy cushion after all; it was an old hat, squashed flat. It was made out of brownish, faded felt, and trimmed with ribbons; two flattened, damp-spotted, once honey-coloured ribbons that now trailed down into the desk's one – slightly open – drawer. Peaches' tail flickered above the drawer too, like a hairy third ribbon. Or a furry arrow?

"What's in here, puss?"

I bent over and tugged at the drawer cautiously – in case I disturbed a nest of snoozing mice or something – and found. . .

1) a roll of brittle plain paper, tied with string

2) a roundish piece of wood, with faded blobs of colour on it, like an old-fashioned palette or something

3) an empty ink bottle, and a scratchy-looking old ink pen

4) a knobbly black twig (Huh?)

But then I realized pretty quickly that it wasn't a twig – it was a piece of charcoal, the sort of thing people drew with long ago, before chalk pencils were invented. My heart pitter-pattered again, same as it had when I scrambled down from my bedroom window just now. *This* wasn't just some mouldy brick garden shed.

"D'you think this was a little art studio or something?" I asked Peaches.

Peaches snored in reply, but as I straightened up, I glanced past his torn and tatty ears, and found my eyes settling on a something peeking out from behind a glass jar of bolts on the bottom row of shelves.

It was a wing.

A delicate, watercolour wing.

Stretching out of the chair, my fingers fumbled around in the dust, and pulled out a tiny tarnished frame, and in it, there was a hand-painted fairy, fluttering amongst flowers. It looked ancient. I mean, *seriously* ancient.

"Thought I saw you lurking in here!"

Lungeing out of my skin was turning into a habit today.

"Just doing a bit of exploring?" Dad smiled, a

halo of sunshine ringing his blond hair as he stood in the outhouse doorway.

"Uh-huh," I shrugged, feeling strangely shy, as if I'd been caught snooping around in someone's sock drawer while they'd nipped to the loo.

"Just thought I'd let you know that the computer's up and running. You've got a few messages. Hey, is this the cat that was in your room yesterday?"

Dad had offered to shoo Peaches out of my bedroom last night – back when he was just some strange, stray cat and not Peaches. I was glad now that I hadn't let Dad chase him away – and I'd have to *properly* introduce them to each other and tell Dad what I'd found out about my ginger shadow (i.e. he was weird, he was a wanderer, he liked custard cream biscuits).

But that would have to wait; just like rooting around some more for hidden secrets (and fairies) in the outhouse.

Right now all I wanted to do was brush the decades-old dust off my fingers, get to that computer, and write a great big techno hello to all my mates. . .!

Chapter 8

Frankie and the secret night out

Already the sun was on full beam outside our kitchen window, and it wasn't even 8.30 a.m. yet. It was going to be *baking* hot today.

And already I was feeling the heat – at least my right leg was. Peaches had wrapped himself so much around it that it was like I was wearing a furry moonboot.

"He really likes you, doesn't he?" Mum smiled, peering under the table at Peaches.

She was on the other side of the kitchen table from me and Dad, sitting in between Jake and Jamie's high chairs like a referee, ready to hold up a yellow card next time one of them aimed a soggy Weetabix at the other.

"He likes the bacon on Stella's plate, you mean!" Dad joked.

"So does Stella!" I said, raising my eyebrows and taking another bite of the ketchup-dripping bacon sarnie I'd just made. That was *one* good thing about this move – back home in London it was all healthy cereals for six days of the week, and unhealthy, fattening fry-ups on Sundays only. But this was Tuesday, and for the last four days, all we'd eaten was junk food. It was a bit like being on permanent holiday.

"So he slept on your bed all night again?" Mum asked.

"Mmm," I mumbled and nodded, my mouth full of sarnie.

Yes, Peaches had slept on my bed all night again, and *hadn't* done a disappearing act by the time morning came, even though my window was left open wide enough for him to escape if he'd wanted to.

"Well, if that cat's going to stay here, we'd better get him some *proper* food," said Mum, matter-of-factly. "I don't care what that old lady told you, it's not good for a cat to live on sardines and biscuits."

"And bacon!" Dad chipped in.

I narrowed my eyes and looked at both of them. Were they saying what I *thought* they were saying?

"You mean," I spluttered, gulping my breakfast down too fast, "I can *keep* Peaches?"

"Well, until he gets bored of us, if what that old lady was saying is true!" Dad grinned.

I was sort of in shock. Back in London, I'd tried

everything to get a pet. "Can I get a dog?" "No – its barking would bug the neighbours." "Can I get a cat?" "We don't have a garden – it wouldn't be fair." "Can I have a hamster?" "Their cages get too smelly." "Can I have a goldfish?" "Er, no." (I think my parents had got so used to saying no when it came to pets that it would have felt too weird for them to say *yes*.)

"Er . . . thanks!"

As I mumbled my stunned thank you, I reached down and scratched Peaches' head, and got a pleased "Prrrp!" in reply. Then he got distracted by a milk-mushy Weetabix that had just splatted from on high (courtesy of Jake) and went off to lick that. I think Peaches was going to like it here.

Glancing back up, I caught Mum and Dad giving each other secret little smiles. Hmm . . . what was *that* all about? And after years of being pet-phobic, how come they were suddenly suggesting we adopt this not-particularly-pretty specimen of cat-ness? Unless . . . unless they were just trying cheer me up, or *bribe* me. You know – Stella's not too happy being dragged here to the seaside, so let her keep the fleabag, if it cheers her up?

Not that I needed too much cheering up this morning. I was well chuffed when I checked my e-mails yesterday and found a flurry of hellos from my friends, all written at various times on Saturday – they hadn't forgotten me after all! Well, maybe Neisha had . . . there'd been nothing from her, but to be fair, she didn't have her own computer and during school holidays had to send and get her messages through her mum's computer at work.

"...the party was great, wasn't it? But ate too much of *everything* and feel sick now, so I thought I'd get up and e-mail you this. Or maybe I just feel sick 'cause I know you're leaving in a few hours! Sniff!" (That was Lauren, at 3.30 a.m. on Saturday.)

"...Seb is *soooooo* cool. Get butterflies in my tummy when I think of him kissing you! You are *sooooooooo* lucky, Stell!" (Parminder, 9.29 a.m., Saturday.)

"You better stay in touch, Stella Stansfield, or I'll never talk to you again! Ha ha ha!" (Eleni, 11.36 a.m., Saturday.)

"...me and Mum just finished tidying up the place. Kept finding streamers in weird places – best one was around the INSIDE of the parakeet's cage!" (Frankie, 12.10 p.m., Saturday.)

Aunt Esme wouldn't have been too chuffed about her precious Peetie being meddled with, but then Peetie had a bite worse than Jamie's, so I'd hate to see the hand of the person who'd decorated his cage when no one was looking. . .

"Oh, Stella – I meant to tell you," said Dad suddenly, a lump of scrambled egg speared on his fork. "I checked the computer earlier 'cause I was waiting for a quote back from a company about recycled floorboards."

Because I'm a very polite girl, I resisted the urge to yawn, and waited for Dad to get to the point.

"Anyway, I saw you got an e-mail from Neisha. Sorry, I should have mentioned it earlier. . ."

As I dived from my chair and disentangled my leg from his clutches, Peaches prrrped a surprised prrrp.

"Sorry!" I called back vaguely as I hurried through to pick up the last of my missing messages.

Hi Stella! Soz I didn't get back to your texts – I'm rubbish, I know.

Neisha's e-mail was dated yesterday, Monday, I noticed.

And couldn't sneak into Mum's work and do my e-mails till today. How's the new place? Hope it's not doing your head in. Things OK here – had fun night out on Saturday, but Frankie'll have told you about that already, I guess. We just hung out near the ponds on the Heath. Loads of people there – right laugh. Parminder dared Lauren to stick her feet in the water (you know how the ponds freak Lauren out – you'd think there were sharks in there or something!), and then Seb ran over and picked her up and pretended he was going to chuck her in! Lauren was going mental, but it wasn't like he was seriously going to do it!

Oops – Mum says her boss has just come in so I gotta go.

More soon!

Neish xxx

It took three read-throughs of Neisha's e-mail for me to work out why it bugged me so much. And then – of course – I realized. I'd spoken to Frankie last night, even if it *was* just a weirdly short, weirdly weird call, and she hadn't said *anything* about hanging out with Seb on Saturday night.

What exactly was my so-called best friend playing at?

"Look, I'm *sure* Frankie didn't tell you because she didn't want to rub it in," Mum suggested, expertly shooting out a hand and pulling the plastic tractor from Jamie's hand before he knew it was gone. "Bet you she didn't want you to feel bad about being so far away from your friends and what they were up to!"

"Maybe," I shrugged, leaning over the twin's buggy to inspect the damage Jamie's tractor had inflicted on Jake's nose (it wasn't *too* bad – only a medium-sized, throbbing red thump).

"The thing is, Stella –"

(Mum suddenly had to raise her voice, as Jamie began a mournful where's-my-toy-gone? howl.)

"– I think you're just feeling a little bit, well, *vulnerable* just now. All this –"

(She waved one hand around, as if she was talking about the shops on Portbore's minuscule high street.)

"– is *bound* to be unsettling for you. And Frankie's never let you down before, has she?"

I shook my head, as we passed a butcher's with a gruesome collection of meat slapped in the window.

"Well, then, just give her the benefit of the doubt. You can ask her all about it this weekend.

And – oh! Hey, look at this!"

Back in London, Mum got her hair cut at this flash, West End hairdresser that was part of a chain run by one of those guys who's always on telly ads flogging their straightening serums or whatever. Even after she'd stopped working ('cause of the twins), she still trekked to the same place, and wouldn't have stepped inside the *local* hairdresser's for a zillion pounds. Yet here she was, cooing over *The Style Compony Hair & Beauty Salon*, which looked about as glamorous as the butcher's next door.

"Stella, could you look after the boys for a sec? I just want to nip in and get a price list!"

Before I could say "OK", she'd disappeared inside, leaving me with the Muppets. It wasn't that I minded looking after Jake and Jamie. They couldn't embarrass me with their wailing (I was too used to it), but what *was* embarrassing was my mum's twittery excitement about this crummy place, a business that couldn't even spell its own *name* right. I mean, if the "Style Compony" was dyslexic on its fancy painted sign above the door, how good were they going to be at cutting hair and doing manicures? I'd be terrified I'd go in for highlights and come out with only one eyebrow.

"Anyway," I mumbled, crouching down and talking to Jake, who was happily smiling despite the throbbing bump on his nose, "what's the point of Mum getting a facial and her nails done when we live on a building site?"

"Hammer go BOOOMM!" Jake roared energetically.

Oh, yes, back home at the building site, a hammer was most definitely going boom. Straight after breakfast, Dad had taken a sledgehammer to a defenceless wall. The noise had been so bad that Peaches had vanished on his travels, and I'd had no choice but to come out shopping with Mum and the Muppets.

"Big lorry, big *LORRY*!"

That was Jamie, who'd stopped crying over his lost toy/weapon now that he had something bigger to ogle at. I felt the lorry before I saw it; the ground was trembling with the rumble of it. Or *them*, actually, since a whole convoy of trucks was thundering its way slowly down the high street, heading in the direction of the beach. Vast sheets of tarpaulin were stretched over the oddest of cargoes – vast, multicoloured arcs of metal dotted with rows of bulbs.

All the Fun of the Fair! read a logo on the side

of the first truck, now signalling right, past the fish and chip shop, to turn on to the prom.

And down at the bottom of the road, where the convoy was headed, I could have sworn I saw a flash of ginger fur disappearing behind the distant *Fresh haddock!* sign propped up on the pavement. . .

"Well! They're certainly very friendly in there!" Mum beamed, coming back out on to the sunny pavement clutching a bunch of leaflets.

I nearly jumped when I saw a small, middle-aged woman waving at me through the shop window: a vision of vivid lipstick, blusher and fluffy clouds of bleached blonde hair just 20 centimetres away from me through the glass.

"The owner gave you a lovely compliment!" Mum beamed, taking charge of the buggy and steering us away. "She said you had stunning hair!"

"Yeah, but I bet they wouldn't know how to cut hair like *mine*!" I grumbled, finding it hard to take a compliment from someone with a candyfloss hairdo (all that was missing was the *stick*).

"How do you know they've got no experience with afro hair?" Mum suddenly frowned at me. "You don't like it if people make assumptions about *you*, Stella, so you shouldn't go around making assumptions about other people!"

Urgh. . . I hated getting told off by Mum. It made me feel about as big as the boys. Feeling my face deepen to scarlet, I kept my eyes fixed on the glimpse of the sea just past the traffic lights and stayed schtum. Even the boys seemed to sense that Mum had snapped at me and shut up. Finally, after an agonizing three second silence, Mum spoke first.

"By the way, you know how you were asking about your grandad the other night?"

I shot her a shy sideways glance and nodded.

"Well, I got thinking last night, and I wondered if your nana had kept any letters from him, or souvenirs maybe."

My heart went *thud!* like something heavy had just dropped in my chest.

"The thing is," Mum continued, "I've still got a couple of boxes of her personal things that I cleared from her house when she died. I can't remember anything in particular being *in* there, but then I wasn't in a great mood when I was sorting through it at the time, so maybe I missed something."

"And you've never looked in those boxes in all

these years?!" I almost gasped, wondering how she could *do* that. Wasn't she in the least bit curious? Wasn't she interested in the possibility of finding out more about her own dad? Her own past?

"I didn't think I could face it before. Thought it would make me a bit sad to go through her things."

There I was, making assumptions again. OK, so Mum didn't feel all that strongly about the father she'd never known, but she *was* cut up about the mum she loved and missed. What a goofball I could be.

"If you find anything, that would be cool," I smiled at her. "But it's OK if you don't."

"Good!" Mum smiled back, as pleased as I was to be friends again. "When I get a minute, I'll check through it all."

Ah, now *that* was the problem.

Between getting the house straight, trying to discourage my dad from demolishing the place around our ears, and stopping the twins from hitting, biting or generally torturing each other, the next time Mum was likely to get a spare minute was probably about a *decade* away. . .

Chapter 9

The way to Sugar Bay. . .

I've got two crystal-clear memories from childhood.

One is of Mum yelling, "No! Don't lick *that*!" when I was about three and curious to see what flavour slugs were.

The other is of a day trip to Southend with Aunt Esme and Frankie when me and Frankie were about four. I can't remember much about the day trip itself, but I remember sitting next to Frankie on the train home, comparing treasures we'd found on the beach. Frankie's included a dead starfish, a big stick and a stone in the shape of a bum (sort of). My treasures were two pockets crammed with seashells and a mangy piece of tinfoil that I was convinced was part of a mermaid's tail, and absolutely *wouldn't* let Aunt Esme take it off me and put it in the bin where it belonged.

Well, I don't think I'd have got all that excited by the glitter of a minging sliver of tinfoil these days, but my pockets were rapidly filling up with sheeny-shiny shells. Don't know why I was bothering to collect them though; if I took them home, Jake and Jamie would probably just *eat* them or something.

After this morning's exciting shopping trip (i.e. going to the chemist's, the hairdresser's and the world's smallest branch of Woolworths), Mum, me and the boys had come home for lunch, only to find that Dad had sledgehammered his way through a water pipe in the wall. I thought Mum might pick up the sledgehammer and do some damage to *Dad* with it, but instead, she helped Jake and Jamie into their wellies, handed them some toast, and let them eat their "lunch" on the move, gleefully kicking around in the puddle on our dining-room/disaster-zone floor. Twenty minutes later, the boys were just going down for their nap when the emergency plumber arrived, so I abandoned my mop, got out of the way, and escaped down here to the beach.

At first, I whiled away the time sitting on the sand texting all of my mates. *Bored, hot, miss u guys. What u up 2? Luv stella.* I tried not to think about the fact that this was the fourth time I'd texted Lauren, Eleni and Parminder, and heard exactly *zilch* back from them since their flurry of Saturday e-mails. (I'd forgive Neisha, since she'd e-mailed just yesterday.)

Texting done, I doodled in the sand with my finger and then got into some people-watching. There were loads of families sunbathing (i.e. going various shades of lobster pink); some small kids happily burying another small kid in the sand (and ignoring his pleas to let him up); a bunch of day-tripping OAPs paddling in the shallows (giggling like they were seven and not 70); a short kid walking a big, hairy Alsatian (or maybe it was the other way around); and I even saw the woman from the Style Compony, letting her high heels sink in the sand as she held the leads of two small dogs that looked like the waddling equivalent of the blonde bouffant on her head (she waved, but I pretended I was watching the OAPs and didn't wave back).

After that, I tried lying down and watching the seagulls swirl around in the sky, but it made me kind of dizzy. So I stood up and started strolling, picking up shells that took my fancy, stopping to gawp for a minute at the fairground lorries unloading in the prom car park, and then found myself slap-bang running out of beach. Towering in front of me instead was a big cliffy bit of rock, partly covered in grass, with a meandering path weaving up it. Holding a hand above my eyes, I squinted at the two signs in front of me, at the top of the short flight of concrete steps that led up from what was left of the beach to the start of the path. One of the signs was made out of metal, and in red lettering on a bright-yellow background, it said *Seaview Holiday Homes* (must have taken the caravan park owners all of three seconds to come up with *that* name). The other sign was wooden, badly faded, and hard to read.

"*Uger ay...*" I mumbled to myself, then bounded up the steps – shells clanking together in my pockets – for a better squint.

Sugar Bay.

While my head was still processing that information, my feet had already made up their mind – the faded arrow next to the faded lettering was aimed up the path and over the hill, and that's where my trainers were taking me.

Five breathless minutes later, I was at the top of the headland, staring at a breathtaking view of . . . caravans. Well, OK, it was caravans straight in front of me, but if I turned around and looked back the way I'd come, there was a pretty, er, *pretty* view of the town and the bustling beach below, stretching right along to the bobbing masts of small boats in the faraway harbour.

"Cawww!"

I flipped my head back round at that ugly sound, and saw one of Portbore's huge seagulls surveying me from the roof of one of the caravans.

"'Cawww' to you too!" I called to it, wondering if it was any relation to the fairy-cake fan from yesterday.

In what felt like slow motion, the big bird extended its wings, flopped off the roof and seemed to be aiming itself straight at *me*. I was just about to panic and break the world speed record for Hurtling Back Down A Windy Path when the bird spun lazily round and with a couple of flaps disappeared over the metal roofs, towards ... well, towards Sugar Bay, as my trainers seemed to know, even if my brain didn't. Stomping my way around a few white, cream and grey caravans, I suddenly stopped dead as the view opened up in front of me.

Sugar Bay curved below like a new moon, the tiny bay as blue as those you see in the Caribbean on holiday programmes on telly. The beach looked like someone (very big) had poured out tonnes of demerara sugar around the edge of the grassy hills that swooped down to meet the water. (Was that how it got its name?) And the weirdest thing about the beach was that it was empty: not an ice-cream van, not a kid, not even a sandcastle was in sight. How come none of the holidaymakers from Seaview was down there? But then maybe the lure of 99 cones, candyfloss and public toilets on Portbore Beach won them over.

Or maybe the house put them off.

The Big House the old lady had told me about yesterday . . . there it was, fancy and grand but falling down, like a cross between a wedding cake and the sort of place the Addams Family might live in. I was kind of spooked by the look of it, but luckily – or *unluckily*, depending on your point of view – my feet were much braver, and started walking down the gravelly path towards it.

As I got closer, I could see red brickwork peeking through the decades-old (centuries-old?) cream paintwork. There were gaping holes in the glass windowpanes – windows like a more glam version of the one tiny window in the outhouse I'd been exploring this morning. (Bored thugs must have been using it as target practice. Then again, it was so old, maybe *generations* of bored thugs were responsible for the damage.) As I got closer still, the garden reminded me of our overgrown jungle too – this one was a muddle of daisies, dandelions, tangled rose bushes and towering purple somethings.

I leant on the ornate, rusted fence that ran round the garden and stared up at the crumbly grandness of it, but for the *brave* part of me (i.e. my feet), that wasn't enough. And so I ducked through the gap where a couple of railings had rusted away, pushed my way through the undergrowth, passed an ivy-covered sign that read *Dan keep out!* (ignoring the fact that there was almost definitely a "ger" lurking under those ivy leaves) and found myself at a window. Only problem was, my eyes were in line with the *sill*.

In a manoeuvre Mrs Kitson my old PE teacher would have been proud of (hey, I was turning into a bit of a gymnast today, if you counted the scramble from my bedroom to the garden too), I launched myself up, scrabbling my trainers on the brickwork and breathlessly thudded my elbows on to the cold, paint-peeling sill.

And I saw . . . nothing. 'Cause right then, my

mobile started ringing and I started slithering, and landed back on the daisies with a thud, and a crunch of shells in my jeans pockets.

"Hi Stella!"

"Mum?" I panted.

"Why are you breathless? Where are you?"

Clambering around a condemned building didn't sound like the sort of answer she'd be delighted to hear, so I told her . . . the truth. Well, it was the truth, five minutes earlier.

"Just walked up the hill to the caravan park, so I could check the view."

"Really? That's nice!"

Let me translate: Mum had just said, "You're kidding? That's brilliant! I thought you hated this place!"

"So what are you phoning for?" I asked, idly plucking at some of the big purple somethings beside me.

"Er . . . do you remember that old-fashioned ironmonger's we passed this morning?"

"Nope," I told her, staring at the rows of bell-shaped blossoms on the long, straggly stalks in my hand.

"Yes you do – it's on the high street."

"Don't remember it," I said warily, wondering

what this was all about. Mum obviously wanted me to pick up something on the way home (again). But I didn't even know what an ironmonger sold. Iron? Had Dad broken something else that only iron could fix?

"You *do*!" Mum insisted. "It's in between the newsagent and the undertaker!"

I don't know if it was the mention of the undertaker that gave me the shivers, but suddenly, I didn't feel in much of a rush to look inside that dark window above me. Suddenly, my feet felt as cowardly as the rest of me and I started picking my way across the garden.

"So you want me to buy something from there?" I asked, wriggling my way speedily through the gap in the railings, and trailing the flowers behind me like a peacock feather.

"Um, yes please. Some stain remover for ink. They're bound to sell it."

"What's Dad done this time?" I grinned, glancing over my shoulder at the house, now that I was a safe, non-spooky distance away.

"It's not your dad. It's, er, Jamie. He found a felt pen somewhere and started drawing. On your duvet cover. Sorry."

You know, I didn't care if they were only two

years old and didn't know any better – Jamie and Jake were going to *have* to stay out of my room, if they wanted to make it to *three*. . .

Chapter 10

Broken shells and cheery "bleep!"s

"Could I have a fuse, please?"

"Certainly," the mild-mannered bald man behind the counter smiled at the woman in front of me. "What size? Three amp, five amp, 13 amp?"

"Er, is there a difference?" the woman asked, sounding flummoxed.

"Well, yes, if you don't want to fit the wrong size to your appliance and burn your house down."

Good grief, this woman sounded as useless at DIY as my dad. But I didn't mind that there was a dithery customer ahead of me in the ironmonger's – it gave me a chance to practise asking what I wanted in my head, in the hope that I wouldn't curl up with shyness and start stammering. (I'm a big fan of supermarkets and mini-markets – you pick what you want and hand over the money, no talking or stammering required.)

It also gave me a chance to gawp around the shop – now that I was here, it looked like the sort of place that might sell huge, toddler-repelling padlocks for bedroom doors. I didn't have enough money on me to get one today, but I'd know where to come back to. . .

"Foxgloves!"

"Huh?"

My mind had been too full of the joy of padlocks to notice that Mrs Fuse had been dealt with and that the baldy bloke behind the counter was ready to help me out. Except I didn't know what he was on about.

"Foxgloves!" he smiled some more, pointing to the long, lanky purple flowers I'd taken with me from the garden of the house in Sugar Bay.

"Oh! That's the name of our house!" I squeaked in surprise at the coincidence.

"Foxglove Cottage? Very nice place – needs a bit of work though!"

I could see a happy twinkle in the shopkeeper's eye, as if he could sense months' worth of custom coming his way now a family of mugs from London had moved into the old, falling-down shack.

"Uh-huh," I nodded, wondering if the lake on the ground floor had been fixed by now – I'd forgotten to ask Mum when she'd called. "Have you got any stain remover, for ink, please?"

I suddenly felt quite proud of myself: I'd been so taken aback to find out what a foxglove looked like and then got caught up in fleeting visions of wearing wellies to breakfast in the morning that I'd forgotten to be nervous in front of this stranger.

"Stain remover? For *ink*? Are you sure that's the one you want?"

"Uh, yes, please," I told him, instantly feeling as flummoxed as Mrs Fuse. What was this guy on about?

"Oh, right. It's just that I thought you were after something to remove *that*."

Omigod, he was pointing at my *chest*!

"Red-brick dust is a devil to get out!" he blustered, suddenly looking excruciatingly shy himself, as if he'd realized the boob (argh!) he'd made. "Like the . . . um . . . like the stamens on lilies! Terrible, they are. . ."

We were *both* blushing now. And then it dawned on me what he was trying to get across. I glanced down and saw that the front of my pale pink T-shirt was covered in vivid, gingery-red powder.

"So, er, been up to Josephs' House, then?" he asked, pulling a box packed with stain removers off a shelf and rifling through it. "Only place around here built of red brick. They imported it specially when they were building the place! Of course they went and painted it when the fashion changed."

Luckily, he was rifling so hard in the box that it gave me precious seconds to figure out what he meant *now*.

"The house in Sugar Bay?" I checked with him. "Is that what it's called?"

"Oh, yes. Magnificent, it must have been, in the old days," the man chattered away, looking relieved to be off the uncomfortable subject of my chest. "Time's running out for it now, of course. It's getting demolished at the end of summer, to make way for luxury holiday chalets."

Can you feel sad for a house? If you'd asked me before, I'd have said I didn't think so, but now there was a tug at my heart at the thought of that grand old place being torn down and carted away in dumper trucks. It was the same sort of painful tug I felt when I thought of dirty, overcrowded, wonderful London and the brilliant friends I'd had to leave behind. . .

But a small "bleep!" soon cheered me up. I heard it just as I stepped out of the ironmonger's shop and on to the sun-bleached pavement, holding the foxgloves in the crook of one arm while I stuffed the stain remover into the front pocket of my jeans, which were already stuffed with (broken?) shells.

From my back pocket, I grabbed my phone, gagging to see who'd texted me.

You have 1 new message.

Top of my wish list would have been a message from Seb, saying *hi, how are you?* (I *wish*!), and bottom would have been Mum texting to tell me the boys had set my room on fire or something. But anything in between – *any* contact with the outside world – would be *bliss*.

Know something u need to know – can't talk now will call u later. N xxx

Neish! It was from Neisha!

Now it was my stomach's turn to do gymnastics; flipping into a few forward rolls and doing a star jump with excitement. Maybe it was some weird psychic thing, but with a sudden rush I knew, KNEW, KNEW that the "something" I needed to know about was connected with Seb. Had he been asking about me? I didn't know whether I felt more like singing or being sick with sheer happiness.

One thing was for sure – I'd be counting the *seconds* till Neisha phoned me. . .

Chapter 11

A watched mobile never rings

Fourteen thousand, four hundred and twenty seconds later, and I was *still* waiting for Neisha to call.

"Stella! Careful!" Mum frowned at me, as she tried to prise Bob the Builder's sponge head out from between Jamie's four front teeth.

Oops. Guess I *had* been rubbing Jake's grubby face with the flannel a little bit too long; I'd probably taken a layer of skin off as well as the different shades of dirt he had smeared on it.

"Sorry," I mumbled, dropping the flannel in the water and staring at my brother's face for signs of grazing or scuffing. But Jake was fine. He just said "Boo!" and then blew spit bubbles out of his chubby, baby lips at me. (Yuck.)

To tell the truth, I hadn't been concentrating much on the twins' bathtime – after doing my mental arithmetic to figure out how long it had been since I'd heard from Neisha, I'd gone on to wonder how many seconds it had been since I'd heard from Eleni, Lauren and Parminder. I'm not very good at doing maths in my head and after a few attempts, I'd settled on twelvety trillion before Mum hauled me up about accidentally smothering Jake with the facecloth.

Then I heard the sound I'd been waiting for. . .

"Can I. . .?" I started, turning to Mum with a hopeful expression at the sound of the phone ringing.

Walking home from the ironmonger's; helping Mum wash and hang out my duvet cover; all through tea . . . I'd kept staring at my mobile, willing it to trill into life. And when I wasn't doing all *that* stuff, I was running through to the cupboard my dad was optimistically calling his "office" and checking the computer in case Neisha had decided to spill her news by e-mail. There'd been nothing. But maybe this was Neish now, calling on the house phone!

"Let your dad get it – the boys, remember?"

The boys. . . How could I forget? It took two of us (i.e. a rotating combination of Mum, Dad and me) to look after them when they were in the bath. That's 'cause something pretty bizarre happened whenever they came in contact with water: it was like they mutated into hyperactive octopuses, capable of chucking *more* toys and inflicting *more* damage on fixtures, fittings and each other than when they were on dry land (which is saying something).

Actually, it was probably Dad's turn to let one of us off the hook with bathtime duties, but our routine had kind of gone out the window – along with our normal lives – since we'd arrived. And last time I saw him, Dad was headed out to the skip with a dripping roll of soggy lino balanced on his shoulder.

I bit my lip, but did as I was told, turning my attention back to Jake and his spit bubbles while I waited to hear Dad answer the phone . . . and then – hopefully – call for me to come and get it?

"Andy?" Mum shouted, as the phone kept ringing.

"ANNNDEEEEE!" Jamie mimicked her, for the sheer fun of having something to yell.

"He must be still out at the skip," I told her, when we heard nothing but silence in reply. My heart was thudding in my chest – I was desperate not to let that caller slip away unanswered.

"The answerphone will click on," Mum said assuredly, standing Jamie up and getting ready to lift him out of the bath.

"ANSRAPHONNNNNNE!!" Jamie threw his head back and bellowed.

"Mum, Dad hasn't set up the answerphone machine yet, remember?"

Mum looked at my imploring face and gave in. "OK, go get it!" she half-smiled, half-shrugged.

I was out like a shot, Jamie's roars of, "GO GET ITTTTTT!!" ringing in my ears.

"Hello?" I panted, after jumping down the rickety stairs five steps at a time.

"Hello! How's my favourite niece?"

Auntie V – great. The only gossip I was likely to hear from *her* was the ridiculous demands of her latest client (there was always some actor wanting flowers/pizzas/Toblerone in their dressing rooms written into their contract). But that wasn't the type of gossip I was interested in tonight.

"Auntie V, I'm your *only* niece," I pointed out, spotting a non-compliment when I heard one.

"Favourite niece, only niece – what's the difference?" she said breezily. "So anyway, how are you enjoying life in your new hovel?"

I couldn't help grinning at Auntie V's cheerful sarkiness.

"The hovel is horrible," I smiled. "It's damp. And smelly. And there's black mould on the bathroom wall, and the bottom of the toilet's all green for some reason."

"Yee-*eewww*," Auntie V grimaced from the comfort of her posh flat in Highgate, with its tasteful antiques and framed theatre posters on the walls.

"Yeah," I added, warming to my theme, "and some plaster fell off the kitchen ceiling tonight, straight into the risotto Dad was making!"

"Oh, that's *gross*, Stella! What did you do, did you have to send out for something to eat?"

"There's only a fish and chip shop here, and they don't deliver!" I laughed, thinking how much Auntie V would loathe Portbore, since it didn't have any of her essentials for life (Chinese takeaways, heaps of theatres, antique markets, posh coffee shops that sold drinks called frappamochachino or whatever).

"How depressing!" Auntie V sighed theatrically. "And what's Portbay like, then?"

"It's Port*bore*, and it's a dump," I set her straight, sort of enjoying being as sarcastic as *she* was for once. It was quite a buzz feeling like I was bantering along with Auntie V, instead of her being my glamorous, confident, mouthy aunt and me being just shy and quiet Stella the non-star. . .

"Poor darling . . . you must really be missing Frankie etc."

I knew Auntie V said "etc." to save time, but it also saved her from remembering details she couldn't be bothered to remember – like the names of all my other friends.

"Yeah, I am. But Frankie's coming at the weekend."

"And so am I!"

"You are?" I gasped, thrilled at the idea of having two allies in the house at the same time.

"Oh, yes – I'm coming to see the slum for myself. But I'm only there on Sunday, for the day – I told your dad that he can't expect me to stay overnight till the place is habitable!"

"Well, you'll never stay, then!" I giggled. "The house was a disaster to start with, but he's making it worse – he flooded the place this morning!"

"Oh, God . . . don't tell me any more, Stella, or I'll change my mind about coming, even for just the day!" Auntie V groaned. "Anyway, is Mr DIY Disaster around? I'd better have a quick word. . ."

"Sure, I'll go and find him," I told her, still smiling.

"No need to find me; I'm here," Dad said softly, from somewhere close by.

You know Aunt Esme's catchphrases? Well, growing up, me and Frankie had one favourite: "Don't do bad things – bad things have a habit of coming back and biting you on the bottom!" We loved it 'cause it sounded so silly, not to mention good and rude (to us six year olds anyway). But *finally* I think I saw the point of that particular saying. After mouthing off so sarcastically to Auntie V, turning around and clocking the look of hurt and disappointment on Dad's kind face made me feel *terrible*.

Yep, I think I'd done a bad thing and just had it come back and bite me on the bottom. . .

Where are u? What's the thing I need to know? Luv S, I tippety-tapped into my phone.

After I'd zapped that text off to Neisha, I bit my lip and stared out of my bedroom window, watching – but not really seeing – the seagulls swirling in the streaky pink, sunset-tinged sky.

I was freaked out, if you want to know the truth. OK, so I'd spoken to Frankie once and had an e-mail and a (mysterious) text off Neisha, but none of my other friends had got back to any texts or messages I'd left on their mobiles the last few days. Er . . . had they *all* forgotten to charge them, or swipe their top-up cards lately? With my heart sinking faster than the *Titanic*, I wondered if – when it came to my gang of girls back in London – little old faraway me was out-of-sight and out-of-mind.

Then I realized – doh! – that I was being paranoid again. This was starting to be a habit, I frowned to myself. All I needed to do to put my angsty mind at rest was call them on their home numbers, instead of their switched-off mobiles.

I was just about to start with Neisha (since she was the one with the hot gossip), when there was a light knock at my bedroom door.

"Come in," I called out wobbly-voiced, feeling myself tense in case it was Dad. I still felt kind of sick at how upset he looked when he caught me whingeing to Auntie V an hour or so ago.

"Hey. . .!"

Urgh, it *was* Dad. Just chuck a bucket of guilt over me right now.

116

"Come and see this, Stella!" he beckoned me.

He seemed OK – not as gutted as he'd looked earlier. I slid off the bed and followed him out of my room, wondering what he wanted to show me, and wondering if I could manage to say sorry to him without a) feeling horribly embarrassed, and b) stammering.

"Check this out!" Dad said softly, opening the door to the twins' room and treading quietly inside, which was actually kind of hard to do considering every floorboard in our house creaked like a cross between a mouse squeak and a loud fart every time you hovered a foot over one of them.

"Aww. . ."

Awkward as I felt around Dad right that second, I couldn't help smiling at my brothers, all tucked up in the cots they were rapidly outgrowing. It's corny to say it, but little kids do look angelic when they're asleep. Well, maybe Jake and Jamie didn't look *angelic* exactly – Jake had a fat finger wedged comfortably up one nostril and Jamie had drool all down his chin – but it *was* very cute, the way they'd stuck their arms through the bars and snoozed off holding hands. . .

"They haven't got a lot to worry about, have they?" Dad suddenly surprised me by murmuring affectionately, wrapping one of his arms around my shoulders and squeezing tight.

I didn't know what Dad meant exactly. And, anyway, I was pretty sure that Jake and Jamie did their fair share of toddler-sized worrying (Jamie: "Is that fat kid going to steal my fish finger again?"; Jake: "Is that skinny kid going to bite me again?").

"What I'm trying to say is, I know it's going to take you a while to settle in here, Stella, and I totally understand that it's not an easy thing to do," Dad carried on, as we both stared down at the snoozling, drooling boys. "But remember it's hard for your mum and me too; once we've got the house straight, I'm going to have to find a new job, and it's not easy for your mum to leave all her friends and London behind. . ."

I suspected that Dad was trying to comfort me. But all it did was confuse me even *more*.

"So, we've all got to give it a bit of time, yeah, Stell?"

Suddenly, I felt kind of *mad* at him for making out that me, him and Mum were all in the same boat, 'cause that wasn't exactly true, was it? After all, *they* chose to move here – *I* didn't.

OK, so now I was simultaneously confused

and mad, and the clash of those two feelings made me plain *nervous*. And what do I do when I'm nervous? Well, I clam up; usually after a tongue-tied stammer or two.

"Um, O-O-O-OK, D-Dad. . ." I mumbled in vague reply, ducking slightly to get out from under his arm before zooming out of the room so fast that the floorboards didn't even have time to squeak/fart. . .

Chapter 12

Peace and toast

"*Huurrrrunggg-uuurrr-uurr-uurr. . .!*"

It was quarter to eight, it was Wednesday morning, it was two days till Frankie arrived, and the loudest snorty snore in the world – snored about two centimetres from my ear – had just woken me up.

"Morning, Peaches," I blinked sleepily at the scruffy lump of cat sprawled across my pillow in a dappled shaft of sunlight. "Where've you been?"

I hadn't seen him since yesterday morning, when Dad had begun demolishing walls and water pipes with the sledgehammer.

"*Humph-urr-urr. . .*" Peaches snored in reply, his chunky hairy legs and uneven whiskers twitching as he chased a seagull or a sardine in his dreams.

Y'know, last night I'd really hoped he'd come hopping in through my window: I could have done with the company (or at least a friendly, furry cuddle), since I was feeling a bit, well, *weird* after that odd, one-sided talk with Dad in the boys' room. But sadly, the only thing that had come through the open window was a breeze that smelled of salt, seaweed and peaches and cream. When I finally fell asleep, my dreams were full of me running along sand-covered corridors in strange, old, crumbly houses, never finding the way out, or the way home...

"Hey!" I muttered softly, pushing myself up on my elbow for a closer inspection of a strange something dangling around Peaches' neck. "That's a bit of a girly collar for you!"

Not that it was a collar exactly; more a chain, a soft-petalled daisy chain. Who'd put *that* around his neck? Some little girl trying to give this scruffbucket a makeover?

"Stella, are you awake?" I heard Mum's voice drift from the other side of my bedroom door.

"Uh-huh!" I mumbled. She must have heard me muttering to Peaches.

"A-ha! I see the wanderer has returned!" Mum smiled, sticking her head around the door and nodding at my fat cat.

"Um, yeah," I nodded, wondering if she and Dad had talked about me last night, after I'd practically walked out on Dad in mid-conversation and hid out in my room for the rest of the night. But nothing in Mum's normal, friendly face gave anything away.

"Listen," she said, tucking a chunk of dark hair behind her ear, "a postcard's just arrived for you!"

"Who from?" I frowned, even though I felt a flutter of excitement.

"Well, you'll just have to come downstairs and see, won't you?" Mum teased. "It's on the kitchen table. If you get dressed first, I'll have a fried egg and toast waiting beside it! Oh, and cat food for your friend, of course!"

Two minutes, clean underwear, my Bugs Bunny T-shirt and denim mini later, I was padding down the stairs (wishing I'd slipped on my flip-flops, to avoid that common condition in these parts: splinters-of-the-toes). Peaches hadn't even stirred when I'd whispered "Tuna Felix!" in his ear, so I'd left him happily sprawled on my pillow.

At the bottom of the stairs I hesitated, almost turning to the computer cupboard on automatic pilot to check my e-mails (if our computer was a human, I think it would have accused me of *stalking* it). But I resisted, lured by the wonderful waft of Sunday-breakfast-on-a-Wednesday and *more* than curious to see who the postcard was from, even though I suspected it was only some *Greetings From Cromer!* silliness from Grandpa and Granny in Norfolk.

"Hi, honey!" Dad beamed at me, as he heaped a mound of scrambled egg on Mum's plate. "One slice of bacon or two?"

Looked like he didn't realize how weirded out I'd felt when we spoke last night – or he was just pretending, at least. Either way, it was fine by me – I just wanted to forget it too.

"Two, please," I smiled shyly, slithering into the nearest chair.

Mum had put the foxgloves in her favourite tall glass vase in the middle of the table, I noticed. Still, the size they were, I couldn't *miss* them, really.

Speaking of missing. . .

"Where're Jake and Jamie?"

"Not awake yet, for once. Great, isn't it?" Mum grinned, looking like she was really going to enjoy eating a mountain of breakfast using a knife and fork, instead of snatching the occasional bite of toast in between feeding, wiping and restraining the twins. "Anyway, there's your card!"

The front of the postcard Mum had just flipped

across the table towards me showed a head-and-shoulders picture of the Queen, complete with round specs, crossed eyes and a moustache hand-drawn on in blue pen.

"Frankie!" I grinned, spotting her handiwork straight away. And sure enough. . .

Big hi from London! Can't WAIT till Friday. The Kentish Town girls versus Portbay – hurray! Frankie xxx

"That's sweet of her, isn't it?" said Mum, meaning – I guess – that it was sweet of Frankie to send me a postcard, not sweet of her to go defacing Prince William's granny.

"Yeah, it is," I smiled, forgiving Frankie instantly for being so rubbish at keeping in touch since I left London. After all, what were a few lame days compared to a lifetime of being a top friend?

"Um, Stella, while we've got a bit of peace, your mum and I wanted a quick word with you," said Dad, plonking a plate of egg, bacon and beans in front of me, even though I'd instantly lost my appetite for them 'cause of what he just said.

Uh-oh . . . what was coming? Was I about to get a lecture about my attitude?

"Stella, like your dad was trying to say last night, we know this move has been hardest on you," Mum began. "And there's not a lot we can do to help make you feel at home here – that'll just happen when it happens."

Y'know, I could feel a stammer tripping about my tongue already and I hadn't even planned on *saying* anything.

"But maybe there is one thing we can do. . ." Dad added, intriguingly. "We know it's annoying for you, now that the boys are finding it easier to get into your room. So yesterday, I was rooting around in the outhouse, and I found these. . ."

Er, I didn't know what exactly I was looking at (or supposed to think exactly). I guess Dad could tell, probably because I wasn't saying anything and was looking as confused as I usually did when my German teacher expected me to understand the dative case.

"They're antique sliding bolts," Mum explained, making sort-of-sense of the two matching, ornate bits of dirty-looking metal in front of me. "They're made of brass; they'll polish up beautifully."

Nope, I still hadn't a clue *what* my parents were on about.

"We're sending all the doors away to be dipped

and stripped soon, Stella," Dad started up again, "and once they're back, I'm going to fit these sliding bolts on either side of your bedroom door – high up – so you can always keep the boys at bay."

As it sank in, I began to smile. They appreciated the fact that I needed my privacy! I'd have been tempted right then and there to give both my parents a hug for being so kind and thoughtful – if they hadn't been responsible for making me move away from London in the first place.

"Tell her the other thing, Andy!" Mum suddenly butted in.

"Ah, yes! Right – we were thinking, till that's done, you could probably do with your own space, for all your art stuff and your bits and pieces."

"So we thought of the outhouse in the garden!"

I blinked at Mum and Dad and then back again. From the smiles on their faces, I think they assumed I was stunned with surprise. Instead I was thinking: "What – you expect me to sit in there, with a bunch of spiders and the dust-mites for company?"

Suddenly I knew what Cinderella felt like. . .

"We can chuck all the rubbish in the skip, and it closes with a hook and eye latch that's too high for Jake or Jamie to reach," Dad chattered away enthusiastically. "And there's even electricity – I fitted a new bulb in the casing and it works fine!"

"And we can clear it out, give it a good going over with a brush and Mr Sheen!" Mum suggested.

Hmm. . . OK, so suddenly I *wasn't* feeling so much like a second-best Cinderella. Maybe having the outhouse as a den could be kind of cool. After all, it had been someone's art studio once, so maybe it could be mine? I could stash my art stuff on the shelves and stick my caricatures around the walls and –

"MEEEEE-*YYYYOWWWWWWWW*!" came a cat-in-trouble screech from upstairs.

In the split-second that Mum, Dad and me stared at each other, we heard another terrible, terrifying sound coming from the floor above.

"Hee-hee-hee!"

Uh-oh – twins on the rampage. . .

Chapter 13

Pocahontas of Portbore

I'd found buried treasure.

It was only buried under layers of dust and cobwebs, but it was still treasure. My haul included: a knobbly bottle with the words "ginger beer" on it in raised glass bumps; a rusted box of half-used watercolour paints; a silver-framed mirror with more dark spots on it than actual *mirror*; a pretty, chipped cup with roses painted on it, some old-fashioned decorated tins advertising stuff like sweets and tea (but which had held nails and screws that I'd chucked away), and a small wooden box with the initials *E G* neatly carved on the top (empty, except for a discoloured gold-ish metal button, which I'd kept).

They were now all on display on my newly scrubbed shelves, along with all my art stuff, a framed picture of Grandpa and Granny Stansfield (taken at Christmas last year, with silly paper hats on their heads) and another one of Nana Jones (taken in the late '60s, with lots of make-up and very hairsprayed strawberry blonde hair).

"Hey, it's looking great in here!" said Mum, appearing in the doorway of the outhouse, one hand on the hip of her jeans. The other hand was holding a jam-jar crammed with pastel-coloured sweetpeas and curly, ferny leaves that she must have picked from amongst the weeds in the garden.

"Yeah, it's all right," I agreed, glancing around at the results of five and a half hours' worth of de-scuzzing the place and feeling pretty chuffed with myself – and Dad, of course. Ignoring proper work in the house, he'd helped me out the whole time, making dozens of trips back and forth to the skip with rusted, mangled gardening tools and assorted useless junk. I'd done all the sifting, sorting, discovering of buried treasure and frantic scrubbing – while Mum kept up a steady supply of buckets of hot, soapy water in the few snatched minutes here and there when she managed to escape the twins.

"That's brilliant!" she laughed, plonking the jar of flowers down on the wooden desk by the window, right beside my carefully placed collection of (the unbroken) shells from the beach. She was pointing at the caricature of the old lady I'd met on Monday. I'd pinned it to the corkboard I'd taken down from my room, right next to my drawing of Neisha and Lauren. Also on the board was the photo-booth strip of me and Frankie, the postcard of the cross-eyed Queen and the flyer for the funfair I'd found in my room the other night, under Peaches' fat tummy. There was also a small space for a Polaroid, or *part* of a Polaroid, if I ever (fingers crossed) happened to find the mangled photo of me and Seb.

"It's just all so . . . *cosy*!" Mum smiled, her fingers stroking the smooth surfaces of the shells, while her eyes darted from the felt hat that I'd dusted off and dangled on a nail on the wall, to the tiny fairy painting hanging pride of place beside the window, right above the desk.

"The rug helps. So does the curtain," I told her, feeling grateful for Mum's donations. The multicoloured rug used to live on Dad's office floor in the old flat ("We'll get a new one once his office here is done up," she'd told me), and the "curtain" was a floaty, chiffon sarong of hers ("Don't think it would fit round my bottom since I've had the boys!").

Then I saw her eyes settle on the circle of ginger

furriness balled up and snoring on the armchair that used to be in her and Dad's bedroom back in Kentish Town ("Our room's smaller here – there's not a lot of room for this chair so you might as well have it for your den.").

"Hmm. . ." she muttered, raising an eyebrow. "Seems like Peaches thinks this place is pretty cosy too!"

Peaches did look very rela*aaaaxxxxeeeeddd* indeed – unlike this morning, when we'd caught Jake and Jamie trying to dress him up in one of their toy's clothes. Or maybe he'd just made a meowling fuss because he wasn't a big Fireman Sam fan and didn't particularly want to wear his helmet.

"Hey. . ." I suddenly began, narrowing my eyes and peering at the fat cat. "What's he got there?"

As Peaches snoozed, I noticed that he was tenderly holding something between his two front paws. It was like he was doing an impression of the boys when they were tucked up in their cots, hugging their Boohbahs close to their chests.

"It's a feather, isn't it?" Mum suggested, peering closer herself. "A seagull feather, by the look of it. Hope he didn't kill one to get it!"

"I doubt it," I laughed, wrinkling up my nose.

"Have you seen the size of the seagulls here? They're bigger than *him*!"

"I suppose!" she smiled. "Anyway, never mind seagulls; have you seen *yourself* recently?"

Stepping sideways, I peered into the splotchy mirror I'd hung up on the back wall and checked out my reflection. Eyes, nose, mouth, hair (held at bay in two short, stubby braids); all of them were where they were supposed to be. But my freckles; they were practically hidden under a dark smudge of dirt smeared *right* across my nose and cheeks.

The stripe of dirt put a dumb idea into my head – reaching down, I teased the feather out of Peaches' paws, stuck it in my hair and turned to Mum.

"Am I a dead ringer for Pocahontas, then?" I grinned at her. "What do you reckon?"

"I reckon I should get the camera!" Dad's bright and sea-breezy voice replied instead. "And speaking of photos, is this yours?"

Standing behind Mum in the outhouse doorway, my grinning Dad looked as dirty and dusty as I did. He leant forward and held out a well-crumpled, jaggedly torn photo that looked tiny next to the big red builder's glove he was wearing.

Seb!

"I just looked in on the boys on the way back from the skip," Dad chattered on, "and I caught them posting cornflakes – and this – down the gaps between the floorboards!"

I grabbed the remains of the Polaroid, my heart thundering under my dust-covered T-shirt.

And there was Seb . . . missing.

All I was staring at was my own face gazing back at me, and a big, ripped space where Seb's should have been. . .

Hi Seb, I typed into the keypad, *it's Stella.*

I sat back on the swivel chair and swivelled a bit, trying to figure out what to write next. I'd got the idea to text Seb when I was in the shower, washing plaster dust – and seagull feathers – out of my hair. As the water hammered down, a thought had drummed into my head: *Just text him! Just say hi! What's the worst that can happen? He doesn't text back, that's all. And best that can happen is that he* does *text back. . .!*

So, in a clean T-shirt and denim shorts, I'd sat down at the computer, checked for new mail (none), and began to text. That was twenty minutes ago and I hadn't got any further than, *it's Stella*, something I actually got stuck on quite a lot.

"It's Stella": that's what Frankie always stepped in and said any time anyone ever asked me my name. Usually people looked at us kind of confused, like they were wondering what the deal was with the ventriloquist act. Whatever anybody else thought, I was always totally grateful to Frankie for saving me the embarrassment of stammering, and giving me a few vital seconds to get over my nerves and talk like a normal person.

But with texts and e-mails, I could be brave. For texts and e-mails I didn't need Frankie. Uh, except I *did*, since I didn't know Seb's mobile number. And if there was *one* person who could wangle that information for me, it was Frankie. . .

Hey, Frankie!

How's things? Is your cousin Tania still at yours? Is she still driving you mad? You can moan to me about her on Friday, when you'll be HERE!!!

Anyway, know you're busy, but just a quickie to ask a big – as in *BIG* – favour. Decided to be brave (like you'd be!) and text Seb! Only trouble is, I don't have his phone no. – so if you see him around, can you

134

ask him for it? DON'T tell him it's for me, though (WAY too embarrassing)!

If you could you would be the BESTEST of BEST MATES, which of course you are already!

See you Friday!

stella

PS Neisha texted to say she had some news – then never got back to me to tell me what it was! Got any idea what she's on about? I'm dying to know!

I pressed the paper aeroplane icon on my computer and watched my e-mail to Frankie ping into cyberspace ... and then felt restless and not sure what to do with myself. So I did what I *usually* did when I was stuck on stuff like homework research, and started flipping around on my favourite sites on the web. First up, I noseyed at a couple of animation sites I liked: one Japanese (Hello Kitty, Neopets, the movie *Spirited Away* – I'm a mug for all things Japanese and cartoony), and one for a mad site with so-bad-it's-good animation of kittens playing in bands.

As usual, it was fun for a while, but the restlessness I was feeling just wouldn't go away, and I found myself staring at a site engine query box and wondering what I should type in next. Then my reflection in the computer screen put an idea in my head; with the sun streaming in behind me, the silhouette of my newly washed, newly springy, light curls looked dark, just like my grandfather's hair must have been. OK, so I couldn't exactly type in "Missing-grandfather-called-Eddie", but at least I could type in *one* detail I knew about his life – where his family came from before they moved to London. I typed in "Barbados".

If those twenty minutes wondering what to text to Seb had dragged, the next hour flew past quicker than a mad gull aiming for a fairy cake. At school, we'd learnt plenty of stuff about the West Indies, and about the horrible slave trade that sent people from Africa to work on the sugar plantations there (especially to Barbados), and all about the *Windrush* and other ships that had brought lots of black West Indians to Britain to live in the 1950s.

All of that had been really interesting, but I'd never thought before about how much it had to do with my missing grandfather, which was basically *everything*. I flicked from one site to another, finding out loads of amazing, fascinating and sometimes kind of *shocking* facts. For example, centuries ago, white officials had these really bizarre, ugly terms for dual heritage children – if I'd lived in those days, I'd have been called a "quadroon", because of my one black grandparent. I mean, "quadroon": it sounds like a mouldy old biscuit made of marzipan or something, doesn't it?

When I thought about it for a sec, it was like I'd been doing non-stop double history lessons all day, starting with hands-on archaeology in the outhouse earlier, and now a chunk of social history on the computer.

Bling!

My fingers hovered in mid-air over the keyboard when I heard the e-mail alert. Frankie – she'd got back to me already!

With a stupid grin splatted across my face, I clicked open her message, and instantly felt the grin melt away.

Hi Stella,
Soz – don't know how to get Seb's number.
Busy with stuff – speak l8r (Friday).

Huh. . .? That was more like *a text* than an e-mail. It was so short and not-very-sweet that I knew something was wrong: was Frankie annoyed with me for asking for her help with the Seb thing? I mean, yeah, it might be mortifying for someone useless like *me* to find out his mobile number, but Frankie was *fearless*. She got a real kick out of charming people and teasing info out of them before they knew what they were saying or doing. What was up with her? How come she could hang out with Seb on Saturday (and not tell me) but suddenly come over too shy to ask him this? And if she didn't want to do it, why didn't she tell me in her usual jokey way? Why hadn't she even bothered to type her name? Where was the smiley we always, *always* put at the bottom of our e-mails to each other?

Up till a moment ago, I'd had my first *almost* good day in Portbore, but now everything had changed; I could sense the black cloud of homesickness and gloom hovering above my head.

"Stella! Tea's ready!" Mum's voice drifted through from the kitchen.

"C-c-c-coming!" I called back, feeling suddenly as queasy as if I was bobbing on a lilo in the middle of a stormy sea. . .

Chapter 14

Chinese whispers in my head

Isn't it funny how boring things can become totally fascinating when you're trying to avoid doing something?

Stuff like cleaning fluff out from under your bed, playing "Boo!" with your kid brothers for two hours solid, checking for split ends . . . all completely snoresville till it's a choice between *that* and *homework*. Then suddenly, it's as if fluff is fascinating, your snot-nosed baby brothers are utterly adorable, and hunting for split ends is the most fun a girl can have.

One day when I was trying to avoid doing my French homework (*quelle barbant!*), I ended up becoming totally fascinated by some dumb telly show talking about that spooky sensation you get where you just *know* someone's watching you. What they were saying was that it's not spooky at all – it's actually pure science. I can't remember exactly *how* the science bit works ('cause, *duh*, I was meant to be doing my French homework), but it's something to do with electrical impulses, the same electrical impulses that help birds fly without bumping into planes or pylons or each other.

Well, I didn't need an electric impulse to let me know I was being stared at right now ... I could see those two liquid green eyes fixed straight on me like laser beams every time I glanced up from my drawing pad.

"You're putting me off!" I mumbled at Peaches, who was curled up on his armchair in the corner of the outhouse.

He just yawned, one yellow fang glinting, and carried on staring. It was as if he knew (by reading my thoughts or by electrical impulse, maybe) that I was trying to do a caricature of him, which was making him look a bit like a furry sack of potatoes with a face.

"OK, fine!" I shrugged, tearing up my unfinished effort and starting again. "Anyway, you don't deserve a picture, not after what *you* did."

Peaches blinked blankly, completely unfazed by the scrunching of the paper or my hopeless efforts at telling him off. But I *had* been grumpy with him this morning, when I woke up (thanks to him snoring) and found dusty red pawprints catwalked right across my newly washed and de-inked white duvet cover. So much for what the baldy bloke in the ironmonger's was saying about the Josephs' house being the only place in the area built of red brick – Peaches had definitely scampered around somewhere built of the same stuff. I mean, even though I'd seen him sunbathing as far as the beach, there's no *way* he could wander as far as Sugar Bay. Could he?

Could he. . .?

I was back at the Josephs' house, and this time, I was ready.

This time, I was wearing my oldest trainers, my scuzziest navy tracksuit bottoms and a wine-coloured T-shirt that wouldn't show red-brick dust too much.

"Where are you off to, then?" Mum had asked, as she pinned the damp duvet cover on the washing line (again), and let it flap about over the top of the weeds.

"Going drawing," I'd told her, holding up the nylon rucksack with my pad and pencils in it.

I'd heard a thump behind me, and wondered if Peaches was planning on forsaking his snooze in favour of shadowing me (I decided to stick a custard cream in my pocket, just in case).

It wasn't like I'd made up my mind to come to the house straight away. After I'd given up on Peaches' caricature, my brain had almost played a game of Chinese whispers with itself.

Firstly, I'd fidgeted with the seagull feather – the one I'd saved from the shower and stuck beside the shells.

Secondly, the feather got me thinking about the seagull I'd tried to draw on Monday.

Thirdly, my thoughts meandered on to fairy cakes. (Of course.)

Fourthly, I started musing about fairies (minus cakes), and ended up staring at the delicate watercolour above the desk.

Fifthly, I'd idly started doodling my *own* fairy (only mine looked less like dainty, wispy Victorian sprite and more like twenty-first century Japanese cartoon-style *funky* fairy).

Sixthly, I got distracted from my funky fairy when a shadow fell over the outhouse window, as Mum pinned up my duvet on the line. It was the pawprints that got me thinking – the washing machine might have tumbled the worst of the red stain out of the material, but with the sun shining through you could still make out those faint, peachy pad-marks.

Seventhly (if there is such a word), scrambling up the side of the Josephs' house for a proper peek inside suddenly seemed like the *exact* thing I should do right now.

And so here I was – thanks to Chinese whispers in my head – dumping my bag down by the dandelions and foxgloves and eyeing up the window above me.

With a couple of grunts, a squeak and an "ooof!", I found myself tumbling over the window sill and on to a wooden floor. It took a second or two for my eyes to acclimatize after the dazzle of the day outside, and for me to sit and get my breath back. Slowly, as the duskiness gradually became less dusky to me, I stared around a vast empty room, as big as my old school gym. But disappointingly, there was no furniture, no trailing velvet curtains at the windows, no ornaments or pictures to give any clues about the history of the house and its once-upon-a-time owners. The only signs that the place had ever been grand were a giant marble fireplace at one end of the room, and walls covered in faded, peeling floral wallpaper. This had to have been a ballroom, where the Joseph family and their friends would've waltzed the night away in big, flowing dresses and moustaches (if you see what I mean).

I pushed myself up and walked towards the huge, imposing fireplace, stepping over a wilting daisy chain on the dusty floor that must have blown in here from outside. But my eyes were on a coloured chunk of something glinting in the hearth. It was just the corner of a tile, one of many that must have been here long ago, and the fragment of yellow and green flower glazed on it made me ache to see what the rest of the tiles and the whole of this room must have looked like, back when it was loved, back when. . .

. . .and then in mid-thought, I felt every hair on the back of my neck stand to attention. Maybe it was those electrical impulses up to their tricks again, but I suddenly didn't feel *alone* any more. Slipping the tile into my pocket I turned slowly, slowly and saw tiny, darting *wisps* of colour and light, fluttering in the gently swirling dust my clumsy entrance had created.

Could it. . .

I mean, could it be. . .

Could it be, well, *fairies*. . .?

Were *these* the current tenants of the Josephs' house, now that humans didn't seem to want it?

144

Uh-oh. I'd come to Portbore and I was going *mad*.

"There's no such thing as fairies," I whispered to myself – and the fairies. But standing there, frozen in shock, I couldn't think of a single explanation for the twinkling dapples of light flurrying and flitting around the room. Or for the tiny, melodic tinkles they seemed to be making.

THUNK!

That wasn't the sound of a fairy, unless it was one who'd borrowed Dad's sledgehammer.

In a panic, I glanced at the furthest away window and saw that a huge gull had landed on the sill and was now settling itself, giving its feathers a shake and eyeing me boldly.

"Caww!" it suddenly cackled, chucking its head back as it squawked.

Like some kind of nervous tic, I almost copied the movement, jerking my chin up a little and then catching sight of . . . the most amazing chandelier I'd ever seen. It was *massive*. The breeze from the open windows was making every one of the hundreds of dangling crystal droplets sway and twist, sending sparkles of kaleidoscopic light dancing around the room.

Ahhhh . . . *now* I got it.

OK, so there *weren't* any real live fairies inhabiting the house. But it didn't matter – my small reserve of courage was fading fast and it was time to leave, before any more tinkles and *THUNK*s frightened me into permanent goosebumps.

"Bye, house," I whispered, hurriedly throwing one leg after another over the window sill, and bounding down on to the warm grass below.

As I grabbed my bag and hurried through the garden, I thought I saw the faintest flicker of something that *might* have been a ginger tail disappearing through the tall grass. But I wasn't in the mood to hang about; if it *was* Peaches, then I'd see him back at home later, where the ear-splitting shrieks of my brothers would keep any spookiness *well* at bay.

But right now, all I wanted was to get to the bustling, tacky beach in Portbore, treat myself to a 99 cone with everything on it, and think about when I might be brave enough to visit the Josephs' house again.

Course I knew that would be the weekend, when the world's most fearless girl would be here to hold my shaking hand. . .

Chapter 15

Nineteenth-century gossip

". . .How I wonder what you are!"

Omigod. If Frankie or Neish or the others could see me now, they'd think I'd gone stark, raving Looney Tunes.

Sitting on my bedroom window sill, swinging my legs and singing "Twinkle, Twinkle Little Star" to a *cat*? They'd disown me. (If a few of them hadn't disowned me already, by the sound of their silence.)

I know it would have looked a bit wet and Walt Disney to anyone watching, but it was nice sitting up here in the warm dark, with Peaches purring companionably by my side. We'd watched the sun set over the sea together, and the lights strung along the prom ping to life. Then – like quiet fireworks – a blaze of coloured bulbs sparked up down by the beach. The official opening of the funfair was the next day, Friday, but I guess the people who ran it knew that there was no better advert than to flick their very big "on" switch.

Then, as if nature was trying to outdo Portbore, a few wisps of clouds floated off to reveal a nearly whole moon and a galaxy of stars.

That's when I got it into my head to sing "Twinkle, Twinkle". And anyway, the line "How I wonder what you are" seemed kind of weirdly appropriate when I was warbling it to Peaches. . .

"Hey, I thought you were scared of heights?" Dad's voice drifted from the doorway behind me.

"Not any more." I turned around and smiled.

"Good! Anyway, if you fell, Peaches would probably cushion your fall!" he laughed, coming over and leaning his long, muscly arms on the window sill beside me.

"Are you saying he's fat?" I asked, wrapping a protective arm around Peaches and pretending to be offended.

"Hey, I guess he's not fat . . . for a baby hippopotamus!"

I took my hand away from Peaches' broad back and gave my dad a punch on the arm.

"Ooh! I take it back, I take it back!" Dad said, acting like I'd hurt him, though he'd had harder punches (not to mention nippier bites) from my little brothers. "Please don't set Peaches' fleas on me! *Please!*"

"Did you come in here to be annoying, or did you have another reason?" I asked, raising my eyebrows at him.

"To be annoying," he grinned, falling down on to his knees and resting his chin on his hands. "As well as the *other* reason, of course."

Before I asked him what that other reason was, I took a quick peek at my dad and realized he looked . . . well . . . not like my dad. *My* dad wore expensive suits and trendy ties. *My* dad managed to look dressed up, even off-duty in jeans, wearing them with "casual" shirts and shoes, never trainers. *My* dad was forty, with a frown permanently in place on his forehead. But *this* dad; *this* dad looked like his clothes had never been introduced to an iron. *This* dad had a T-shirt with Nirvana written on it. *This* dad had been smiling so much the last few days that he was going to give himself laughter lines, but there wasn't a forehead frown in sight.

"So? What's your other reason?" I asked, waving a curious moth away from my face.

"I got talking to one of our neighbours today. Her name's Maggie – she's a retired teacher who moved to Portbay ten years ago."

Why was Dad telling me this? Had he arranged something hideous, like for me to have extra tutorials with her over the summer holidays?

"Anyway, I was asking her about the old couple who used to own this place," he continued.

OK, maybe I was safe. This didn't sound like it was leading to holiday tutoring. I already knew that Foxglove Cottage used to belong to an old couple who'd moved into a retirement home or something. It had been left to grow damp and crumbly for a few years, till the owners' son decided to sell up. (Bet no one in the town would touch it with a bargepole; bet he had to wait till the mugs from London with more-money-than-sense came along. . .)

"So?" I prompted him, while Peaches lazily swatted at the moth with one enormo paw.

"*So*. . ." Dad waffled on, ". . .she was saying that the few years she knew the couple who lived here, she never heard them talk about art, or saw them drawing."

"Then whoever owned the cottage *before* them must have used the outhouse as a studio!" I suggested, not having to try *too* hard to work that one out.

"Uh-huh." Dad nodded and agreed. "But it

would have been a long, long time ago. Maggie said the old guy had lived in it all his life. He'd been born here, just after his parents bought the place."

How amazing – to spend all your life in the same house, to live out all your history in one place. Maybe it *wasn't* such a crummy idea to do the place up after all. But who was the mystery artist who'd used the outhouse as a studio? By the old-fashioned look of the fairy painting, the ancient art materials and the fragile felt hat, I realized something.

"So I guess the artist must have been someone who –" I began, stopping to check that the maths I'd done in my head was right, "– who must've lived in the house maybe as much as a hundred years ago!"

"I guess so," Dad nodded, casting his grey-blue eyes up to the stars outside in the night sky. "Anyway, Maggie told me some interesting things about the town, too."

"Oh, yeah?" I said warily, wondering if Dad was using the excuse of this chat to give me a subtle lecture about Portbore's good points.

"Yeah. Lots of smuggling and piracy went on round here centuries ago, y'know!"

"I *do* know," I told him matter-of-factly. The mad old dear with the fairy cake had already filled me in on *that* particular snippet of local history.

"And she said we have to check out a place called Sugar Bay."

I didn't say anything, but was aware of a pair of green eyes glancing up at me.

"She says it's a beautiful little cove, just on the other side of the caravan park on the headland," Dad carried on, unaware that I knew it pretty well. "There's an old, dilapidated mansion there, apparently; built by some rich plantation owner in eighteen-hundred-and-something, who settled here from Barbados. Guess he must have made his fortune in the sugar trade."

Peaches had looked dopey and sleepy for most of the time I'd known him so far, but I swear his ears did a three-hundred-and-sixty-degree swivel right then – same as *mine* would have, if I had swivelling kind of ears.

"That must be why it's called Sugar Bay!" I gasped, the realization dawning on me, as vivid as the sun zooming back up in the sky and nudging the moon out of the way.

"I suppose so!" Dad agreed, nodding at me. "Anyway, *here's* a bit of interesting historical gossip for you: the plantation owner and his family caused quite a stir in Portbay at the time because they brought a young black servant boy back with them from the Caribbean."

"Really?" I murmured, feeling goosebumps prickling all over my skin at that piece of information.

"Mad, isn't it, to think that some teenage boy was the talk of the town, just because of the colour of his skin!" Dad laughed. "Mind you, a glimpse of a lady's ankle would have been front page news in those days!"

Ha! The citizens of Portbore didn't just get their knickers in a twist over nothing in the nineteenth century – hadn't the sight of my stripy socks sent a ripple of *shock* around Shingles café just the other day?

"Anyway . . . this time tomorrow, Frankie will be here!" said Dad brightly, changing the subject. "Looking forward to it?"

"Oh, yes," I grinned, forgetting all my niggling worries about my best friend.

After all, when Frankie breezed into town, frumpy Portbore wouldn't know what had hit it. . .

153

Chapter 16

Mrs Sticky Toffee and the tooth fairy

Tippety-tap, tippety-tap, tippety-tippety-tippety-tap!

What was making that sound? It took me a few minutes to work it out.

Tippety-tap, tippety-tap, tippety-tippety-tippety-tap!

Libraries are meant to be silent, right? Well, not this one. A small transistor radio on the shelf behind the desk was tuned into some station that should've been called Crummy FM, and corny old Frank Sinatra was currently crooning out a tune (help – I felt homesick for Clive our singing neighbour!).

Not only was Frank crooning, but the librarian – busy putting away a pile of books – was keeping time by *tap*-dancing his way between the shelves. (*Tippety-tap, tippety-tap, tippety-tippety-tippety-tap. . .!*)

Nuts. Seriously nuts.

Still, the backgound noise was a blessing in

disguise – you'd never notice me snoring with all that racket going on. And I was *seriously* in danger of snoring for two reasons. First, I'd hardly slept last night 'cause of Peaches snoring, Frankie coming and thinking about that servant boy from Sugar Bay and the hard time he'd got in this town. Second, the book I was flicking through was as boring as watching my dad strip wallpaper in the hall (his riveting project for today).

Point of Interest No. 3: The crazy golf course – with its Treasure Island theme – has been popular with locals and tourists alike since it opened in 1962.

What a dazzlingly fascinating fact (not). Good grief – it might be home to loads of weirdos, but this town was obviously *so* boring that no one had bothered to write a decent history of it.

I mean, get this; I was sitting at a desk in the library with the one, single, solitary guidebook to Portbore, and I'd read leaflets about plaque at the *dentist* that were thicker than this. It was full of these "Points of Interest" that were about as interesting as a verruca. What other thrilling points of interest could I expect?

. . .No. 51: The third lamppost on the left as you walk along the prom has long been a favourite with local dogs.

As for the one place I was dying to know more about. . .

Point of interest No. 5: Sugar Bay – Once known as Smuggler's Bay, due to the fact that this hidden cove was perfect for smugglers unloading their stolen wares. Its name was changed when the Grainger family moved from Barbados to the area and in 1840 built a grand house with the profits of the fortune they'd built in the sugar trade.

And that was *it*! No info about the family, *or* their servant, or why exactly the house had been left to moulder away. They hadn't even got the family name right – what was with "Grainger" instead of "Joseph"?

What a waste of time. I hadn't written a *thing* in the notepad I'd taken along; instead of jotting down fascinating historical facts, I'd just covered the pages in *doodles*. It was Mum who'd suggested that I come to the library to learn more about the

Josephs' house, but I think I'd learned *less* (if that was possible), *and* got more confused into the bargain.

"Ooh, now *that's* more like it!" said a familiar voice close by, as I was enveloped in a whiff of toffee. It reminded me of happy, sticky days eating sticky toffee pudding with Frankie in Aunt Esme's cosy kitchen.

"Um . . . hello!" I said shyly, turning to see the old woman from the beach. Against the dark wood of the bookshelves her lime-green coat and pink meringue hat looked more vivid than ever.

"You know, that's *so* much prettier than the style you were doing before!" the old lady smiled, not bothering with a hello herself.

Her dainty cream handbag swinging from her wrist, she tapped a wrinkled finger on one of my doodles. It wasn't bad, actually; it was another of my funky fairies, complete with dragonfly-meets-Batman wings.

"Don't know about that cropped top and tummy button ring, though!" she murmured, turning her head this way and that as she studied my drawing. "But I guess I'm just a bit out of touch with the fashions that fairies are wearing these days!"

Was that an attempt at a joke, or was she just

mad? To be polite, I forced a smile. I figured that if she'd been joking, then it was the right response, and if she was plain mad, then it was probably the safest thing to do.

"So, what's this?" she queried now, breathing toffee fumes over me as she shifted her gaze to the so-called book I'd been flicking through. "Doing some homework about your new home town?"

Urgh. I didn't want to think of this as homework and I didn't much want to think of Portbore being my new home town either, thank you very much.

"I was trying to find out about the Joseph family and their servant," I told her, pointing to the poor-quality black-and-white print of the old house at Sugar Bay.

Mrs Sticky Toffee frowned for a second and then had an "aha!" moment. "Ah, now, you're barking up the wrong kettle of fish, there, dear!" she announced. "The family weren't called Joseph; they were the Graingers – Mr and Mrs Grainger and their daughter Elize."

So the book had been right *after* all? Hey, now I was even *more* confused. "But why is it called the Josephs' house, then?" I blinked at her.

"It's not *the Josephs'*, dear – it's just *Joseph*, as in, Joseph's house. The locals have always referred to it as that in honour of the Grainger's servant, Joseph."

"Really?" I asked in surprise, wondering how I could have been so dumb as to mishear the name in such a small but important way.

"Oh, yes! Of course, back in those days, practically no one had set eyes on a black person before. The townspeople of Portbay were terribly proud to be the first place on the south coast to have someone of colour in their midst. He was quite the celebrity!"

Well, knock me down with a seagull feather. Last night, I'd been tossing and turning, thinking that poor servant boy had been made to feel like an outsider, some kind of *freak* here, and all the time the locals had thought of him as *special*. Special enough to call the old house at Sugar Bay after him, and not the master who'd built it. Wow.

I was about to ask why, if Joseph was so famous, there was nothing in the local library about him, but with a rustle of her raincoat, Mrs Sticky Toffee was on the move.

"Oops! Would you look at the time ... I'll be late for my appointment to get my bunions done!"

Er, I hadn't a clue what bunions were exactly,

and I didn't know what you might get *done* to them, but whatever – they sure didn't sound like something I'd want to know about. Just as she was heading for the door, Mrs Sticky Toffee glanced over her shoulder – almost catching me wincing – and said. . .

"If you want to know more about Joseph's house, have a look in the museum, dear!"

Museum? I didn't even know Portbore *had* a museum. But then it seemed like there was plenty about Portbore that I didn't know about. . .

And then I remembered my manners and went to wave bye . . . but Mrs Sticky Toffee had already vanished, off to get her bunions "done". (Bleurghh. . .)

"I hope she's not the tooth fairy!" a man's voice cheerfully announced. It was the tap-dancing librarian, hovering beside me with an armful of books.

"Excuse me?" I asked, completely stumped.

"Well, she shouldn't be offering sweets if she's the tooth fairy, should she!" he beamed at me, before click-clacking off to the desk to stamp someone's book out.

Was that another sort of strange joke? Or another sign of madness?

Just as I was trying to decide which one it was, I spotted something on my notepad. I'd doodled my funky fairy with arms outstretched, and now she seemed to be holding something out to me.

"Er, thanks," I mumbled to no one in particular, as I picked up the toffee and started unwrapping it. . .

Chapter 17

The truth about the texts (or lack of 'em)

My heart was in my mouth.

I'd missed her call from the train – my mobile had gone missing and only reappeared when Dad was lassoing Jamie into the double buggy beside Jake and felt the unusual bump in Jamie's nappy.

"Hi – s'me! Frankie! I'm on the train now, and I think it's running on time, so see you at half-six!" I'd heard her say, once I'd given the phone a wipe with a Wet One and listened to my messages.

It had been chaos when I'd come back from the library this afternoon. I'd planned to spend a bit of time making my room look less like a half-built hovel for Frankie coming, but instead I'd had to help wash and brush away Jamie and Jake's latest disaster. When Mum had put the washing on, she hadn't spotted the twins adding the entire contents of the box of washing powder – plus the box – into the porthole door of our Zanussi. Actually, the first Mum and Dad knew about the mutant foam tidal wave that was oozing out of our drain, down the driveway and covering a whole section of Dingle Lane was when I ran in and told them. (I'd been walking up the lane on the way home and couldn't figure out why cars were coming towards me covered in floaty layers of foamy bubbles.)

So, *first* there was the big clear-up, and then there was *another* panic when Dad tried to blow up the inflatable spare bed and found he couldn't 'cause Jamie had bitten straight through the rubber tube of the pump. Dad had tried to repair it with tape, but it didn't work – the bed flopped limply across the floor, as if a hamster with asthma had tried (and failed) to blow it up. He went next door to see if our neighbour Maggie happened to have a spare pump (or failing that, a spare cage for the twins), and ended up wheeling back a fold-out single bed that she'd been happy to lend us.

By the time he'd dragged it upstairs to my room, we were already late leaving for the station. Then we were later *still* 'cause I had to run indoors to find a Wet One for my phone. I guess we must have really looked like the Barking Mad Family from London as we raced along the road in the direction of the station, Dad pushing a double buggy of squealing, delighted boys at top speed.

We needn't have hurried. The train turned out to be running ten minutes late, due to the wrong sort of track on the track or something. Actually, it was a pity Frankie's train had been held up, because for the first time today I'd had time to worry. No sooner did my heart rate start to slow down after our sprint to get here, then it started tappity-tapping faster than a librarian's shoes at the thought of how exactly Frankie was going to *be*. 'Cause no matter how much my mum tried to stick up for her, Frankie had acted so off-hand on the phone and by e-mail this week, that I wasn't sure what to expect. Only her cheeky postcard had sounded like the Frankie I knew and adored. So which Frankie was going to get off the train. . .?

It didn't take long to spot her – amongst a sea of bobbing, white-haired pensioners stepping on to the platform, you couldn't really miss a pretty black teenage girl with tiny braids flying as she ran full tilt, arms outstretched, yelling, "Stell-*AAAAAAA*!". . .

*

"WOOOOF!" barked Jake. "WOOF! WOOF! WOOF!"

The big hairy Alsatian tied up in front of the

café just about jumped out of its hairy skin, but I think that was less to do with my brother's "uncanny" dog impersonation and more to do with the fact that Jake was slamming his hands over and over again against the plate-glass window.

Some concerned-looking bloke behind the counter – who might have been the owner of the Shingles café – appeared to be as alarmed as the dog outside on the pavement. They weren't the only ones; every customer in the place on this busy Friday night was staring at us. I was just glad I was facing the window and had my back to their disapproving glances.

"Wanna see the DOGGIE!" Jake yelled above the sound of his heavy-duty glass thumping.

"I'd better take him outside; try and calm him down a bit," Dad mumbled, screeching his chair back and making a grab for Jake.

"Hmm," Mum nodded wearily.

She was doing her best to seem cheery for Frankie's sake, but the boys efforts at causing maximum mayhem today had kind of ground her down, I suspected.

"Can you girls keep an eye on Jamie while I nip to the loo?" Mum asked, once the café door had clanged shut behind Dad and Jake.

"Sure. . ." I nodded, wishing Mum and Dad hadn't decided to take us straight here for a "treat" instead of going home for our tea.

"No problem!" Frankie smiled at Mum, chomping on her last mouthful of carbonara.

But before Mum had got two steps from the table, a terrible wailing started up.

"Mummmmee-EEEEEEEE!" sobbed Jamie, holding out his arms as if she was abandoning him to the Childcatcher from *Chitty Chitty Bang Bang* instead of his own sister.

Once Mum had sighed, grabbed Jamie and trundled off to the loo with him on her hip, Frankie rolled her eyes and grinned at me.

"Couldn't you trade 'em in for something quieter, like a couple of goldfish, maybe?" she joked, even though she'd known the twins since they were two days old and thought they were pretty entertaining, really.

"Don't suggest that to Mum – the mood she's in today, she'd probably think that was an ace idea!" I joked back.

This was great. Not the boys showing us up, I mean – just Frankie being here, and . . . well . . . being Frankie. I needn't have worried about how she'd react to me when she stepped off the train;

166

the second I felt her hug the breath out of me on the station platform I knew we'd be fine. And in between Jake and Jamie's food fights, fist fights and screaming matches here in the café, me, Frankie, Mum and Dad had jabbered away like crazy, catching up on news of the move and how Aunt Esme was doing and loads more.

Course, in front of Mum and Dad, I didn't moan too much about the boringness of Portbore, and Frankie didn't ask – but there'd be plenty of time to catch up on that later, when we were on our own.

"What are *that* lot staring at?" Frankie suddenly frowned over my shoulder. I turned around and saw a bunch of about five teenage lads at the back of the caff, huddled around Cokes, grinning and staring our way.

"I was going to tell you about them!" I turned back and whispered across the table, though there was no way the boys could have heard me above the din of the music from the jukebox, the chattering of families and the violent hiss of the coffee machine. "I'm *sure* they're the same lads that were in here on Sunday, taking the mickey out of me!"

"Oh, yeah?" Frankie bristled. "Well, we'd better

give them something to look at, then!"

Uh-oh. With Frankie, you never knew what to expect. I felt a familiar flutter of panic as I watched her stand up – dressed in a white vest top and pink combats – and wondered momentarily if I had time to bolt outside or slither under the table before she did whatever she was going to do.

But just like always, fear froze my muscles and I wasn't going *anywhere*. Instead, I watched as Frankie put one hand on her hip and blew the most exaggerated kiss in the lads' direction with the other. Ha!

I *had* to see their reaction. Sneaking a backward peek, I spotted a couple of them pull faces and give embarrassed laughs, but Frankie's full-on cheekiness had done the trick. Every one of the lads had turned awkwardly away from us and started looking very interested in the table.

"*That* was easy!" Frankie said with satisfaction, sliding gracefully back on to her seat, and stealing an uneaten carrot off Jamie's plate. "Boys can never handle girls who are more full-on than them. So . . . who do you want me to sort out for you next, Stella?"

Frankie pulled her knees up and rested her trainers on the table, biting the end off the carrot with a loud crunch.

"Um, no one, I don't think," I said, realizing that the only people I really knew so far in Portbore were Mrs Sticky Toffee and Peaches, and Peaches didn't really count as a person (or a normal *cat*). "But hey, I wanted to ask you, Frankie . . . what's going on with Lauren and Eleni and Parminder?"

At the mention of our other friends' names, Frankie stopped crunching and dropped her feet back down on the floor with a thud.

"What do you – *cuh* – mean?" she asked, choking slightly on her carrot.

"Well, it's just that I've tried phoning them and they never get back to my messages, or my texts or e-mails. I mean, I heard from Neish – like I told you in my e-mail, she texted me about some gossip or something on Tuesday, but I haven't heard from her since. . ."

Frankie looked positively weird for a second, like one of those policemen on TV shows that arrives to break bad news but faffs around before spitting it out.

"What?" I laughed nervously. "Have they all been abducted by aliens or run off and joined a cult or something? Is *that* why they've been so lousy at keeping in touch?"

The fooling around there; that was just my way of trying to keep calm . . . I could feel the flutter of a stammer threatening.

And then finally Frankie spoke.

"The thing is, Stella," she said with a sigh, staring off at the waitresses stacking dirty trays on the counter. "They've felt funny about speaking to you."

"Funny? Funny *how*?" I blinked at her, flutters of panic rattling around in my chest again.

Frankie shuffled in her seat looking uncomfortable, like she was struggling to come up with an answer to my question, or just finding it hard to say the answer out loud. "Funny, 'cause they know something . . . and don't want to be the one to tell you."

I didn't like the sound of that one tiny, little bit.

"What? What *sort* of something?"

Frankie frowned, and my heart flopped even nearer to the floor.

"It's just that . . . well . . . it's *Seb* – OK?" She was staring at me now, sort of annoyed, as if I'd forced her to do something she didn't want to do.

"O-O-O-OK," I mumbled, feeling very, *very* far

from OK myself.

For a split-second, I almost started nervously joking again; nearly asked if it was *Seb* who'd been abducted by aliens or run off to join a cult or something terrible like that. . .

"Look, Stell – he's going out with someone. None of the girls wanted to be the one to break the news to you. They knew you'd be gutted."

Neisha nearly did, but must have lost her bottle after she texted me, I thought numbly for a second, as the news sank in.

Outside, I could see Dad hovering warily, as Jake patted/thumped the nervy Alsatian on the head. And the bellowed roar of "IWANAN-ICECREAM!" coming from the direction of the loos meant that Mum and Jamie were on their way back to the table. But it was as if I could see and hear my family through a fog – Frankie's words were the only thing I could concentrate on, like they were TeChNiCoLoUr in my head.

"Wh-wh-wh-who is she?" I asked, sounding like a puzzled owl, not a traumatized 13-year-old girl.

"No one," shrugged Frankie, ducking away from a waitress – the grumpy red-haired one I'd seen before – as she started clearing away the plates. "Just some girl. She was hanging around Seb the

171

night after your party – we saw them up at the Heath."

So *that's* why she'd kept Saturday night a secret. Like Mum had suggested, Frankie was only trying to protect me.

"You all right, Stella?" she asked, biting her lip.

I was just about to answer her when a ball of lightning dressed in Gap Kids jeans hurtled into the waitress's legs, sending her – and the stacked tray she was carrying – flying.

"*Jamie!* Look what you've *done*!!" I heard Mum's shocked voice shout out.

Gazing across the table, I could *just* about see Frankie's face through the strands of soggy spaghetti that were dangling in front of my eyes. She was trying really, *really* hard not to laugh.

"Say sorry to the poor waitress *right* now, Jamie!" Mum ordered my brother.

"Sowwy, lady!"

"*And* your sister!"

"Sowwy, Stewwa!"

Ignoring Jamie's apology, I watched – through eyelashes dripping with white sauce – Frankie's shoulders heave as she struggled to keep her sniggers in.

"Hey, Frankie," I suddenly asked her. "What

were you saying about me being all right?"

And with that, she exploded, sending infectious giggles splurging across the table and setting me off too.

After all, it was hard to stay tearful and tragic with leftover carbonara dolloped on your head.

Though in its *own* way, that was pretty tragic too. . .

Chapter 18

Sad, sad, sad or funny, funny, funny?

"You have *got* to be kidding!" Frankie growled.

"Yo ho ho! Yo ho ho!" a jovial voice replied.

"I'm sorry, Stella, but I'd rather eat my own *arm* than go in there!"

"In there" was the Treasure Island crazy golf course.

"Yo ho ho! Yo ho ho!"

"I don't know what *he's* 'yo ho ho'-ing at!" Frankie grumbled, staring at the life-size fibre-glass pirate in front of us. "They should change the tape in the machine so he says 'sad, sad, sad', 'cause that's what this place is!"

"I dunno!" I laughed. "It's pretty funny, Frankie!"

From what we could see of the golf course over the perimeter hedge, it was packed full of miniature galleons, gaudy treasure chests, plastic palm trees and lots of people having a laugh. One little kid nearby was cheering his dad on as he putted a golf ball into the mouth of a pirate who was buried up to the neck in sand. Another kid was stroking the parrot sitting on the shoulder of a mean Captain Hook-a-like. A guy in his twenties was groaning as his golf ball disappeared into a shark-infested puddle. It hadn't been my idea to come here – Dad had dropped us off on his way to a timber yard he'd heard about – but now that I could see it for myself, I suddenly understood why the crazy golf course had been so "popular with locals and tourists alike" for the last however many years. Yeah, it was totally naff, but kind of cute too.

"*Funny?* Are you having me on, Stell?!" Frankie pulled a horrified face. "This place is as corny as Kellogg's Cornflakes!"

Er . . . wasn't that the point? For it to be corny, I mean? Crazy golf was hardly ultra cool or cutting-edge. What did Frankie expect? A *Matrix*-themed course, with state-of-the-art special effects and a full-size statue of Keanu Reeves saying "I am Neo"? Still, I didn't say all that stuff out loud to Frankie. She was in one of those moods where everything (and everyone) was fair game for a sarky put-down. Normally I didn't mind them – the moods or the sarky put-downs – 'cause they were pretty entertaining. But today I was feeling sort of sensitive, I guess: the news about Seb had left me with an ache in my chest, as if I had a big, tender bruise on my heart. . .

I really wanted to talk to Frankie about all that again, but hadn't had the chance since she first blurted it out to me in the café yesterday. Thing was, once we'd got home last night, I ended up suspecting that my parents were missing the company of their friends more than just a little bit, 'cause they *sure* made a fuss of mine. They hardly left me and Frankie alone for a minute. I mean, OK, it *had* been a laugh: all of us showing her around the house (Dad posed cheesily with his sledgehammer), eating ice-cream (Mum took out the good Ben & Jerry's stuff once the twins were safely asleep), and sniggering about the spaghetti incident (it *was* funny, though I didn't plan on going back to the Shingles café for the next century or so). But by bedtime, I was aching to get Frankie on my own, to finally get a chance to talk about Seb and the girl who'd turned his head two seconds after I'd left town. But when I came back to my room after brushing my teeth, Frankie was already asleep – arms, legs and braids flung star-shaped across the borrowed single bed.

I'd stayed awake in the dark for ages after that, curled up on the top of the duvet, staring out through my open window at the spangles of lights from the funfair down at the beach. The whole time, running through my mind like the lyrics of some song, was, *Hey, bad timing! Love S xxx* . . . the message scrawled on the back of the mangled Polaroid. I didn't get to sleep till Peaches silently bounded through the window, snuggled himself into a cosy circle behind my knees, and soothed me with his purry snores.

And then after breakfast this morning, I sneaked Frankie away from her fan club (i.e. my family) and took her out to check out my den. I thought *that* would be the perfect place to have a little privacy and discuss the Seb situation, but I got the feeling Frankie didn't want to. Straight away, she was off – grinning, noseying, teasing, filling the conversation with so many jokes and jibes that there wasn't *space* to change the subject.

"Wow!" she'd gasped, when I'd shoved open the stiff door and ushered her into the den. "What a dump! Hey, isn't this where the plague started?"

"God, what a swot you are!" she'd announced, staring at the sheet of paper I'd printed off the website about Barbados and pinned on my corkboard. "Doing history homework in the holidays? You're mental!"

"Now, Stell," she'd grinned, grabbing the floppy felt hat off its nail and plonking it on her head, "I *know* you're not as hip to fashion as me and Neish and everyone, but honestly, granny chic? I don't *think* so!"

"What's this?" she'd asked, picking up the chunk of tile I'd taken from Joseph's house as a souvenir. "Are you turning into one of those mad old women you see on telly documentaries who hoard junk? *They've* always got skanky, manky cats too!"

She's mucking around and slagging off Peaches 'cause she's just trying to make me laugh and keep my mind off Seb, I'd realized, as I watched Frankie warily pick up the chipped rose-patterned cup and study it like she was examining a test tube full of snot. . .

"Stella," Frankie said sternly now, resting a hand on the face of the "yo-ho-ho"-ing pirate, "*please* tell me there's something more exciting to do in this town!"

"Um. . ." I mumbled, looking off down the prom for inspiration and not finding any. I guess I *could* have suggested paddling with the pensioners or feeding fairy cakes to seagulls, but Frankie probably would have snorted in my face.

"Oh, poor Stella!" Frankie suddenly sighed, stepping away from the pirate and coming over to wrap her arms around me. "You really *have* moved to the most boring place on earth, haven't you. . .?"

I felt a bit dizzy, then realized I'd been holding my breath. (Idiot.)

Taking a big lungful of air now, I watched fascinated as dust swirled around our ankles – not 'cause it was dust, but because I realized it might have lain undisturbed here for *years*. Me and Frankie, we were treading up the creaky, once-grand sweep of stairs, and excitement was fizzling up my spine like bubbles in a fish tank. This was much, *much* further than I'd got before. In a few seconds, we'd be discovering whatever secrets there were to discover in the upstairs rooms, and I couldn't *wait*.

Frankie, meanwhile, couldn't care *less*.

". . .so anyway, they're all going down to Camden Market this afternoon, and get this – Lauren's going to try and pretend to be sixteen, 'cause she's dying to get her belly-button pierced and the place there won't do you under sixteen unless your parents are up for it, and you *know* what Lauren's parents are like!"

I'd decided to show Frankie that Portbore wasn't *totally* boring, and brought her to Sugar Bay, to Joseph's house. Now we were here, I got the feeling that she thought exploring an old decrepit building was about as interesting as finding out how cement's made.

"Eleni said she'd do Lauren's make-up for her to make her look older, but Neish said no, that's a dead giveaway. She's right, isn't she? 'Cause it *does* look like you're trying too hard if you wear loads of make-up, doesn't it? Specially in the daytime!"

"Yeah, I s'pose," I muttered, turning my head this way and that as we reached the first-floor landing and saw several doorways leading off it.

"Parminder's got a bet on with Neisha that Lauren doesn't get away with it," Frankie chatted on, leaning her elbows on the banisters while I darted off to look in each room, where I found nothing but emptiness, bare floorboards and great views from the windows in every one of them.

Over the years, someone – lots of someones? – had obviously stripped out anything original to the house or personal to the family, and I couldn't believe how sad and disappointed that made me feel.

"If Parminder wins, Neisha's got to buy her a copy of *Heat* every week for a month," Frankie babbled away from the landing, "and if *Neisha* wins, she gets to borrow Parminder's hair straighteners for a fortnight."

Only vaguely listening to my best friend, I found myself in the smallest of the bedrooms, as bare and empty as the others. I was about to turn and leave when I spotted something that made me start . . . and then smile. In America, taking a "kitty-corner" is a phrase that means not taking the obvious, straight-ahead route. I think it has to be named after cats, the way they weave their way across a garden, like their paws are following some twisty path that's invisible to the human eye. Well, some cat (some fat ginger cat?) had been kitty-cornering its way right across this room – pawprints lightly stamping a winding trail through the dust over to the window. So I followed, doing some kitty-cornering of my own. (It was just as well that Frankie couldn't see me, or she'd think I'd gone completely barking and jump on the first train out of here. . .)

"Anyway, Lauren was saying that it was a pity

I couldn't go with them today," Frankie's voice drifted through, "'cause if she bottles out, the rest of them will just let her get away with it, but if *I* was there, she'd be too scared not to do it!"

Resting my hands on the window sill, I stared out at the most amazing view of sea, sand, sky and whirling seagulls, and my head went completely buzzy at the idea that someone – long, long, *long* ago – had slept in this room and woken up to this exact same view every day.

"Hey, what're you doing?" asked Frankie, her footsteps now stalking me into the room. "Listen, no offence, Stell, but this place is a bit of a snooze. Can we go somewhere else?"

Just as she spoke, my fingertips sensed grooves in the sill. I glanced down, and saw a name . . . and then another; decades-old graffiti carved in the painted wood. In wobbly, swooping lettering, I made out the first name: *Elize*. The second was *Joseph*. Alongside there was fainter etching that was harder to read.

"'Friends for eternity, 1841'," I mumbled, my heartbeat thundering like it was in training for the hundred metre sprint at the Olympics.

"What?" mumbled Frankie, through a yawn.

"Listen, I know somewhere else we can go!" I

grinned, ignoring her question.

"Oh, yeah? Where?"

"The museum!"

"You have *got* to be kidding!" Frankie growled, for the second time today. . .

Chapter 19

A feeling of déjà view. . .

"Look at the *state* of this! Did that minging cat of yours sleep in my overnight bag or something?" moaned Frankie, picking rogue ginger hairs off her black sleeveless top.

I'd been charging ahead of her, along corridors packed with cabinets of blunderbusses, nabbed loot, and general gruesome info about smugglers and pirates (all to be looked at another time, when I wasn't so distracted). But at the mention of Peaches I stopped, and let Frankie catch up.

"Hey, what are you doing, you nutter!" she laughed at me.

A family studying pirate paraphernalia started staring at *us* instead of the exhibits. Maybe it was because Frankie was dressed like she was a dancer for a particularly cool R'n'B act, and would have looked more at home on *MTV* than in Portbore Museum. Or maybe it was because I was sniffing her top. . .

"Nope, Peaches definitely didn't sleep on your stuff," I told her, detecting no telltale sweet scent.

"Better watch out!" said Frankie, nodding towards the puzzled family. "They'll call security and get us chucked out!"

"What – for inappropriate Sniffing of Clothes in a Public Place?" I joked back, straightening up and heading off along the corridors at high speed again.

"Er . . . what exactly are we looking for?" Frankie panted, struggling to keep up with me.

"Not sure – but I'll know it when I find it," I said vaguely.

And then I nearly missed it, I was hurrying so much. But *something* made me pause in one particular doorway. Slowly – forgetting to breathe again for a second – I stepped inside, staring all around me at this strangely familiar room, with its wine-coloured, flocked wallpaper and ornate antique furniture.

"So? What's this, then?" asked Frankie, stumbling in behind me.

I was pretty certain I knew what it was, but went over to check out the plaque on the wall anyway.

"'Ballroom, circa 1850'," I read out the heading. "'This grand room was replicated from Joseph's house, Sugar Bay, using antiques and artefacts taken from the original building.'"

"All I heard was *Ballroom blah, blah, blah. . .*" Frankie shrugged. "D'you fancy translating?"

"It's a room from the house we've just come from!" I explained excitedly, to a frankly unimpressed Frankie.

Actually, it was the huge room I'd first scrambled into, earlier in the week. But instead of just dust, daisy chains and dapples of light, there was a grand piano, swanky velvet sofas, paintings on the wall and tall candlesticks on the fireplace.

"Look!" I gasped, hurrying over to the marble fireplace and gazing down at the flowery yellow and green glazed tiles in the hearth.

"OK, I'm looking at a *floor* . . . so what am I supposed to see exactly?"

"Those tiles! There's the chipped one – I've got the corner of that on my desk, beside the shells!" I carried on, ignoring Frankie's lack of enthusiasm.

Poor Frankie – she and museums went together like mince and trifle. We'd passed the Shingles café on the way; I should have left her there with a copy of *CosmoGirl* and a doughnut till I was done here.

"Omigod . . . Frankie! Check it out!" I suddenly gasped, staring up at the family portrait hanging above the fireplace. "It's *them*! In *this* room! I mean, the *real* room!"

"'The Grainger family, 1840'," Frankie read from the brass plate next to the painting. "Great. Anyway, listen . . . I saw a seat out in the corridor and my feet are tired with all this rushing around. So I'll meet you there, yeah?"

I think I said yeah, or fine or whatever, but I was too busy gawping at the sight of the stern-looking Victorian parents posed on the sofa, with a pretty dark-haired girl standing obediently behind them. It *had* to be their daughter Elize, and she must have been about ten. And in the background, holding a tray, was a boy not much older, in a red velvet jacket with brass buttons. Joseph. . .

I stared at the two young faces – one dark-skinned, one light – and tried to figure out the feelings going on behind them. The boy Joseph might have been holding an upright, uptight pose, but the painter had made his dark brown eyes bright and alive. Same with Elize's earnest expression – her mouth might not have been smiling but her eyes sure were.

"Lovely painting, isn't it?"

The voice belonged to a woman in a navy blazer. Spotting the "curator" badge on her lapel, I panicked for a second, thinking that Frankie had been right and we were about to be chucked out. Or maybe she'd heard me saying the thing about the tile and was going to demand I hand it over.

"Do you know the house?" she asked, not seeming to mind that I was staring at her like a fool in my panic.

"Mmm," I nodded nervously.

"The museum was very lucky that Miss Grainger donated the contents of this room when she finally moved out – everything else had to be sold. Vandals have made a bit of a mess of what little was left, I'm afraid!"

"Miss Grainger. . . That's the girl, isn't it? Elize?" I asked, curiosity getting the better of my nerves, now that I realized the curator hadn't heard a word I'd said to Frankie, *or* had any plans to order me to collect my loud friend and *leave*.

"Elize, yes!" she beamed, looking as chuffed as my old maths teacher did when I managed to figure out a percentage problem without taking as long as normal (i.e. *for ever*).

"So why did she move out?"

"Well, when she was young, her father gambled away most of the family fortune, and it was always a struggle to keep the house going after that. But Elize – Miss Grainger – somehow managed for years, until it finally became too much for her. She moved away in 1900, when she was quite an old lady – she was about 70, I think."

"What happened to her after that?"

"She moved to a small cottage in the town. It must have been very upsetting for her to see her former home go to rack and ruin after that."

So now I knew what had happened to Elize. But what about her "eternal" friend?

"And what about the servant boy – Joseph?" I asked tentatively.

The curator woman seemed very impressed with my local knowledge. I half-expected her to give me a certificate or a gold star or a *hug* or something. Still, all I was interested in was finding out if Elize and Joseph stayed as close as they were when they were children, back when they carved their names in what must have been Elize's bedroom, just a year after this portrait was painted.

"Joseph? Well, Mr Grainger left him some money when he died. It was enough for Joseph to give up working at the house and leave Portbay.

He was still only a teenager, and I suppose he wanted to see something of the world."

"And nobody heard from him again?" I asked, thinking fleetingly of my grandad, Eddie.

"I don't think so," the curator shook her head. "But people in the town were rather sorry he'd left. They started referring to the old place as Joseph's house after that, even though Miss Grainger and her mother still lived there."

So "eternity" had turned out to be pretty short-lived for Elize and Joseph. But then I supposed that if people gave my Nana Jones and Grandad Eddie a hard time for dating in the 1950s, then how hard would it have been for the servant and the master's daughter to be buddies a whole century earlier?

"At least they were friends for a while," I said out loud, trying to remind myself of that.

"Elize and Joseph, do you mean?" asked the curator. "Funny you should say that – I've always thought that too, looking at this painting. They've got the same mischief in their eyes, don't they?"

I wondered if I'd tell her about the carvings in the window sill, and then decided to keep it as my own secret for a little while. Maybe over the summer, I'd borrow Dad's camera and take a picture of it, and take it here to the museum so they could put it in a display cabinet for all the world (or at least all of Portbore) to see. . .

"Hey, Stella, can we go now? *Please?*"

I turned round and saw Frankie slouching miserably in the doorway, blowing a giant pink bubble from her mouth.

"Yeah, let's go," I nodded at her, knowing I'd better get her out of here before the bubble burst and she ended up getting gum stuck all over some priceless antique smuggler's swag bag or whatever.

Then the nice lady curator really *would* chuck us out. . .

Chapter 20

Up, up and away-hey-HEY!

"Uh-*ohhhhhhhHHHH*!"

"On a scale of one to ten, Stell," I heard Frankie gasp, "how scared *are* you?"

The coloured lights of the fairground were falling away *frighteningly* fast.

"TEN!" I squealed, holding on so tight to the safety rail folded over our laps that my knuckles were practically *bulging* out of my skin. "What about yooooo-*ooohhhhhHHH*!"

"Nine!" she squeaked back, gripping her hands around the rail every bit as tightly.

Just nine? Well, Frankie always *was* braver than me. And I was kind of relieved to know that she was as freaked out as *I* was about this Big Wheel ride. I took back everything I said about it being a breeze after the London Eye. I mean, yes, the London Eye is high tech and huge, but you're in an enclosed glass pod practically as big as a bus, moving so slowly that you have to keep checking

192

your view of the scenery outside to make sure you've actually *moved*. But this thing; it really hadn't looked that bad when we were standing underneath it a couple of minutes ago. Now that we were up here, though, my insides were swirling around in plain, old-fashioned, non-high-tech *fear*.

THUNK!

"Omigod! What was *that*?" Frankie gasped, as the wheel juddered to a halt, leaving our gondola gently rocking in the evening sea breeze.

"It's OK – look, they're just stopping to let more people on to the next lot of gondolas!" I told Frankie, proud of myself for daring to peek down over the rail – and my dangling legs – to figure out what was going on.

"Don't do that! You're making it swing more!" Frankie begged, sounding suspiciously like a "ten out of ten" on the fear scale to me.

"Look, it's OK – we're moving again!"

"Whose idea was it to come on this thing anyway?" asked Frankie, her voice high and shrieky like she'd just had a suck on a helium balloon.

"Yours!" I laughed at her, forgetting to be worried for a second.

THUNK!

"I wish they wouldn't do that. . ." Frankie moaned. "Y'know, we should have stayed on the dodgems – those lads in the red car were quite cute!"

"Huh?" I choked in surprise. "But you just spent the whole time staring daggers at them and psyching them out!"

"Well, I was only doing it for *your* sake." Frankie shrugged. "Just want everyone in Portbore to know not to bother you."

Hmm . . . I appreciated Frankie acting all protective, but I didn't really *love* the idea of her permanently scaring people away from me, not if I had to *live* here (like it or not).

THUNK!

"Oof!" we both groaned as we came to a standstill again.

"Hey – I don't know what I've hated more today," Frankie began again brightly, once we'd started moving. "Getting my best clothes covered in red dust and cat hairs, hanging about that *borrrrring* museum, or risking my life on this giant bike wheel!"

Things Frankie could usually make me feel: proud, happy, excited, embarrassed (sometimes). But I'd added two new feelings to the list this week: confused (when she blew hot and cold by phone and e-mail) and irritated (that was such a new feeling it had only happened right *now*). Why did she have to have such a downer on Peaches and Portbore?

SCROINGGGGG!

"This is getting ridiculous!" Frankie grumbled, as we thudded to a metal-screeching halt. "How many more people have to get on before they run this ride properly and we can get off?!"

"Frankie," I said warily, "I don't think this is a proper stop. It didn't make the right noise then. . ."

"It didn't?"

"No. It was more of a '*scroing*' than a '*thunk*'."

Normally, saying something daft like that would have given us both the giggles. But when you're dangling worryingly high in thin air, it doesn't exactly feel too normal.

Still, I dared to bend forward again, taking it slowly, slowly this time, to avoid any rocking. We were at the very top of the wheel now, bang on 12 o'clock. And oops . . . the ground seemed freakily far away.

"What's going on?" asked Frankie, leaning as far back as possible on the padded vinyl seat.

"There're some fairground blokes down there, and they're looking a bit worried and sort of . . .

shouting at each other."

"Oh, God. . ." groaned Frankie. "I can't look. I'm going to shut my eyes till they get this thing moving again!"

I wasn't exactly ecstatic about being stranded up here either, but I didn't feel like closing my eyes. The view was just too . . . *wow*.

Directly below, the muddle of music and spangles of coloured lights was kind of mesmerizing. I leant on the rail, ignoring the stressed-out fairground guys, and instead watched as the Saturday night crowds weaved and wound around all the brightly lit attractions. For a second I thought I might have seen a pink meringue hat bobbing amongst all the hairdos and baseball caps, and turned to point it out to Frankie, but she had her eyes shut so tight that I didn't think she'd thank me for forcing her to stare over the edge at the headgear of some mad old lady.

When I turned back, I couldn't see Mrs Sticky Toffee or her meringue hat any more, and didn't know if I had in the first place. There was such a jumble of colour and movement going on down there that a giraffe could wander by in search of the Ghost Train and you wouldn't be sure you'd really seen it.

"What's happening now?" Frankie hissed through clenched teeth.

"Nothing much," I replied, straightening up and gazing around.

More twinkling lights surrounded us in the dark night – none quite as dazzling as the hundreds of coloured bulbs blinking below, but all just as beautiful. To the right, the town spread out, dots of yellowy-white light spilling from every house and streetlamp. To the left, the inky blackness of the sea was broken up with distant sparkles from faraway ships. Over on the headland, even the caravan park looked *almost* picturesque, when all you could see of it was a soft glow peeping out of a myriad of windows. And then above us, there were stars. . .

I tell you something, if I'd been an alien hovering over Portbay tonight, I'd probably think it was the most magical place on –

Bleep!

Much as I was loving the view, I guess the noise I most wanted to hear was the mechanical grind of the Big Wheel starting up again. But failing that, the *bleep!* of an incoming text message was pretty cool too.

"Don't! You're making it wobble again!" Frankie

begged once more, as I let go of the rail and fished my mobile out of my pocket.

"Oops, sorry! Hey, brilliant – it's from Neisha!" I grinned, happy to see our mate's message pop up on the illuminated panel. "She says. . . *Hi – is F there?*"

"I'm here all right," grumbled Frankie, through fear-gritted teeth.

"Look, don't worry," I tried to reassure her, simultaneously texting, *Yeah, F's here – having a mad time!* back to Neisha. "The fairground guys'll get us down soon!"

"They'd *better*," Frankie grumbled unhappily, "or they might end up with hotdog on their heads. . ."

"Huh? You haven't *got* a hotdog to chuck at them!"

"Yeah, but I might hurl the one I ate earlier if they don't hurry up. . ." she groaned miserably.

I was just about to ask her how she could be travel sick when we weren't even *moving* when a familiar bleep interrupted me.

"*Great! So u r not 2 freaked @ Seb news?*" I read aloud, my eyebrows slowly meeting in confusion. "*What* Seb news? Is Neish on about the girl at the Heath?"

I was just about to text back when the phone suddenly disappeared out of my hands.

"*Frankie!*" I gasped. "What did you do *that* for?"

"'Cause I know what Neish is on about, OK?"

"Er, OK," I frowned at her. "So . . . are you going to tell me what it is, then?"

"I'm. . . *I'm* going out with Seb, all right?!" she blurted out, looking half-tearful and half-defensive. "Neish must have thought I'd told you already!"

"*You* and *Seb*?!"

Urgh – tonight was getting more surreal by the millisecond. . .

"Yeah! Me and Seb!"

I felt as wobbly light-headed as I had when we came off the Waltzers earlier.

"But . . . but *you* said it was just some girl hanging out at Hampstead Heath!" I blustered, trying to make sense of something that made no sense at all.

"*I* was the girl hanging out at the Heath!"

"But . . . how? I mean. . . I mean. . . Well, *how*?"

Maybe I wasn't sounding too fluent in English, but Frankie managed to decipher what I was trying to babble.

"Look, I didn't plan for it to happen, Stella! I knew you always liked Seb – *obviously*. It's just that *I* liked him too, but I never ever said 'cause you got in there first. And I didn't know *he* liked me that way too, not till I ran after him when he left your party, when I was trying to get him to sign the photo as a surprise for you."

My limited powers of speech had dried up with the shock. Frankie felt the silence and filled it with more explanation.

"But Seb said he didn't want to write anything on the photo, 'cause he'd come to the party for *me*. He came 'cause he fancied *me*. And I just thought of you and felt terrible and couldn't say anything back. And then he sort of asked me to come up to the Heath the next night and hang out and . . . and . . . I *did*, and he's *lovely* and I like him so, *so* much, Stella, and I'm so, *so* sorry!"

My mouth might not have been working, but my mind certainly was. So *that's* why Seb always made a point of talking to our gang – he was really just talking to Frankie. And the two of them getting together; *that* must have been why Frankie had been off-and-on weird with me this past week.

"All this time you liked Seb too?" I mumbled.

"You should have told me! We tell each other everything!"

I couldn't figure out which was freakier – Frankie going out with Seb behind my back, or Frankie keeping something from me. We were supposed to be mates for ever, no secrets allowed, right?

"I was just looking out for you, like I always do!"

"Huh?" I blinked at her. "How is that looking out for me?"

Hurt, or maybe anger, flitted across Frankie's face.

"Stell, I've *always* taken care of you. I never let anyone hurt your feelings – not even me. So *that's* why I never blabbed about fancying Seb too!"

I crinkled up my nose, not really pleased at hearing her make out like I was some kind of injured bunny who needed constant protection. My silence – and nose crinkling – just seemed to make her *more* hurt and angry.

"You think it's always easy for me, don't you, Stell? Same as Lauren and Neisha and everyone. People look at us and think, Stella, she's the shy one, and there's Frankie, all loud and mouthy. *She's* all right. No one asks me if *I'm* feeling OK or sad or lonely, ever. It's like you leaving London,

201

everyone's, 'Poor Stella – what's it going to be like for her?' But how come it's never, 'Poor Frankie – how's it going to be for her, with her best friend moving away?'"

Now it was *my* turn to feel kind of angry and hurt, and maybe a bit guilty too. I mean, yeah, for the last few months, I'd been all wrapped up in coming here to Portbay, and I guess I hadn't thought about just how bad it would hit Frankie, but now it sounded like she resented me for not noticing how she'd been feeling. But what was I supposed to be – a mind reader? Was it *my* fault if she kept it all to herself?

And never mind that – there was still the fact that she went out with Seb about five seconds after I left town, and there were still a couple of questions about that that I needed answers to. . .

"Seb came over to me at the party and told me that he'd always thought I was kind of cute!" I blurted out.

"But you *are* cute, Stella!" said Frankie, rolling her eyes. "He was just being nice and giving you a compliment 'cause it was your leaving party!"

Talk about feeling gutted. . .

"But what about the Polaroid?" I frowned at Frankie. "He wrote that message on the Polaroid!"

Frankie bit her lip and stared at me . . . and the truth flooded into my befuddled brain.

"*You* wrote that, didn't you?"

"Well, I didn't want to disappoint you! I did a pretty good job of disguising my writing, didn't I?"

My so-called best friend suddenly seemed to realize that she had no hope of an answer to that question and wordlessly handed me my phone back.

And that's how we stayed for endless minutes, silently stuck in mid-air, with no way to escape each other, though that was the exact thing I was sure we both wanted to do. . .

"*CAWWWW!!*"

"Stella!" Frankie screeched, as loudly as the seagull that had swooped in front of us, bobbing on lazy currents of air and amusing itself with our predicament.

"It's all right – it's just a gull!" I snapped at her. "It won't hurt –"

Before I could explain that there was no danger of the bird dive-bombing us, the dopey thing only floated over and landed with a gentle thud on the back of our gondola.

"Eeek!" squeaked Frankie, yanking the hood of

her top up and pulling the drawstrings so tight that only her panic-stricken eyes peeked out.

The bird blinked blankly at her, wondering what all the fuss was about.

"What does it want?" a shaky, muffled voice came out of the hood.

"A fairy cake, I think."

"A *what*?"

And then I had a vision – if an alien *did* happen to be hovering in the vicinity right now, what would it see? One freckle-nosed, grumpy girl (me), Kenny from *South Park* (Frankie) and a large dorky bird (the fairy-cake fan), swaying gently in mid-air on a jammed fairground ride. It was too ridiculous for words. Actually, it was too ridiculous to keep a straight *face*. . .

"What are you laughing at?" Frankie muffled from inside her hood, probably alarmed that I'd turned psycho and was about to chuck her out of the gondola or something. But I was giggling too much to explain to her, and a few worried seconds later, I saw her eyes crinkle up with giggles too.

And you know a couple of somethings that occurred to me then? The first something was that already, although I'd only been here in Portbay a week, London – and Seb – seemed as far away as the stars spangling above me. It was just that Frankie's confession didn't *bother* me as much as I thought it would. Well, not the one about Seb, anyway. The stuff about how she wasn't as tough as she made out bothered me quite a *bit*, which brought me on to the *other* something: Elize and Joseph had lost touch; Nana Jones and Grandad Eddie had lost touch. Losing touch with people that mattered was awful, and no *way* was I going to let that happen to me and Frankie. No stupid boy with some stupid lopsided grin in stupid London was going to come between me and my oldest, bestest mate. . .

"Frankie?" I said, when the giggles eased off.

"Uh-huh?" she mumbled, tugging the cord on her hood loose.

"From now on, no more secrets. We tell each other everything. *Everything*. OK?"

"OK!"

The seagull flapped away when me and Frankie started hugging, probably off to see if it could find any leftover toffee apples or Portbay rock or whatever weird food was its second favourite after fairy cakes. . .

Chapter 21

Fluffy burgers and undercover freckles

Ah . . . it was a perfect party, on a perfect summer Sunday afternoon. Smoke was billowing from the barbecue, neighbours were chatting, small children were headbutting each other and the sun was glinting off the skip. . .

"So what do you think of the house, Auntie V?" I asked, as my aunt glided over towards me and Frankie with a paper plate in one hand and a look of pure horror on her face.

"Well, Stella, my little star, it's nice . . . if you like cowsheds," she shrugged, placing the plate on the nearest window sill with a clang of silver and amber bracelets. I noticed she'd only taken one, neat bite out of her burger.

"Listen, girls, I'm only going to tell you this once," Auntie V suddenly lowered her voice to a whisper. "Stick to the hotdogs – the burgers are like burnt dog food!"

Frankie and me swapped glances and tried not

to giggle. Not just 'cause it was funny the way Auntie V was slagging off Dad's barbecuing skills (specially when she was smiling and waving to him at the same time), but because we knew *another* reason not to touch the dog-food burgers. This morning, we'd been too busy e-mailing Neisha and the others (telling them everything was out in the open and everything was cool) that we hadn't gone with Dad to pick up Auntie V from the station. Once we'd pressed the last "send" on the last message, me and Frankie ambled through to the kitchen – and caught my harassed mum washing fluff off the frozen burgers under the kitchen tap.

"The boys got hold of them," Mum had explained, red-faced, to us. "They were rolling them along the floor having a race!"

"Who won?" Frankie had joked, till she'd spotted Jake and Jamie pouring half a mug of cold tea into one of her trainers. . .

"We'll stick to the hotdogs, then!" I smiled at Auntie V, pretending to take her advice.

I wish I'd given her a bit of advice too – don't wear white trousers near small boys. I don't think she'd spotted the greasy handprints around her knee, where Jake had hugged her as soon as she'd arrived.

"You know I love them dearly, Stella," Auntie V began chatting again. "But your parents are insane. Who has a house-warming party in their driveway, with a skip full of rubble in full view?"

"Yeah, but they couldn't have it in the back garden," I started to defend Mum and Dad. "They haven't cleared it yet and I think they're scared there're bear traps in there!"

"Good to see you've still got a got a sense of humour, Stella," she turned and smiled, scrutinizing my face. "I was worried I'd find you in floods of tears today, stuck here in Cowshed Town, so far away from Frankie etc.!"

"It won't feel like they're too far away, not when we can e-mail and stuff," I told her.

"And Stella can come to London to visit us!" Frankie chipped in.

"Or you and Neish and Lauren and everyone can come down *here*!" I pointed out to Frankie.

"What, so we can play crummy crazy golf or something dullsville like that?" Frankie grinned at me.

I think it was going to take her a few visits to get used to Portbay, like I had. Mad as it sounded, I wasn't in too much of a hurry to rush back to Kentish Town – not when I had gallons more to find out about this weird place that was now home.

"You know something?" Auntie V suddenly said, narrowing her eyes and putting a hand out to stroke my curls. "All this sea air seems to suit you, Stella. You're sounding – I mean, *looking* really good."

"Now, you've got to watch the truth; it has a funny habit of slipping out, even when you hold it back!": that's another of Aunt Esme's favourite sayings. And my *real*-life aunt might have just corrected herself, but I knew what she meant, and I knew Auntie V was right. I *was* sounding better. I'd always been able to chat away easily to my parents and Frankie, but since I'd been here, I wasn't just saving my words for *their* ears. And the words I was saying didn't start with a stammer . . . well, not as often as they used to.

And I liked that. A *lot*. I liked the fact that I could be a whole new Stella in this town. I wasn't Stella the non-star, and I wasn't Frankie's silent, shy friend. To anyone who might be interested, I was the new girl from London, with too many freckles but really great hair. . .

"Hey, I think your dad's waving you over!" Frankie suddenly nudged me, pointing to Dad's blond head sticking up above a sea of bobbing, chatting neighbourly faces.

I started over towards him, Frankie following. In our wake, at the cracking sound of another headbutt, Auntie V lunged across the driveway shouting, "Animal! Gonzo! Would you two *stop* doing that!"

"Stella!" Dad beamed, waving a barbecue fork around with a blackened sausage stuck on the prongs. "This is Maggie, the lady I was telling you about, from next door!"

Oh, yeah, the ex-teacher. She was slim, grey-haired and sporty-looking. Er ... I *really* hoped that friendly smile aimed in my direction didn't mean she was about to offer me extra tuition *after* all.

"Hello, Stella! Your father said you were keen to find out about the artist who lived in your cottage. And I thought this might just solve the mystery!"

Gingerly, with a quick glance at Frankie, I took the old yellowed newspaper she was holding out.

"I found it in my loft yesterday, when I was storing a few things. It was used to line an old chest of drawers. . ."

Frankie leant her chin on my shoulder as I opened up the crackly, fragile paper. The date at the top of the front page read, 12 July, 1930. I didn't know what I was looking for at first, but with a nudge from Maggie, I turned to the second page of the *Portbay Chronicle* and saw a grainy black-and-white photo of a very, *very* old lady, sitting in a pretty garden with an easel in front of her, a floppy felt hat shading her eyes from the summer sun. On the easel was a familiar half-finished painting of a fairy, and on a small table by her side was a pretty china cup and a wooden box for her pencils. Because of the angle, you couldn't see the letters *E G* carved on the top of the box, but I *knew* Elize Grainger's initials would be there.

"'*A Hundred Years of History! Miss Grainger celebrates her centenary with her favourite hobby, painting*'," Frankie read aloud. "'*It may be a far cry from her former palatial home in Sugar Bay, but for the last thirty years, Miss Elize Grainger has been very happy in the much smaller but nonetheless most commodious surroundings of Foxglove Cottage.*' God, they were pretty fond of using big words in those days, weren't they? I mean, what's 'commodious' supposed to mean?"

Frankie was still asking her question when I mumbled my thanks to Maggie and ran off around the side of the house in the direction of the garden. . .

*

"That smelly cat isn't in here, is it?"

"No," I told Frankie as she followed me into the outhouse. "And he's *not* smelly. Well, he *is*, but in a good way. . ."

Frankie didn't look convinced – just like Portbay, it was going to take a bit of time for her to fall for Peaches' scuzzy charms.

After walking in warily, Frankie pulled up the armchair that Peaches liked to sleep in and sat down beside me at the table. (I didn't dare think about the fact that she was wearing her new black trousers. . .)

"So what's that you're looking at?" she asked, pointing at the chipped china cup and wooden box I'd taken down from the shelves.

"*This*, actually," I told her, holding up the blackened brass button that had been in the box when I first came across it. "I think it belonged to—"

"Joseph! The servant guy, right? He was wearing some fancy jacket with buttons like that in the painting, wasn't he?"

So Frankie had been paying more attention than

I thought at the museum yesterday! Or maybe it was just that she'd tried *really* hard to listen this morning, when I'd taken her out to the den and explained why the house at Sugar Bay had fascinated me so much. And I knew Frankie really did understand now, specially when she got all choked up as I finished carving *Stella + Frankie, m8s 4eva, 2004* on the rickety window sill of the outhouse.

"She must have kept this as a memento of her old friend!" I said softly, turning the button over in my fingers.

"I guess. . ." nodded Frankie, her braids swaying across her shoulders. "Hey, you'll have to get this newspaper story framed, and the photo your mum dug out last night!"

Oh, yes, today I'd found out a chunk of the history of the house, but last night – after we'd finally been set free from the Big Wheel – me and Frankie arrived home to discover that Mum had unearthed a chunk of history about *me*.

"Stella, I swear I never knew they were there," Mum had told me, as she stared at the photo she'd handed to me. "Ever since I was little, I remember my mum wearing heavy make-up. I always thought it was just her style; I didn't know she was slapping it on to cover her freckles!"

The black-and-white photo of Nana Jones in all her 17-year-old freckly glory was now pinned to my corkboard, till Woolworths opened tomorrow morning and I could get a decent frame for it.

"He was pretty cute-looking, your grandad, wasn't he?" Frankie commented, leaning forward and squinting at the handsome young guy hugging my Nana Jones so proudly, laughter dimples visible in his dark skin.

"Yep," I nodded, just as happy and delighted as I had been last night that Mum had finally found one of those elusive "spare moments" and come across this photo that she'd never known existed in Nana Jones's stuff. And it was great that it had nudged her memory a little.

"Of course! I *do* remember my mother saying he worked on a fairground. That's why he was only there for the summer, then moved on!"

"Weird coincidence him working on a fair when we've just been to one!" Frankie murmured, her eyes skimming over the gaudily painted Waltzers in the background, covered in ornate decorations of fat cherubs and flighty fairies.

"Isn't it?" I agreed, though I didn't think that for a *second*. Secretly, I didn't believe in coincidences any more, not since I'd come to Portbay. . .

"Prrrp!"

Uh-oh – Frankie had better prepare herself for Peaches and his Amazing Shedding Hair. Any second now he'd come bounding through my still-to-be-repaired broken windowpane (minus the lethal shards, which Dad had removed, only causing himself one deep cut and a few scratches).

And then I heard another familiar voice, and peered outside.

"Er, hello there, pussy!" Auntie V was saying, veering away as Peaches tried to curl himself and his ginger fur around her legs. "Have you seen Stella etc., hmm? I've got to tell them it's safe to come back now – the new neighbours have eaten all the dog burgers!"

I grinned, partly at Auntie V's joke and partly because I *really* liked the sound of what she'd just said: Stella etc.

OK, so at the moment, Stella etc. consisted of me (Stella), and an ugly, fat, funny-smelling cat called Peaches. But give me time (like a whole summer holiday), and who knew who'd be part of the "etc."?

I couldn't *wait* to find out.

"Oh, there you are!" said Auntie V, sticking

her head around the outhouse door and frowning through her smile, as if she was terrified that a family of spiders might drop into her serum'd hair. "Jake and Jamie just fed the cheesecake your mum made to the collie from across the road, so your neighbour Maggie's brought around a tray of biscuits that she just made. Coming to get one?"

"What kind are they?" asked Frankie dubiously. "I hate biscuits – they're so boring."

"Well, they're not *biscuits* exactly," Auntie V shrugged, oblivious to the cobweb that had attached itself to the side of her head. "They're old-fashioned, and in those funny paper cups. What are they called again? Fairy cakes! Yes, *that's* it!"

"My favourite!" I grinned, following my aunt out into the sunlight.

Walking around to the front of the cottage, I heard Frankie curse as Peaches lovingly wound his way between her legs, shedding hairs and practically tripping her up with every step.

And me? Well, I was busy scouring the sky for signs of seagulls with a sweet tooth. . .

From: Frankie
To: *stella*
Subject: Re: Helloooooooooooo!

Hi Stella!

No worries about missing my phone call – if you had to help look after the Muppets, then you had to help look after the Muppets. (By the way, tell your mum that the bite-mark on my arm has practically healed. And tell Jamie I'm going to bite him back when he's big enough!)

But seriously, thanks for sending me that stuff Stell – that first week you left was weird for us both in different ways, wasn't it, and it's great to hear it all from your side. I'd love to sit down and write things from my side now too, but I won't because I'm way, way too lazy. Ha!

Nothing much happening this end. Well, OK, things are going brilliantly with Seb, but I'm not going to go on about that 'cause I still feel a bit weird about the whole thing with you and me and him. I know it bugs you when I say that, but tough. Double ha!

Miss you ☹, but m8s 4eva ☺!
Frankie

PS Tell Peaches that I still keep finding his hair everywhere!

PPS Send more attachments – I need to know PROPERLY what's going on. Like who was that boy who answered your mobile the other day, hmm? You'd better tell me more SOON, Stella!!

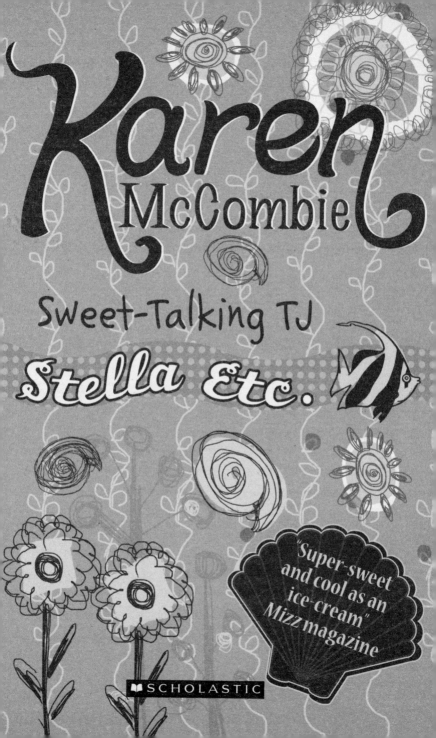

Karen McCombie

Sweet-Talking TJ

Stella Etc.

"Super-sweet
and cool as an
ice-cream"
Mizz magazine

SCHOLASTIC

Contents

From:	*stella*
To:	FFFrankie
Subject:	Hope you're bored 'cause here's more stufff to read!
Attachments:	"Sweet-Talking TJ"

Hi FFFrankie!

Wow . . . Lauren just e-mailed THE most boring e-mail I have ever had in my lifffe. I really miss you lot in London and love hearing fffrom you, but did Lauren *really* need to tell me the shape she fffiled her nails into? I wrote back and told her that ifff she was really fffed up, she should ask her mum and dad ifff she could come and visit me, and we could just have fffun, hanging out at the beach fffeeding fffairy cakes to the psycho seagull and stufff. She hasn't got back to me yet – d'you think I scared her offf by mentioning the psycho seagull?!

Talking about e-mails, in the last one you sent, I couldn't fffigure out what you were on about in your PS – the bit about "who was the boy that answered your mobile?". It did my head in fffor ages, and then it suddenly hit me, and I realized. . .

Hey, you know something? I'm not going to tell you here, 'cause that'll spoil the surprise. I thought it'd be better ifff I wrote the whole thing down, starting fffrom the night after you got the train back to London, 'cause that's when . . . oops! Nearly blew it again!

Look, just read the attachment and it'll all make sense. (Er. . .)

Miss you ☹, but M8s 4eva ☺!

stella

PS It took me ages to input this because Peaches is sprawled out and snoring *right* in fffront of the keyboard. I have to hit the "FFF" key really hard 'cause of a wodge of ginger fffur stuck under there. . .

Chapter 1

Fuzzy eyeballs

Y'know . . . when you cross your eyes, things look really different. (Including you; it makes you look like a right idiot.)

At this moment, my idiotically crossed eyes were gawping across the jumble of tiled rooftops outside my bedroom window, vaguely focusing on the faraway fairground down by the beach. When I squeezed my fuzzy eyeballs together, all the jewel-coloured bulbs on the Big Wheel looked blurrily beautiful, like gently pulsating lights on some alien spacecraft, hovering in the sunset over Portbay. . .

Hey, that was pretty poetic.

Or maybe it just sounds like the rantings of a nutter; I don't know.

Blame my sudden genius/nutter rantings on the fact that it was nine-ish on Sunday night and I was *completely* pour-me-into-bed tired after the weekend. It had all been a bit like the roller coaster me and Frankie had whizzed around on last night, hanging on for dear life and not knowing whether to shriek in total fear or burst into a bad case of the giggles.

So how'd you describe the weekend I'd just had?

Put it this way, if I saw the words "GREAT", "TERRIBLE", "EVEN *MORE* TERRIBLE", "EMOTIONAL", "FUN", and "ZONKED" on a form with tick boxes, I'd tick *every* single one.

I'd tick "GREAT", 'cause Frankie had come to visit me here at the new house (and new town).

I'd tick "TERRIBLE", 'cause she'd acted weird, making me homesick for London, homesick for Seb (the boyfriend I *might* have had), homesick for all my old friends, and homesick for the best, most brilliant mate that Frankie (usually) was.

I'd tick "EVEN *MORE* TERRIBLE", 'cause of Frankie admitting last night that she was the girlfriend Seb definitely *did* have (urgh). And the fact that she admitted it while we were marooned at the top of a broken-down Big Wheel ride didn't exactly help (but that's another story).

I'd tick "EMOTIONAL", 'cause of Frankie and me falling out, then making up again, promising to be friends for ever, and never to let boys and long distances get in the way.

I'd tick "FUN", 'cause of this afternoon's house-warming party – having Auntie V here, as well as Frankie, was ace. And then, through our new neighbour, I got to find out lots of info on the mysterious person who used to live in our house.

And finally, I'd tick "ZONKED", 'cause of all the post-party tidying that had to be done, *and* 'cause of all of the above added together. . .

"Hey, Stella – that was your Aunt Vanessa on the phone!" I heard Dad call up from downstairs. "She's just got back home, but she told me to let you know that she and Frankie managed to get a seat together on the train back to London!"

Actually, I'd just e-mailed Frankie about twenty minutes ago, asking how the trip home had gone (probably had a million spelling mistakes in it I was so tired). I was glad to hear it went OK – even if I wasn't hearing it from *her*.

"Great!" I called out in reply.

I could make out Mum shushing Dad from somewhere, annoyed with him for risking waking the twins. Ha! If they were half as tired as I was, you could yell the theme tune of *EastEnders* through a megaphone at them and they wouldn't move a muscle.

I should've given in and headed for my bed

and early snoozeland too, but I didn't have the energy to get up from my kneeling (OK, *slouching*) position on the floor of my room. So I just let my elbows slither further apart on the windowsill and stared – kind of contentedly – into space.

That was until my hazy view of the twinkling Big Wheel was suddenly obscured by a huge black shadow. . .

OK, OK, so it was more of a huge, *ginger* shadow. A ginger shadow that looked fuzzy even once I'd uncrossed my eyes.

"Hi, Peaches!" I smiled at the huge scruffy cat that had silently hopped up on the windowsill and settled its purring self *right* in front of my face.

"Prrrrp!"

I couldn't be absolutely sure what "prrrrp!" meant, but I had a funny feeling that it translated as "I've been curled up in your den in the garden, hiding away from your demented little brothers".

I couldn't blame Peaches if he *had* hidden away; at this afternoon's house-warming party, the twins had somehow managed to eat a whole trifle between them when no one was looking, and spent the next hour roaring around on a sugar high, causing mayhem and resisting all attempts to be caught and have the cream and coloured sugar sprinkles washed off their faces/hands/ hair/clothes.

"Hey, I saved you some leftover hot dog," I told my cool cat, taking my elbows off the sill to make more room for His Tubbiness. "It's in your bowl in the kitchen. I even washed off the mustard so you don't burn your tongue!"

Peaches' green eyes stared deep into mine, as if he was slowly devouring that edible piece of information. Then he stretched forward, catty nostrils working overtime, until he gently touched his inquisitive nose on to mine, making my eyes go crossed all over again.

By the time I blinked my eyes into focus, he was gone, bounding out of the open window, landing on the kitchen roof with a powder-soft *doofff*, and then padding and pouncing off somewhere wherever. And there I was, left lounging on my bedroom floor, wondering what exactly I smelled of (leftover hot dog?) and if I'd just been given the feline version of a nose-rubbing Eskimo kiss.

"Except the *proper* name for Eskimos is Inuits," I murmured to myself, some module we'd done in geography about societies around the world popping pointlessly into my mushy brain. Of course, I'd learned that at my *old* school, back in London. After the holidays, I'd have a new school, a new geography teacher, and new classmates (gulp). Only five weeks to go (double gulp). . .

To take my mind off that distressing thought, I grabbed a hunk of my T-shirt and sniffed hard, trying to suss out what exactly had got up Peaches' nose just now. Aha – it seemed that today's party and the tidying-up afterwards had left me with barbecue-scented hair and a general waft of Fairy Liquid. Nice. . .

Bleep!

It was only a tiny, high-pitched noise, but the sound of that incoming text message acted like a big, flashing, neon "GO!!" to my nervous system and I practically *scrambled* over to my bed, grabbing the flashing phone that I'd tossed on there earlier.

Remember – every day! was all it said, but it made me smile. It was from Frankie, that was for sure, reminding me of the promise we'd made to each other on the platform of Portbay station, earlier this evening. From now on, we'd keep in touch – by text, e-mail, letter, phone, jokey postcard or carrier pigeon – every single day, so that the distance between us didn't matter.

"M8s 4eva!" I keyed back to her, thinking how strange it was that she was back in London, and how strange it was that I didn't ache to be there too, considering how bad I felt about being dragged to this bizarre-o little town only a few days or so ago. But then, so much had changed in such a tiny amount of time: last Sunday, I'd been so miserable about moving to Portbay that it felt like someone had cut out my heart and stuffed a sack of sludge in its place. Then all the weird and kind of wonderful stuff started happening: Peaches moving in, like he'd always lived here; meeting the mad old lady (Mrs Sticky Toffee) with her even madder "pet" (a bad-tempered seagull with a sweet tooth); discovering Sugar Bay, and the secrets of the old, not-so-grand house there.

Amazingly, tonight, instead of yearning for my old life in Kentish Town, I was yearning for tomorrow to come, just to see what other secrets and surprises Portbay had in store for me. . .

Well, my newly reactivated brain might have been mostly full of vibey thoughts, but a tiny part of it was alerting me to an odd noise coming from somewhere outside.

"Bark!" [thump] "Bark!" [thump] "Bark!"

Dropping the phone back down on the duvet, I got up and wandered over to the open window.

"Bark!" [thump] "Bark!" [thump] "Bark!"

At the end of our overgrown tangle of a back garden, just over the tall brick wall that you can hardly see for tangle, there's a tiny lane that ambles between all the mismatching houses and cottages in our corner of the town. Right now, just above the top of the wall, I could make out a furry brown head – which appeared with a bark, before disappearing with a thump.

What's that dumb dog up to? I wondered to myself, watching its Jack-in-the-box routine.

And then I got it: Peaches.

In the couple of minutes since he'd flounced off the windowsill and left me to my mobile messaging, Peaches had perched himself comfortably on the garden wall, all the better to peer at passers-by – human and canine – on this warm, summer's evening. And now he was being peered at himself, by an over-enthusiastic four-legged "friend".

For a second there, I panicked, feeling a protective flurry of worry for Peaches, but then I realized I was wasting my time. I mean, I guess that any *normal* cat – faced with barking and big teeth at close quarters – would now be off like a shot, hissing and spitting, doing the whole arched-back thing. But not my Peaches. He was calmly squatting, paws tucked under his ample belly, watching this frantic, manic dog with nothing more than mild interest, the way you might let your eyes settle on a meandering dust-speck if you were spectacularly bored.

"Bob! C'mere! Leave the puss alone!" I heard a boy's voice suddenly urge.

I was glad to hear that someone was in charge of the mental mutt, but it couldn't have been a very grown-up or tall someone – I couldn't see a hint of anyone above the adult-sized wall.

"Bark!" [thump] "Bark!" [thump] "Bark!"

"Bob! I said *down*, boy!"

Whoever the kid was and however young he was, the dog thankfully did what he was told and gave up with a gruff "Awww, spoilsport!" grumble.

"You idiot! Don't you remember the *last* time you tried to lick a cat?" I heard a voice chatter, as the kid and "Bob" set off down the lane. "It took *months* for your nose to heal. . ."

As the voice, the dog-panting, footsteps and claw-taps faded away along the cobblestoned lane, I gazed down at Peaches, who at that exact same second turned and looked up at me. And *winked*.

Wow, that cat sure was weird. . .

Chapter 2

Bob, the boy and the dive-bombing bird

Well, shock, horror: Jake and Jamie were playing nicely.

OAPs strolling past us on the beach cooed at the boys, who were happily digging and patting at their sandcastle, chubby hands clutched around plastic buckets and spades.

"Aren't they adorable!" said one older lady, stopping to smile down at the general cuteness.

"Like little angels!" said her friend, tilting her white-haired head.

"Mmmm!" I mumbled in reply, shading the sun from my eyes with my hand as I smiled up at the two elderly ladies who were obviously besotted with my brothers. Ha! They wouldn't have called Jake and Jamie angels if they had seen them this morning, having joint toddler tantrums and then a kicking competition, all over a quarrel about a piece of jammy toast.

("Er, Louise..." my dad had grinned at my

mum, as they each grabbed a twin before the boys put any serious dents into each other, "can you just remind me – *why* did we decide to have more kids after Stella?")

"Are they brothers, or just little friends?"

"Brothers. *My* brothers," I replied, not surprised at the woman's question, since the twins weren't identical, and none of the three of us looked particularly alike. "They're twins, actually."

"Twins? Oh, how lovely!" said her friend. "Twice the fun!"

("Do you think it's too late to take them back to the shop and get a refund?" my mum had joked drily to my dad, hoisting a wriggling, ranting Jake in the air earlier.)

"So boys, what are your names, hmm?" the first lady asked, bending over and ruffling the nearest two-year-old head, which happened to be Jamie's. My heart was suddenly in my mouth: my mate Eleni back in London has this sweet little Jack Russell called Dixie that no one can resist petting when her family takes him for a walk. Then Eleni or whoever always has to launch into this big apologizing thing after Dixie has nipped a chunk out of the well-meaning stranger's hand. The trouble is, Jamie isn't as fussy as Dixie; stranger,

235

sister, friend, foe, fellow toddler, OAP . . . he'll bite anyone if he's in the mood. I held my breath and silently prayed that he *wasn't* in the mood.

"NEMO!" yelled Jamie, grinning widely enough to show off his fine rows of baby teeth. (Good: *showing* was cool; *using* wasn't.)

"GONZO!" yelled Jake, throwing his head back for full roaring effect.

"Oh, um . . . those are *very* unusual names!" muttered the lady who'd asked the question. In that split second, I could practically read her thoughts: "I don't know; parents these days! Why can't they give their children *sensible* names?" But before I could explain that Jamie was obsessed with his new bucket and spade set (decorated with scenes from Disney's *Finding Nemo*), and that Jake was just yelling out the nickname my Auntie V has for him (after a character from the old Muppets TV show), a sudden honk distracted her.

"Maureen – I think that's our bus driver tooting. We'd better get a move on!" said Maureen's friend, nodding at the day-trippers' coach up on the prom.

"Yes, we better had. Well, bye, dear! Bye, er, boys!"

The three of us – me, Nemo and Gonzo –

waved at the departing ladies, as they struggled to hurry across the hot golden sands that seemed to swallow up their sandals with every step.

"Big ladies go wibble-wobble," Jamie/Nemo announced, loudly enough for a bunch of nearby bikini'd sunbathers to start sniggering.

Yikes.

When I saw the four girls push themselves up on their elbows and look over at us, I felt myself blushing, and quickly rummaged around in the sand for my half-buried sunglasses to hide behind. It wasn't *just* the fact that my brothers were embarrassment on four legs, it was more the fact that I recognized those girls: they were the same crew that did a stare-a-thon on me that first time I went into the Shingles café with Mum and the boys. And let's just say that from their sneers, they sure let me know *exactly* what they thought of me. (Clue: not much.)

"Er, whatever . . . and little boys go dig, dig, right?" I said, turning and trying to restart the twins' interest in their sandcastle, before they embarrassed me any more.

Luckily, digging *did* seem more interesting than shouting after wibbly-wobbly big ladies, and the boys went back to creating what looked like

Camelot to *them*, and a big mound of sand to everyone else. And luckily, the girls from the café slid back down on to their towels and carried on burning themselves pink.

Which gave me the chance to pull out my mobile and talk to a friendly face, even if I couldn't see it.

"Frankie? S'me!" I smiled, turning my head away from the direction of the café crew so they didn't get a chance to earwig on my conversation.

"Hey, Stella! I was just going to e-mail you!"

"Yeah? What were you going to say?"

"Just thanks for the e-mail you sent last night – I picked it up this morning. And just to tell you that I ended up sitting with your Auntie V all the way back on the train last night."

"Too late – I knew that already. Dad spoke to Auntie V last night!" I told her, ruffling grains of sand through the fingers of one hand and idly people-watching from behind the safety of my sunglasses at the same time. (Facing this way, I could see a family racing each other squealing into the sea; the blokes up in the prom car park dismantling the fairground rides; a bored-looking indie kid boy kicking along the sand with a hairy dog and a singing, skipping little girl in tow.)

"Yeah? Well, that's saved valuable writing time, I guess! So what're you up to, Stell?"

"I'm at the beach, babysitting the boys."

"Why? What are your mum and dad doing?"

"Dad's heavily into his DIY today—"

"He's wrecking the house some more, you mean?" Frankie said cheekily (and truthfully).

"Yep. And Mum's at the hairdresser."

I was hoping that Mum wouldn't be too long; it wasn't that I was stressing out about looking after the boys or anything, it was just that I was itching to get to Woolworths and check out their photo frames, dull as that might sound to anyone else. But it wasn't dull to me; I'd promised myself that I'd get a nice frame for the black and white snapshot Mum had come across at the weekend. For the moment, it was pinned to a corkboard in my den in the garden (i.e. the outhouse Dad had helped me clear out). But it was too precious to leave like that; because a) it was the one and only photo I had of Nana Jones and Grandad Eddie together, and b) it was the one and only photo of people in my family who looked *anything* like me.

Y'see, I hadn't inherited my dad's tall, blond looks, and I didn't look much like my mum, with her olive skin and long, dark, straight hair. (At least, I *hoped* it was still long, dark and straight when the hairdresser had finished with her.) But anyway, I'd gone a bit shivery on Saturday night, when Mum shoved the photo under my freckly nose, 'cause *there* was my pretty Nana Jones (aged seventeen), with a mass of freckles sprinkled over her *own* pale nose, and there was her boyfriend (Grandad Eddie, aged eighteen), a handsome young black guy with his hair like a dark halo against the brightly painted backdrop of the fairground where he worked.

It was just a pity that I couldn't meet them in person, to talk about how much of a pain freckles are with my Nana Jones, and ask Grandad Eddie if he liked my golden-brown version of his own dark afro curls. But neither of them was around, mainly 'cause one of them died years ago (Nana Jones) and one of them had vanished (Grandad Eddie, about six weeks after the photo had been taken and *before* Nana Jones could tell him that she was expecting my mum).

Still, you can't change what you can't change, as Frankie's mum used to say; and she's very fond of her sayings, is Frankie's mum. I was just thrilled that my mum had come across the photo at all, and that I had this tiny but important piece of my own history. . .

"Bob! *No!*"

"Who's that?" Frankie asked, her natural nosiness picking up on the boyish, shouting voice close by me.

"Er . . . I dunno," I said, hardly able to talk about someone who was only standing about a metre away. And then I heard a boy in the background at Frankie's end too.

"Hey, Stella – Mum's just let Seb in. Look, can I call you back later?"

"Sure, talk to you later," I nodded to no one in particular, wondering how long it would be before Frankie stopped feeling awkward about mentioning Seb, since (amazingly) it didn't really bother me much any more.

"*Bob!* What did I *say*?"

Pressing the end-call button on the phone, I immediately zoned in on the look of alarm on both my brothers' faces as a *very* large, *very* hairy Alsatian loomed over them, lifted his leg and prepared to pee over Camelot.

"Down, *now!*"

"Hurfff?" gruffed the dog, as it lowered its leg and stared up dolefully at the boy hollering at it.

"*Naughty* Bob! *Naughty* Bob! Bob's a very *naughty* dog!" a blonde little girl sing-songed to the Alsatian, who turned its hairy head and gazed at her with mild confusion.

(Uh-oh – all the commotion had got the café crew up on their elbows for a nosey, I couldn't help but notice out of the corner of my eye.)

"C'mere!" the boy ordered, trying to sound stern and pointing to his side. I wasn't sure if he was talking to the pooch or the little girl (his sister?), but as the girl took no notice of him and kept skipping barefoot, daisy-decorated sandals swinging in her hand, I guessed it was the pooch.

Like a kid who's just been told off, "Naughty Bob" reluctantly ambled where he was told, by the boy's side, his head held sulkily low. Meanwhile, the little girl started skipping around the sandcastle, merrily singing her "Naughty Bob" song, while the twins stared at her with the same mildly confused expressions the dog had on its fuzzy face just now.

"Sorry," the boy said, with a cute grin a mile wide. "Thought you were about to get a moat around your castle then!"

Pretty funny.

"I guess!" I laughed, scrambling to my feet to

talk to him (and keeping my back to the café crew so they couldn't put me off). "He's cute!"

As I patted the hairy bundle of dog, I was chuffed to notice that there was no sign of my first-time-speaking-to-someone stammer. Though to be honest, *that* only tended to rear its head when I was nervous – in front of anyone remotely older than me, or especially when it came to people around my own age. But now that I was standing up next to this lad, er, make that *towering over* him, I sussed out that he could have only been about ten, or maybe eleven, which made my lack of stammering make sense, if you see what I mean.

"Yeah, he's great, but he's just a bit thick!" the boy continued, rubbing the top of the dog's head so hard it shook, which earned him a tongue-lolling smile from "Bob".

Bob . . . of course.

"Y'know, I *saw* you last night. Or at least a bit of your dog," I said, rewinding Bob's Jack-in-the-box trick in my head. "He was barking at my cat in the alleyway behind my house!"

The boy frowned for a second, pushing the floppy fair hair back off his face as he tried to figure out what I was on about. It didn't take too long.

"Ah, right! That cat – what's its name again? Peaches! He's living with you now, is he?"

"Uh-huh," I said nodding, remembering what Mrs Sticky Toffee had said about Peaches' wandering spirit. It still seemed funny to think that people around the town knew Peaches already, when I was just starting to feel like he belonged to me. Or more like *I* belonged to him. . .

"So you've moved in to that old dump in Dingle Lane?" the boy asked bluntly, the smile freezing on his face when he realized what he'd said.

"Don't worry," I told him, smiling so he knew I wasn't horribly offended. "It *is* a bit of a dump! But my dad's doing it up, so it should be pretty nice . . . by the time I'm thirty-five, maybe!"

Hey, I made a joke! And I got a laugh! Back home in London with my old gang, it was always Frankie or Neisha or one of the other girls that made the jokes and got the laughs, never shy old *me*.

"Yeah – that place could be OK," said the boy, trying to sound positive and undo the boo-boo he'd made. "I, uh, probably should just keep my mouth shut, but I sneaked in there once, when it was empty. There was a broken window. Had a nosey around and everything!"

That was a bit weird to hear too. I mean, our house had sat unloved and unlived-in for *years* before my mum and dad bought it, but it was funny (peculiar, not ha-ha) to think that this lad might have wandered around my room before I'd ever set eyes on its peeling walls.

Still, what did it matter? Hadn't I gone noseying around the old, deserted, dilapidated mansion in Sugar Bay, once or twice – OK, make that *three* times – this last week? What *did* matter was that this was the first conversation I was having with someone even *vaguely* near my own age since I'd moved here, and I didn't want it to stop. I was just about to try another joke – something pathetic like asking him if he'd needed to call Jungle Rescue to find his way out of our hugely overgrown garden – when a funny (peculiar) thing happened.

"Don't move. Please!"

The boy hurriedly stepped directly in front of me, and was hunkering his head down into his shoulders, like he was trying to do a turtle impersonation and make his head disappear into his scruffy, khaki, army-style shirt. Confused, I cast my eyes right (nothing, apart from vaguely curious café crew, who were whispering amongst themselves), and then left (and just saw my brothers, who were now skipping Pied Piper-style behind the little girl, followed by Bob, who was sniffing madly at what looked suspiciously like a bit of jammy toast peeking out of Jake's pocket).

"What is it? What's wrong?" I asked, feeling suddenly like a human shield.

"It's just some lads I know. Er, mates, I s'pose. Just don't want to see them right now."

I couldn't figure out *why* you might not want to see your so-called mates, but what I *could* figure out was that they must be somewhere directly behind me. With a quick swivel of my head, I turned and spotted four guys, slouching grouchily along the prom.

"They're your *mates?"*

I turned back to face the cowering boy whose name I didn't know yet and frowned. OK, so I didn't know a *lot* of stuff about him, but it didn't seem, well, *right* somehow that those slouchy, grouchy lads could be people he'd hang out with. For a start, they were a lot older than him (they were at least fifteen, I reckoned), and second, they looked like *trouble*. (Actually, what they also looked like was familiar, weirdly enough. . .)

"Yeah, well . . . kind of. It's just— Oh, God, not *now*!"

I heard the flap of wings a millisecond before the ear-splitting cawing started up.

"Gerraway! *Gerroff!*" the boy yelped, stumbling about and doing plenty of flapping himself, as a huge seagull began dive-bombing him.

"Shoo!" I said feebly, then stopped as a flash of recognition hit me. Was it the same one I kept seeing? The one with the sweet tooth (sweet beak?) that Mrs Sticky Toffee fed fairy cakes to?

Maybe I should do a Bob and grab that jammy piece of toast off Jake and see if I can lure it away, I thought frantically, wondering what exactly this big bird had against this potential new friend of mine.

Speaking of Bob. . .

"Bark! Bark! Bark!" Bob woofed madly, leaving the Pied Piper trail and coming to the rescue of his master.

And then I heard *another* noise above the shouting, cawing, barking commotion: cackling.

At first I suspected the café crew – who, sure enough, were sniggering themselves stupid again – but the source of the cackle was *way* too deep and blokey for them. I turned and saw the gang of lads, now leaning on the blue prom railings, presumably to stop themselves from falling down laughing at the sight of their mate's predicament.

"Hey, Deejay!" one of them yelled over. "Got to watch out for that seagull, mate! The size of you, it could lift you up and carry you away!"

The rest of the lads went into cackling overdrive at that dig – and *that's* when I knew where I recognized them from. They were the boys who'd laughed at me in the Shingles café last weekend, when I ended up with Jake's tomato sauce handprints on the front of my T-shirt. *And* they were the same ones Frankie had blown a cheeky kiss at and made a fool of when she was here. . .

Anyway, never mind me: the cackling definitely got a reaction from the boy. He flushed through eight shades of pink as he glanced at the lads, then at the café crew, then at me.

"Ellie, come on – let's go!" he suddenly ordered his skipping, singing maybe-sister, while the seagull circled higher, out of Bob's barking way.

"'Deejay. . .?" I muttered to myself, my eyes fixed on the boy's speedily retreating back, as he scarpered along the sands, head down and cheeks vivid. Behind him, his maybe-sister and his dog skipped and galloped. Above them all, the seagull swirled ominously.

What would that day-tripping old lady make of someone landing their kid with a name like "Deejay" – specially if she thought Nemo and Gonzo were bad? I couldn't help wondering.

"Bye, doggie!" Jake called after them in a disappointed voice.

"Bye, girl!" Jamie called out, ditto.

My brothers looked like they hadn't a clue what had just gone on. Well, I might have been eleven years older than them, but I didn't have much of a clue either. What in Bob's name was all that hiding, teasing and dive-bombing all about?

Hey, it looked like it was just another weird day in bizarre-o Portbay. . .

Chapter 3

A lot of naff, with a touch of twee

I'd been worried that Mum would go into the hairdresser's with a semi-decent, semi-grown-out haircut, and come out looking like she was wearing a bad wig for a joke.

The reason I didn't hold out much hope for her getting anything remotely resembling a half-decent haircut was that the woman who ran the place had hairsprayed blonde candyfloss perched on her head, which was strangely similar to the doggy hairdos of the two pet shih-tzus flopped on the salon floor. Also, the fact that the owner seemed oblivious to the spelling mistake on her shop sign didn't make me trust her judgement too much either.

But now I took it all back: the Style Compony had actually done a pretty good job.

"Quite nice, isn't it?" Mum asked, glimpsing the reflection of her long, layered, dark bob in the window that we and the buggy were parked in front of.

"Yeah, it is nice," I nodded, taking a lick of the ice-cream cone she'd just bought me. "But I'm still planning on sneaking down here one night with a ladder and some paint and putting that sign right!"

"What, doing some spelling graffiti, you mean?" said Mum, grinning at me over the top of her lemon sorbet.

It was fun just hanging out with her, talking rubbish, mooching around the few shops that Portbay had to offer. The thing about Mum is, she's great (and really groovy, according to all my friends), but hanging-out time together – just me and her – was always pretty limited. *Pre*-twins, it was 'cause she worked long hours in the marketing department of the same magazine compony (sorry, *company* – it's catching!) that Dad used to work for. And then *post*-twins ... well, one sweet-natured little baby would have kept her busy enough, I guess, but *two* boisterous babies meant there were times when I didn't really get a look-in. Still, to make up for dragging me away from London, Mum seemed to be making a big effort. Or maybe she was just a bit more relaxed here in Portbay. And it sure helped right now that both the boys were sound asleep and drooling in their double buggy, after a hard morning's work creating their mega sand mound (without moat).

"Anyway, you still haven't chosen your favourite," Mum reminded me, nodding at the display inside the window, which we'd been gawping at before her reflection caught our attention.

The shop we'd stopped at was the Portbay Galleria, although it should really have been called the Portbay Nafferia, since every piece of locally made art and craftiness lovingly exhibited could have won top prizes in a national Naff competition, with consolation prizes in the "Twee" and "Rotten" categories. There were dozens of seashorey landscapes, all duller than the last one. There were clay figurines of jolly fishermen, jolly smugglers, and jolly pirates, who all looked like the same jolly guy; with the sculptor swapping a sword for a swag-bag, or an eyepatch for a fish, depending on which character he was trying to capture. (Mum said she hoped he never got muddled and ended up sticking a haddock instead of a parrot on the pirate's shoulder.) There were sets of crystal fish, which consisted of hunks of crystal with googly plastic eyes and the odd fin stuck on. There were bits of driftwood carved into shells, shells glued together into something that *might* have been a frolicking seal (or haddock), and even bog-standard stones with the word "Portbay" painted on them, specially made for those tourists suffering from a severe lack of taste.

"I think the lampshade made out of dried seaweed is my favourite," I decided finally. "Think of the pong once you've had the light on for a while!"

"Yeah, well that *is* bad," Mum agreed, "but the worst one's *got* to be the painting of the mermaid, hasn't it?"

Actually, Mum was right. There were a few paintings by the same artist – of the usual fishermen, pirates and smugglers mostly – but they all had one thing in common; terrible fingers. Since drawing's just about my favourite thing to do, I know how hard hands can be, but if I was as bad as *this* artist, I'd stick to bland landscapes, or make the people in my paintings hide their hands behind useful props, like boats, treasure chests and large parrots. I mean, the muddle at the end of each arm was distracting enough when you studied the fishermen, pirates and smugglers, but it looked particularly awful on the serene mermaid, perched on her rock, scales shining, hair tumbling . . . and a bunch of sausages in her lap.

"Looks like there hasn't been a good local artist in this town since Miss Grainger!" said Mum, talking about the old lady who we'd just found out owned our house, decades ago.

Once upon that faraway time, Elize Grainger had used my den as an art studio, and I had one of her delicate fairy paintings – discovered and dusted off – up on the wall in her honour.

"But never mind Miss Grainger – *your* stuff's miles better than most of this lot, Stella!"

As soon as Mum said that, a faint haze of lime and sugar-pink caught my eye in the glass of the window. Spinning around, I expected to see Mrs Sticky Toffee strolling along the prom, her meringue netting hat keeping the sun off her head, her shiny green raincoat flapping in the breeze, swinging her tiny bag crammed with sweet treats for any human/cat/seagull she happened to come across. Whether the mad old dear knew it or not, she'd got me kind of interested in this town and all its stories, and since I'd got Mum's attention, I'd have loved to point her out.

But there was no one there. Well, no one apart from a whole crowd of holidaymakers, I mean, and the only pink on view was a few lobster-shaded people who'd lain on the beach too long and were too stupid to use sunblock.

Speaking of which. . .

"Hey, look at this," said Mum, pushing the buggy along the pavement and reading a notice that was just being stuck up on the shop door. "Fancy joining the local Knitting and Crochet Society, Stella?"

Mum was only fooling around, but right at that moment I found it hard to smile, since the person Sellotaping the sign on the other side of the glass door was one of the sunbathing café crew from earlier. What was she doing? Did she have a holiday job here or something? It would have to be a pretty laid-back job, if the boss let you have sunbathing breaks with your mates. . .

"I'd rather have a hole drilled in my head," I said, talking about joining the Knitting and Crochet Society, but the same could have been said about the idea of hanging out with this girl and the rest of the café crew. The girl probably thought the same thing about me; the second she clocked me standing outside, she turned her pretty, but pretty *sulky* face and walked away into the depths of the shop.

"Well, what about Dog Training classes?" Mum suggested, pointing to another sign. "You could take Peaches along and say he was a rare breed of Himalayan lion dog!"

"Or I could take Jake and Jamie – it would be handy to teach them to walk on a lead!" I joked back, relaxing now that I wasn't being given the evil eye any more.

"Ah, now *this* actually looks vaguely interesting," said Mum, leaning closer to read yet *another* sign. "Did you know it's the Portbay Gala Week in a fortnight's time?"

"Er, no. . ."

I was only half-listening – my attention had been grabbed again by something reflected in the window.

"There's going to be lots of events taking place all over town. Could be a laugh! Oh, and what's this? *'Tiny Acorns Play Workshop for 2 to 5 year olds'*. That could be fun for the boys, couldn't it?"

"I s'pose. . ."

I'd kind of zoned out of what Mum was saying as I watched a gang of lads stomping along the sands in a laughing scrum. I could've been wrong – since I couldn't see him – but I had a feeling that Deejay was somewhere in the middle of that scrum, mainly 'cause his blonde maybe-sister and

Bob the dog were tagging along behind, a safe distance away. That was odd: half an hour ago he couldn't get away from those lads fast enough. . .

Remember that boy's voice you heard in the background today? Well, his name's Deejay, and he's only a kid, really, but we got talking and he was a laugh, I wrote in my head, thinking of the e-mail I'd send Frankie once I got home. *But there's something weird going on with him and these older lads he's hanging out with – think they're the same ones you blew a kiss at in the café when you were here – and I really, really want to know what it's all about. . .*

And then I pressed the "delete" button in my brain and wiped my unwritten message. From the way she'd acted on the phone earlier, it was pretty obvious that Frankie was still hung up on guilt about dating Seb – which made me worry that if I wrote all that stuff then she'd jump on the word "boy" and get all excited at the prospect of me having someone *else* to have a crush on, ignoring the fact that Deejay was a) a stranger, and b) only came up to my *knees*.

No, I wouldn't mention him to Frankie till I knew more, except I wasn't exactly sure *how* I could make that happen. . .

Chapter 4

The sound of quiet hammering

Super-cool Peaches was acting like an idiot kitten, skittering around my bedroom floor. Well, I guess Peaches was a bit too tubby to do anything as kitten-like as skittering; I guess you'd probably call it waddling-at-high-speed.

Deejay has to be a nickname, right? I thought to myself, as I stepped out of Peaches' way and grabbed a clean, sand-free T-shirt from my drawer. *His friends must have given it to him, 'cause he's really into music or something. . .*

Speaking of music, while I got changed and mused over the boy at the beach, I had a CD on, really low, since the twins were still out for the count. (Mum and me had more or less *tipped* them out of their buggy and into their cots for their afternoon nap when we got back home.) The volume wasn't up loud enough to drown out the slow, tinny, tiny *tap-tap-tapping* coming from downstairs though. Ever heard of someone hammering quietly? Well, I think that's what Dad was trying to do now, as he worked on dismantling our old bathroom. Who knew what *that* was going to look like when he was finished, since DIY and Dad went together like bananas and Bovril. Back in London, he couldn't tell which end of a screwdriver was which, but since we'd moved here, he was determined to reinvent himself as Bob the Builder. I just worried that we'd end up with a shower that pumped out arctic-cold water and a toilet that flushed every time you turned the taps on. . .

Clunk!

"What've you got there, Peaches?" I asked, bending down with a frown to see what he was batting about between his paws. I wasn't scared it was a mouse or anything with a pulse – living things don't usually tend to go *clunk!*

Peaches stopped, panting slightly, and gazed up at me with his knowing green eyes. Between two fat, furry front paws was a marble; shiny clear glass with a twist of ribboned green through the middle. The *clunk!* had been the sound of the marble hitting my mobile, which must have fallen out of the sandy shorts I'd kicked off a couple of minutes ago, and scooted just out of sight under the bed.

"Thanks for finding that," I told Peaches, as if he knew what I was on about. "I'd have been in a panic later, thinking I'd lost it or something!"

Just as I went to straighten up, a gleam from the marble made me stop. It dawned on me that it was the sort of small, shiny, irresistible thing that one of my brothers would spot straight away and shove up any nostril going.

"Sorry – I'd better take this," I said, pinching up the marble. For a second, I held it just in the middle of Peaches' forehead, so that he looked like he had one of those spooky third eyes that you get in old Buddhist or Hindu paintings. (I couldn't remember which – I'd have to ask Parminder next time I spoke to her; *she'd* know. Er, except she's Sikh, I think.) All I *did* know – sort of – was that third eyes were meant to represent spiritual powers, like telepathy or something.

It suits you, I told Peaches in my head, testing his telepathic powers. His Ginger Tubbiness looked up at me with all three eyes, and I *know* it was a trick of the light, but I could have *sworn* he blinked all three. . .

And then the message service on my mobile chose that exact moment to ring, just about startling me out of my skin.

"Hey, Stell! It's me, Lauren!" my friend's recorded voice chirped in my ear. How had I missed her call? Must have been after I chucked off my shorts, when I was in the bathroom washing sand out of my ears. *"Just bumped into Frankie and Seb on the High Street a few minutes ago, and she said she'd been talking to you this morning."*

From somewhere downstairs, there came a sudden loud crash, followed by a reverberating clank, and then a very odd strangulated sort of roar. What *was* Dad up to? I walked over to the door to close it, so I could hear Lauren's message better.

"Did she tell you that I'm definitely going to go through with getting my belly button pierced tomorrow afternoon? Eeeeeeek! I'm excited but scared. You know me and needles!"

Oddly enough, as I got to the door, I realized that the only noises coming from downstairs were Dad's quiet hammering and the clatter of cutlery in the kitchen as Mum sorted out lunch. So where was that clanking, roaring racket coming from?

"So what are you up to right now – you're not hanging out at that dumb, deserted house again, are you? Beware of the ghosts of Elize and Joseph! Hee hee!"

Lauren was joking about Joseph's house, the old, dilapidated mansion in Sugar Bay – Frankie must have told her all about it. At the weekend, Frankie'd tried her best to seem interested in all the history mystery stuff I'd found out about the family that used to live there, but I could tell she found it about as exciting as watching nail varnish dry, specially since Lauren was now talking about it like it was an episode of *Scooby Doo*. . .

"Anyway, I'm really glad everything is cool between you and Frankie after the weekend – we all hated knowing about her and Seb and not being able to tell you. And it's brilliant that you're so cool about it too. Um, you are, aren't you?"

As I listened to Lauren's byes, I made a mental note to phone her back after lunch and tell her yeah, I really, *really* was OK about Frankie and Seb, hoping that all my *other* mates in London weren't fretting that I was just putting a brave face on. . .

I switched off the phone and walked over to the window. Uh-oh: more clanking, a loud THUD! and then a long, drawn-out *screechhHH* . . . all weird and all coming from the house across the back lane from us, I was now pretty sure.

Which is why ten seconds and a short cut

(learned from Peaches) later, I was lowering myself off the kitchen roof and down the old coal bunker, ready to go investigate further.

"Hey, Miss Mountain-climber!" Mum called out of the back door, having heard me slip out of my bedroom window and pad over the ceiling above her. "Lunch'll be ready in about five minutes, so don't go too far!"

"OK! Just going to check something out!" I said, giving her the thumbs-up, while carefully taking giant steps over the knee-high jumble of wild flowers, regular flowers and nipping nettles. A few well-placed bounds, and I was at the back wall, scouring the ground for old pots or bricks I could stand on.

CLANK!

Drat – who knows what was lurking underneath the undergrowth (rusting cars? Roman ruins? bottomless wells?) but one thing was for sure, there were no useful pots or bricks.

CLANK! CLANK! *ScreeeeeeecchhhHHHH!*

Course, there was always the old chair in the den; I could go and grab that and get a better look over the wall. . .

THUDDY-THUDDY-THUD-THUD, *booooooinnnggg!*

As the noises got more mental all of a sudden, I ditched the idea of getting the chair and just *jumped*, trying to sneak a peek over the wall, over the lane, and into any of the windows of the house opposite. The *first* time, I didn't jump high enough and only got an attractive, close-up view of the moss near the top of the wall. The *second* time, I managed to focus for a millisecond on the upper half of a downstairs window. The *third* time, I thought I saw a vague shape of someone through the glass, and then instantly realized – mid-jump – that if *they* saw *me*, I'd look exactly like Bob the dog had last night.

"Stella, what are you up to?" Mum called out from the open kitchen window.

Poor Mum; she must have thought her one and only daughter had completely flipped, watching me pogoing at the bottom of the garden one minute, and then cracking up at some private joke in my mad little head the next.

It was one of those daft moments that I'd normally have loved to tell Frankie about. And I guess I could still have e-mailed her about it in a little while, but somehow the silliness of it all might not have seemed so funny, with her being so far away. What I could really use was a here-and-now friend to share dumb, daft moments with.

Deejay. . .

Still standing by the wall, my mind somehow slithered back on to the boy from this morning. Could he possibly be a possible friend? Still, he was a bit young. But then, he wasn't 112 or furry, like Mrs Sticky Toffee or Peaches – the only other locals I'd got to know in Portbay so far.

Speaking of a furry local, Peaches chose that moment to appear from nowhere in particular, and began happily curving himself around my bare legs.

"Maybe you can read my mind, fatso," I muttered, heaving him up into my arms and getting a nose full of ginger fluff, "but I wish you could laugh at my jokes!"

"Ha ha HA!" came a rumbling guffaw that sent the hairs on my neck standing to attention.

Through my fingers, I felt most of the fur on Peaches' back do the same thing. His deep green eyes looked at me; my light-brown eyes stared back at him, and I knew – telepathically or not – that we were thinking the same thing: *Huh?*

"Take that! And THAT!"

Rat-a-tat-TAT! Thumpety-thumpety-*thump*. . .

I didn't know about Joseph's house, but I

suddenly started to wonder if the cottage over the lane from us was haunted – by the ghosts of psycho sumo wrestlers, by the sound of it. . .

Chapter 5

Stalking Deejay

"Well, if someone wants to go clanking and thunking around their own house, it's none of our business, really, is it?" Dad had said yesterday, when we were having our lunch, listening to the clanking and thunking and everything else going on in the background.

"Yes," Mum had agreed, picking a large lump of plaster out of Dad's hair before it fell in his minestrone soup. "Between the boys thundering around and your dad demolish— er, working on our place, we can hardly moan about someone *else's* noise, can we?"

My parents were really, seriously, *annoyingly* un-curious about the goings-on in the house over the lane, but I guess that had something to do with living in London for so long. Every area has its own, unique customs, and in London, people have this habit of pretending that weird stuff is normal, especially on the tube. I mean, you could find yourself sitting opposite someone who's dressed in a deeply loopy way, but the rules are that you must carry on reading your copy of *Mizz* or whatever and act like you come across people wearing wellies, a kilt and Stetson *all* the time. It's the same with neighbours; where I used to live, no one would have dreamt of telling Clive our singing neighbour to get back inside and stop howling ancient Frank Sinatra hits out of his window – no matter *how* much him and Frank were doing people's heads in.

Anyway, all of yesterday afternoon, I hung out in my den in the garden, aiming to do lots of drawing but instead getting distracted by the many mysterious noises coming from next door. "You need binoculars," Lauren had suggested, when I called her back yesterday afternoon. "Then you can spy on your neighbours from your bedroom window!" There were only two problems with Lauren's suggestion: 1) We didn't have binoculars, and 2) I wasn't an expert on legal stuff, but I was pretty sure spying on your neighbours through binoculars was ever so slightly against the law.

Then today, bizarrely enough, there wasn't a clank, *aaaarrrgghhh!*, THUNK! or screech to be heard. Maybe sumo-wrestling poltergeists have

Tuesdays off, I don't know. But without strange noises to listen out for, I felt at a loose end, and decided to stuff a pad and my chalk pencils into my backpack and go and find something to draw. (Or maybe find a shop that rented binoculars. . .)

I'd never fancied anyone with a pierced lip, black eyeliner and a Marilyn Manson T-shirt before. But the lad leaning on the counter, chatting on the phone, was seriously cute (in a scary way).

"So I says to *him*, 'You don't want to use Logic Audio 5.5 with OSX 10.2, 'cause it doesn't support VST plug-ins!'"

I hadn't a clue what he was on about, but the longer the scary/gorgeous guy waffled on in strange techno-speak, the longer I got to sneak a peek at him, from above the row of vintage comics I was pretending to rifle through.

He was about seventeen, had spiky black hair (dyed), great cheekbones and a (ouch!) pierced lip. He'd have been the-one-everyone-fancies in a boy band, if grunge/goth lads ever formed themselves into boy bands, and I didn't think they did.

So what was I doing, gawping at a lad who was definitely not my type? Well, it was all Bob the dog's fault, kind of. I'd been scuffing down the High Street, on the way to the beach, when a mournful "Howwww-ooooo!" grabbed my attention. And there was Bob, down an alley I hadn't noticed before, sitting outside a shop, beside a metal board sign that read "The Vault – Rare Grooves and Vintage Comix".

Feeling like it might be my destiny to detour, I ambled up the alley, scratched Bob's head, decided that there was a dyslexic sign writer on the loose in Portbay ("Comix"?), and then took the plunge and wandered inside "The Vault" to see if Bob's owner happened to be in there. Not that I had a clue what to say to him if he was.

Coming in from bright sunshine outside, it had taken my eyes a while to adjust to the gloom in The Vault. The Vault wasn't a vault, by the way (though it looked and smelled like one). It was just your standard shop, but one that could definitely have done with a *Changing Rooms* style transformation. Maybe Laurence Llewelyn-Bowen and the design team could have zoomed around and replaced the black paint on the walls, ceiling and shelving racks for something more vibrant and soothing, like a nice sorbet pink. Maybe they could've replaced all the rock/metal/grunge posters on the walls with a few nice framed pictures of kittens. Maybe there could've been a vase with scented roses at the cash desk, instead of the plastic skeleton-on-a-Harley-Davidson-motorbike that the scary/ gorgeous guy was fiddling with while he talked on the phone.

But then I guess the people who wanted to shop here for second-hand albums, CDs and rare "comix" liked it just the way it was. They probably thought that it felt very authentic and gritty and real, even if – only two minutes down the road – everyone was strolling around eating 99s with raspberry sauce and comparing sunburn marks.

"But then he says to *me*, 'Yeah, but, Sigh, man – VSTs are old news. You want Audio Units plug-ins.'"

"Sigh"? The scary/gorgeous grunge boy was called "Sigh"? What was it with teenagers in this town and their weird nicknames? And speaking of people with weird nicknames, where was Deejay? I hadn't spotted him at all, but he *had* to be here, if Bob was impatiently waiting and "Howwww-ooooo!"ing outside.

As an old Nirvana track suddenly blasted through the shop's speakers, the top of someone's floppy head of fair hair started bouncing up and down in time behind the "M–R" alphabetized CD section. It was *him*, I was sure. But he was so short that I had to stand on my tiptoes and strain my neck just to see him properly. Which is when he saw *me*.

"Hi!" I saw Deejay mouth, over the bass-y boom of "Smells Like Teen Spirit".

"Hi!" I mouthed and waved shyly back, trying to lower myself down very slowly so that I looked more like a regular girl than a curly-haired, nosey-parker giraffe.

Help – he was walking over. Which is pretty much what I *wanted* to happen, but now I panicked about a) what to say to him, and b) whether I was going to say whatever I said to him with or *without* a stammer. . .

In the three seconds it took for him to reach me, I stuck what I hoped was a friendly smile on my face and did a quick inventory of Deejay: that floppy fair hair, still bouncing when he walked; a grin a mile wide; jeans and baseball boots; a faded grey T-shirt with the slogan "I'm with Stupid!" printed in dark blue with an arrow pointing to the right.

"Like the *X-Men*, do you?" he asked, nodding his head at the magazine I hadn't realized I was holding.

"Yes," I told him.

I hated the *X-Men*. Neisha made us watch the first one on DVD 'cause she's got this thing about wanting to be Halle Berry, and I hated it so much that when she suggested we all go and see the follow-up, I told her I'd rather change both my brothers' nappies for a *month* than sit through another load of super-heroes with numpty names saving the planet or whatever *again*.

"I don't really like them," said Deejay, shrugging.

(Drat!)

"Did you see Nightcrawler in the *X-Men 2* movie?" he asked (I shook my head). "It was just a bloke with black face paint on! How's *that* meant to be scary? My mum looks scarier than that first thing in the morning!"

Listening to him, it dawned on me that Deejay maybe wasn't as young as I'd first thought. Close up, he looked and sounded maybe about thirteen, same as me. Maybe Deejay wasn't so much a kid and was just plain *short*.

"Howwww-ooooo!"

"Hey, I meant to ask you yesterday," said Deejay, casting a wary glance towards the door, where Bob's hairy face could be seen peering in.

"Where've you moved from?"

"London. Kentish Town," I told him (where I used to be known for my stammer, I *didn't* tell him).

"Howwww-ooooo!"

"Yeah? Wow – this place must be pretty boring compared to London!"

Deejay sounded genuinely interested, but he couldn't help fidgeting at the sound of Bob's yowling.

"I dunno," I shrugged.

I hadn't planned on liking Portbay when I first arrived, but what I *did* like was that I could reinvent myself here; not have to be just Frankie's shy best friend, or hide me and my stammer behind all my other brilliant but loud girl mates. Course it would be handy to have someone to show my reinvented self off *to*. Auntie V always used to ask me how Frankie etc. were, just 'cause she could never remember (or be *bothered* to remember) Eleni, Parminder, Lauren and Neisha's names. And here in Portbay, I needed a new "etc.". Could Deejay be it?

"Howwww-ooooo!"

"Look, I'd better go – Bob'll be in here in a second, and Simon barred him after he peed on a pile of *Star Wars* box sets," said Deejay agitatedly. "Anyway, I've got to go and pick up my little sister."

"Oh, OK," I replied, half-taking in the fact that "Sigh" must be "Si" as in "Simon".

I was stupidly disappointed. Not about the scary/ gorgeous guy having a less intriguing nickname than I'd thought, but disappointed about Deejay leaving five seconds into our conversation. I don't know what I'd hoped for exactly, but maybe I'd kind of *half*-hoped that me and him could hang out for a bit, and I could ask him stuff like *why* he was hiding from his mates yesterday and *why* a seagull had a grudge against him. Maybe I could have told him all about my friends back home, and how this shop reminded me of loads of stores and stalls in Camden Market near where I used to live, and maybe I could have even worked up to admitting that I'd lied about liking the *X-Men* and I didn't know why.

But Deejay was already heading out of the door, squeezing past a sulky girl in a black leather jacket, stripy black and purple tights, Doc Martens and – eek! – a pink tutu, who pushed past him like he wasn't even there (hey, he wasn't *that* small).

I nearly burst out laughing when I saw Deejay

pull a face behind her back, but I didn't think that was a great idea, since she looked like she wasn't the sort of girl who could take a joke. (Hey, maybe if he'd stuck around I could've asked why so many girls in Portbay looked so sulky, *and* what that tutu was all about.)

"Uh. . ." Deejay called out, just before he stepped out of the gloom and into dazzling daylight. "You don't fancy meeting up tomorrow afternoon, do you? I could show you around . . . if you want!"

If I wanted? If I *wanted*? It was the exact, specific, *precise* thing I wanted more than anything. A mate to hang out with? Yes, please!

"Why not?" I said, deciding to play it cool and not come across as a desperate, clingy saddo.

"'Bout two o'clock, then? Down on the prom, by the water fountain?"

I had no idea where that was exactly, but that wasn't going to stop me.

"Sure!"

Deejay nodded in reply to my stupid, overeagerly nodding head, then waved as he and Bob sloped off together.

And then I realized that I knew Deejay and Bob's names, but they didn't know mine. Hey, perhaps I should have a go at reinventing my name before I met up with them tomorrow. I could call myself something cooler, like Halle, or Brodie or Courtney. . .

But it would kind of blow my cover if me and Deejay (and Bob) *did* happen to become proper mates and my parents or my brothers called me by my real name in front of him. And anyway, I'd only recently managed to say it out loud without stumbling all over it.

Nope, tomorrow Stella Stansfield would be officially introducing herself to Deejay and Bob – and I couldn't *wait*. . .

Chapter 6

The 1% idiot factor

Mum and Dad were delirious.

They tried to pretend they weren't, but they *so* were.

I kind of wished I hadn't said *anything* about Deejay and meeting up with him tomorrow; they'd quizzed me so much about it all through tea that it had started to do my head in. I mean, I *know* they were excited about the idea of me having an actual, living, human friend in the town, but I was getting fed up with saying "I don't know", every time they asked questions like "How old is he?", "Where does he live?", "Do you think you'd like to invite him round here?", "Does he know how relieved and grateful we are?" (OK, so maybe I made that last one up. But I bet one, or more like *both* of them thought it.)

Thumpetty-thumpetty-thumpetty-DOOF.

After escaping from Mum and Dad and their well-meaning, we're-so-happy-for-you grins, I was now kneeling on the floor, staring out of my bedroom window, with only Peaches and the stars for company. I'd been thinking about how happy I was to have made a potential friend today, while Peaches had been contentedly purring, drooling and padding his claws into my knees. But both of us stopped thinking, drooling and clawing the second we heard that noise.

"It's like a riddle in a Christmas cracker, isn't it?" I whispered to Peaches, as though whoever (or whatever) lived in the house at the bottom of the garden could hear us, as much as we could hear them (it). "What goes *thumpetty-thumpetty-thumpetty-DOOF*? Only we don't know the answer. . ."

"Prrrrrp," prrrrrped Peaches, agreeing with me.

Though there was something I *did* know about the odd occupants of the place; when I'd come home this afternoon with no drawings but tales of Deejay, Mum had blurted out a snippet of info direct from our next-door-neighbour Maggie. She'd said nobody lived in that cottage permanently – it was just rented out to holidaymakers in the summer.

I squinted at the closed curtains, and tried to figure out what would have brought a family of sumo-wrestling poltergeists to Portbay. Couldn't they have stayed at *home* and rattled things? Maybe they just fancied a bit of sea air while they were swirling furniture around the room, you never know. . .

Bleep!

A text – great. Not that I could find my phone at first; it seemed to have a habit of wandering off this week.

"You found it for me yesterday, Fatso, so got any ideas today?" I asked Peaches, scrambling round my room and hoping it would bleep again so I could play a game of "You're getting hotter!" and track the stupid thing down.

Peaches yawned, his one, long yellow fang glinting by the light of the small lamp by my bed. (The small lamp was the best way to illuminate my room – overhead lights and full sun showed up the semi-stripped flowery wallpaper and lumpily plastered walls that were probably *last* on Dad's list of things to fix around here.)

At first I thought Peaches was turning his back on me and settling down for a snooze. Well, he *was*, but his tail was stretched out, straight as a furry arrow, flicking in the direction of my trainers. Since I didn't have anything else to go on, I thought I might as well try there, and sure enough, my mobile was nestling in one trainer, along with a blue Smartie and a Duplo brick. Looked like one or both of the twins had been in here while I was hanging out in The Vault this afternoon. . .

Hi Stell! Talked 2 Lauren yet? Got to ask about her nu piercing – ha! Wot u up 2? Lol Neish x.

Uh-oh, I winced, reading Neisha's text. I'd forgotten Lauren was going for that today. I didn't much like the sound of that "ha!".

Something must've gone wrong, I realized, about to phone Neisha straight back and ask. But then I stopped. It's just that if I got talking to Neish, she'd ask me what I was up to, and then I'd end up telling her about Deejay – and I wasn't sure I wanted to, not yet anyway. It's just that even though I hoped it would have got back to the others (via Lauren) about me being absolutely, honestly *fine* about Frankie and Seb, I still had a funny feeling they'd get overexcited, get the wrong idea about Deejay, and think he was a budding *boyfriend* or something. So I copped out and texted Neisha back (*"Wot happened? Tell, tell!"*), and decided I'd go downstairs soon and drop Lauren an e-mail to see what was going on with that tummy button of hers.

281

I guess this holding back on talking about Deejay had something to do with Frankie's mum. Frankie's mum – otherwise known as Aunt Esme, otherwise known as my ex-childminder – used to love spilling her pearls of wisdom my way, mainly 'cause if she tried it on her own daughter, Frankie tended to roll her eyes and shake her head. But one of Aunt Esme's sayings had come into my head now: "Stella, my sweetheart, 99% of the time, you got to trust your instincts. But always hold back till you check for that 1%. . ."

Well, 99% of me had a good feeling about Deejay, and only 1% worried that I'd got it wrong and he was an idiot. So until I met up with him tomorrow and sussed out whether he was an idiot or not, I'd do like Aunt Esme said and hold back on telling any of my friends back in London about him, before they'd practically married me off to him, just like Mum and Dad had done. . .

"*La, la, la, la, la-LA-LAHHHHHH!*" a megaphone-loud voice boomed from somewhere across the lane, jarring me out of my thoughts.

OK, that was it. I didn't care whether Deejay was a solid gold ace person or a nutter; as long as he owned a pair of binoculars he was prepared to lend to me, I'd be his friend for *life*. . .

Chapter 7

I must have made a mistook

"Oh, hi!" I smiled shyly.

"Hiya!" grinned Deejay, surprising me by coming up to the water fountain via the beach, while I'd been glancing nervously up and down the prom for him.

"Hurrrufff!" said Bob, stopping to scratch some sand out of his huge ear with a mighty rear paw.

"D'you fancy walking along by the harbour?" he asked (Deejay, I mean, not Bob).

"Yeah, sure," I said with a nod, not wanting to admit that I didn't even know that Portbay *had* a harbour. I'd only explored what lay beyond one end of the beach (Sugar Bay). I'd never gone very far along in the other direction.

"I mean, I know it smells of fish and everything, but there're these winding stairs there that take you up to the main road and the crazy golf. That's like, if you *fancy* playing crazy golf."

"Yeah! That's fine!" I told him.

I knew the Crazy Golf course – me and Frankie had passed it on Saturday. It was all themed like something out of *Pirates of the Caribbean*, which I thought looked fun, but Frankie decided was naff. So we hadn't gone in.

"I'm Stella, by the way," I said, suddenly remembering that Deejay still didn't know this one vital piece of information about me.

"I'm TJ," said, er, Deejay.

Oops. . .

It was a simple case of mistaken identity. Or looking at it another way, it was me being an idiot and getting it all wrong. Again.

The thing is, when I get nervous – apart from stressing about stammering – I tend to mishear things. Like at primary school, when I got summoned to the headteacher's office this one time. With the blood thudding at breakneck speed through my panicked head (what had I *done*?), I could have *sworn* she'd shouted, "Come in!" when I knocked on her door. It was only when I barged into her office and caught her flossing sweetcorn out of her teeth that I realized she'd said, "Coming!" (It turned out that she'd called for me so she could tell me one of my pictures had been entered for a local art competition. Bet she wished she could withdraw it after that. . .)

And last week, I'd got the name of the prom café wrong (it was called the Shingle café, not "Shingles", as in the disease, though I'd never stop thinking of it that way). And *then* I'd got the name of the old mansion at Sugar Bay wrong; I thought it was called the Josephs' house, and guessed that was the name of the rich family who'd built it. But it's actually called *Joseph's* house, in honour of Joseph, the young black servant boy who came back with the family from Barbados, where they'd had sugar plantations, back in eighteen-hundred-and-something-or-other.

Then yesterday in The Vault, there was that whole, dumb Sigh/Si/Simon muddle in my head.

So I'd made another mistook and got yet *another* name wrong; what was new?

"*Tee*jay?" I said, frowning and slightly flustered, as we strolled along the prom.

"TJ – just the initials 'T' and 'J'."

"Oh! I . . . I thought it was something else. . ."

"Like what?" TJ asked, padding along beside me in his baseball boots, his head just coming up to my shoulders.

"I, um, wasn't sure," I said, waffling a bit and trying not to make too much of a fool of myself in front of my potential new friend (and his dog, who was tagging along by his side, like a big hairy minder). "Those guys shouting at you on the beach on Monday . . . I couldn't figure out properly what they were calling you."

"Well, it was *kind* of a miracle that they were using my proper name," he shrugged, his hands thrust deep in his jeans pockets. "Normally, they just call me Titch, or Lofty. Or Knee-high. Or Bug."

"Huh? But I thought they were your friends?" I said, horrified to hear that roll call of nasty nicknames.

"Uh, *sort* of. They never used to bother with me, but they've been getting more matey recently. Dunno why . . . but I s'pose it's good, 'cause they're a couple of years older than me, and they're kind of *cool* at my school. But sometimes they're a bit, well, *y'know*. If you see what I mean."

Yes – straight away I was pretty sure I did know, even if TJ wasn't explaining himself in a sparklingly clear way. I guessed that he meant that he was flattered that a gang of older, cocky, tough lads were paying him any attention. But he was also pretty wary of them; you could tell that from the way he was speaking about them just now, and from his body language on Monday (i.e. when he tried to use me as a human shield).

"How old are they anyway?" I asked, realizing this could be a subtle way to solve the mystery of just how old TJ was.

"Sam, Ben and Marcus are fifteen. I think Aiden might be sixteen now."

Fifteen . . . he'd already said they were a couple of years older, so that made TJ thirteen, same as me. He was just straightforward *short*, then.

"I saw you . . . well, I think I *almost* saw you later, down on the sands – you were right in the middle of those lads," I told him. "Your dog and your sister were following behind you."

"Yeah, they were just fooling around. Said they fancied playing beach volleyball, and I could be the ball. . ."

At first I thought TJ was joking, since he seemed to be a smiley, jokey kind of person. But I realized that although he *did* have a frozen-looking smile in place, he must've been pretty humiliated by the volleyball jibe, from the way he was examining the cracks in the pavement so intently.

Hey, maybe it was a good time to change the subject.

"So . . . what does TJ stand for then?"

"Nothing, not any more!" he said with a shrug. "I've just been TJ for forever. *Everyone* just calls me TJ. Even teachers."

"But it must stand for something! Thomas James?" I guessed, thinking of the most common names I knew that started with those letters.

"Nah," said TJ, shaking his head and grinning.

"Toby Joshua?"

"*Toby!* Give me a break!" he laughed.

"OK, OK. Well, how about. . ." I tried to think of the fanciest, most fanciful name I could come up with. ". . .I know! Tarquin Jethro!"

This was fun; having someone to fool around with. It was only when I noticed TJ doing that crack-in-the-pavement staring thing again that I realized he might *not* be having fun.

"You're not *really* called Tarquin Jethro, are you?" I asked, hoping I hadn't put my foot in it and guessed his actual name at the same time as taking the mickey out of it.

"No," said TJ, with a shake of his head, his floppy hair falling round his face. "It's just plain TJ."

We'd been hanging out for all of three minutes and already I was wondering if my 99% gut reaction had been totally wrong. I mean, TJ had gone from grinning to gloomy to grinning to gloomy again.

I tried to think of something to say that might get the grinning version back again, but I was suddenly so nervous that I worried that anything I might try and say would have a stammer at the beginning of it. So I shut up.

Cool way to start a new friendship, huh?

Above us, under a baby blue cloudless sky, a life-size plastic palm tree flapped its fronds in the sea breeze.

TJ had one elbow leaning on the beak of a luminous pink flamingo (fake), and was doing his best to put me off.

"You've got *no* chance."

"Wrong!" I said, tightening my grip around the club and aiming for the pirate's head. "Bet you a bag of chips I can get it in his mouth!"

"Bet you a bag of chips with onion rings you *can't*!"

Phew. I still didn't quite understand what had gone on when we first met up earlier, but I was having a *way* better time hanging out with TJ now. After strolling through the harbour (v picturesque, v fishy, v sure I spotted Peaches sitting on a boat washing his scruffy fur. . .), we'd ended up as planned at the Treasure Island crazy golf, and so far we were neck and neck, taking about fifty trillion putts to get about three-quarters of the way around the course. Me and TJ, it turned out, were both *equally* rubbish crazy golfers, and were having a *ball* being so rubbish. The only one who *didn't* seem to be enjoying the afternoon was Bob, who kept peering mournfully over the perimeter hedge, watching our every move, guilt-tripping us into remembering that dogs were (most cruelly) not allowed in Treasure Island.

"Urgh!"

That was me, groaning as my ball ricocheted off the pirate's nose.

"Ha ha ha!" cackled TJ, doing a quick victory dance at the side of me. "One order of chips and onion rings, please, with plenty of salt 'n' vinegar!"

Grinning grimly, I glanced over at the takeaway van parked outside the entrance. Perched on top of it, I noticed, was a large seagull, staring intently our way. I decided not to mention it to TJ – there was no point getting him wound up, if it was just any old gull, and not the dive-bombing nutter-bird. And who wanted to spoil a great afternoon now? Not me.

Actually, we had Lauren to thank for getting us

over that bumpy start earlier – not that she *knew* it. While we were walking along in silence, she'd texted me to tell me *today's* bad news: that not only was yesterday's belly-button piercing lopsided (thanks to her screaming and jumping at the wrong moment), but now it had gone septic too. After I read that out to TJ, I'd gone on to explain my disastrous attempts to cheer Lauren up when we were e-mailing last night. When I told him I'd written *"Hey, it's OK – maybe you'll start a new fashion for squint piercings!"*, he'd laughed so much he got hiccups and kind of frightened Bob.

After that, *nothing* got in the way of us talking like we'd known each other for ever, rushing to fill in the details of our lives. *I* told him about Mum and Dad and the twins, and how I had to help look after them; *he* told me about his mum (an actress) and his kid sister Ellie (the little blonde singing girl) and how he had to look after her a *lot* of the time. *I* told him how much I'd hated the idea of moving from London to here, but how OK I felt about it now; *he* told me about the school I'd be starting at, and said it was "all right". *I* told him about Frankie and the other friends I'd left behind in Kentish Town; *he* told me how he got on with loads of people at school, but wasn't close to

291

anyone in particular, since they *all* took digs at him about his height. *I* talked to him about Sugar Bay; *he* told me him and Bob walked over there all the time. *I* asked him if he knew any of the weirdos I'd come across in the town so far; *he* told me he wasn't sure about Mrs Sticky Toffee (but hey – what thirteen-year-old boy is interested in bizarre old ladies?), but he certainly knew the tap-dancing librarian I'd spotted stamping out the books in the library last week – he was TJ's sister's Saturday morning tap and jazz dance teacher.

I sucked in all the information like I was a girl-shaped sponge. Course, there was *other* stuff I wasn't so keen to hear: like the sniggering café crew down on the beach? Well, TJ said their names were Rachel, Brooke, Hazel and Kayleigh, they were totally in love with themselves, and were the main clique in what would be my year at school (oh, *great*). The one I'd seen hovering at the door of the Portbay Nafferia was Rachel, apparently – her mum owned the shop (and was responsible for all that bad taste craft tat, then).

"Right! Move over!" said TJ, nudging me out of the way and getting ready to take his aim at the pirate's mouth.

"Yeah, yeah, Tiger Woods!" I goaded him, using

the name of the *one* golfer in the world I'd actually ever heard of.

Just as TJ was about to take aim, there was a swoosh of air, a flap of gigantic wings, and a large seagull pooped *right* in front of the toe of TJ's left baseball boot.

So, it *was* the same gull with a grudge.

"What's that bird got against you?" I asked, watching as it soared skyward, whirling impossibly high on some unseen current of air.

"I whacked it with a pebble once," said TJ, glancing up warily in the air.

"You did *what*?"

To tell the truth, I was kind of *shocked* to hear him admitting a case of animal cruelty so easily.

"Not *deliberately*, Stella!" said TJ, turning and staring appealingly at me. "I was out at Sugar Bay a couple of months ago with Bob, and I was just skimming stones off the waves. And then one of the stones pinged off a big hunk of rock, and – *blam!* – it hits this seagull flying past. . ."

"What – and it's had it in for you ever since?" I asked, incredulous.

"Uh-huh. Every time I come down near the sea, it goes for me, and—"

Midway through his sentence, TJ caught sight

of something. The something happened to be the digital clock fixed on the side of the lookey-likey Spanish Armada galleon where you bought your crazy golf tickets and hired your clubs.

"Urgh – I didn't realize it was that *late*!" he mumbled, shoving his golf club at me. "I've got to run – I was supposed to pick up Ellie ten minutes ago!"

"Um . . . you don't fancy coming round to mine tomorrow, do you?" I heard a confident-ish voice shout out after him. (Oo-er, it was mine!)

"What time?" he called out, skipping backwards towards the entrance.

"One-ish?"

"Yeah! Sounds OK! See you then, Stella!"

And with the briefest of "see you!"s, TJ took off like (a short) Cinderella, even though the clock on the galleon had just struck ten past four, and not midnight; and even though Cinderella didn't tend to be pictured in the fairy-tale books wearing jeans, baseball boots and a Strokes T-shirt.

"See you!" I smiled, as I watched my new best friend dash off, followed by a galumphing great dog and a low-flying, slow-flapping seagull. . .

Chapter 8

The amazing, inflatable cat

Once upon a time, long, long ago, Elize Grainger would have sat in her tiny studio (now my den), gazing out of the small window at her prettily planted garden (now our jungle).

Taking a break from working on the flower fairy watercolours she did so well (like the one I'd hung on the wall), the elderly Elize would take a sip of tea from her delicate, rose-patterned china cup (now dusted off and displayed on one of my shelves) and muse over the faraway days of her childhood. There were those hazy memories of running wild on her parents' plantation in Barbados, followed by happy times in the Big House in Sugar Bay, with the family's trusty servant and her best friend Joseph to keep her company on long walks along the beaches of Portbay. . .

Between exploring the old mansion, finding stuff when I was clearing the den, mooching around the museum, and getting a copy of an old local paper from our neighbour, I'd pieced together plenty about Elize Grainger's life, and vaguely imagined the rest. But I wondered what she'd think if she could gaze around her old studio now. Maybe she'd be thrilled that I'd restored it a little. Maybe she'd be chuffed to see her own knick-knacks displayed. Maybe she'd be pleased that another artist (i.e. me) was following in her footsteps, even if I wasn't sure what she'd make of *my* take on fairies (i.e. the funkier the better). One thing was for sure, I don't think she'd have taken too kindly to having a farting dog slobbing out on the floor. . .

"Oh, God! I'm sorry!" said TJ, wincing and flapping his hand in front of his face. "I ran out of his dog biscuits this morning and had to give him a tin of tuna instead. It *always* does that to him."

A sprawled Bob snoozed on, unaware of the whiff he'd just caused.

"It's OK – I've got two little brothers, remember?" I told TJ, wafting the den door back and forward to let some air in. "You need a gas mask when you're changing their nappies sometimes!"

"You'd need to give me a gas mask and a million pounds before I'd go near a dirty nappy!" said TJ with a wicked grin, as he turned his attention to my corkboard. "Hey, look at that – did you do this?"

"Yeah," I nodded, feeling a bit shy as he studied my best attempt at a modern-day fairy. "I like a lot of Japanese animation and stuff. . ."

"A ninja fairy – cool!" he grinned, studying the mutant butterfly wings and big dewy eyes I'd drawn on the little figure. "She looks sort of like your mum!"

I hadn't thought of it that way, but I guess my mum *did* have a pixieish face, specially with her new haircut.

Speaking of Mum, I thought she'd been very restrained when TJ had turned up a little while ago, with Ellie and Bob in tow. I'd been sure she was going to throw her arms around him and give him some reward money for being friends with me, but instead she'd just smiled a lot and forced tonnes of biscuits on him, which hopefully came across as being in the normal range of mum-ly behaviour. (Thank goodness Dad was away choosing toilets or whatever at the plumber's yard; he'd probably have mortified me by asking TJ to be an honorary member of the Stansfield family or something.)

"And you did that too?" he asked, pointing to a cartoon drawing of two girls, one with huge ears, one with a huge nose.

"Yeah – those are two of my friends from London; Lauren and Eleni. Eleni thought it was pretty funny, but Lauren wasn't too chuffed with it!" I explained, stepping closer and gazing over TJ's shoulder (and head) at the caricature, and at the board pinned full of bits of my life. "And that's Frankie."

"Yeah, I know."

Er. . .

How *exactly* could TJ know that the mad-looking girl fooling around in the photo-booth strip of snaps was Frankie? I mean, *yeah*, so I'd talked about her yesterday, but. . .

"Poo! Smelly!" said TJ's kid sister, appearing in the doorway and doing a quick mini tap-dance on the worn, flat doorstep. "Do you know something? Because my name is Ellie, I get called 'Smelly' at school sometimes, but only by boys, and *they're* smelly. Aren't they?"

Before I had a chance to answer, Ellie broke into another tap move and another snatch of conversation.

"Was this someone's little house? It *looks* like it was someone's little house. It's nice but it's a bit dark. You could paint it a bright colour!

What's your favourite colour? Mine is lilac. That's a proper colour; that's a kind of purple. *And* it's a plant. My mummy said she nearly called me Lilac when I was born, which would have been good, 'cause it wouldn't have rhymed with 'smelly'."

Yeah, but the smelly boys at school *sure* would have had a field day teasing her about having a name like Lilac. . .

"Hey, Ellie – I thought you were supposed to be playing with Stella's little brothers?" said TJ, widening his eyes enthusiastically.

As an older sibling, I could tell straight away that TJ had just spoken in code. What he'd *actually* said was: "I like you a lot, Ellie, but you are doing my head in. Please, *please* go away."

"Yes, but I just came out to say hello! So hello! And bye*eeee*!" trilled Ellie, spinning around on her pink and white trainers and bouncing towards the house.

"She's cute!" I said, as soon as she'd skipped out of hearing range.

"Yeah, cute as a migraine!"

"That bad?" I laughed.

"Well, *you* try getting woken up by her singing along to her *Lion King* video at twenty to seven in the morning!"

"Today, you mean? Or every day?"

"*Every* day," sighed TJ, flopping down on the chair by the desk, like he was exhausted by the very memory. "I mean, it's the holidays, isn't it? But Ellie's always been the same; the *milli*second she's awake, she's up and doing stuff. With me, it takes about an hour just to get both my eyelids to move up and down at the same time. . ."

"And has she always been into the dancing and stuff?"

"Uh-huh. She sings along to ads on the telly, and tap-dances to the theme tune of every programme going. Soaps, the news, weather jingles, whatever."

"Does it drive your mum mad too?" I asked, stretching my leg out and ruffling Bob's fur with my bare foot. TJ hadn't mentioned a dad so far, and I hadn't liked to ask.

"Are you kidding?" said TJ, as his eyes drifted along the rows of trinkets (a few of mine, a few of Elize's) that I had stashed on the shelves of the den. "If you want an idea of what my mum's like, just think of Ellie . . . but aged 36."

"What – she dances along to the weather report too?"

"Near enough! Like I told you, she does all this

amateur dramatic stuff, so she's always wandering around, rehearsing her lines or belting out some dumb song."

She'd been a proper actress in London, TJ's mum: he'd said so yesterday, when we'd been swapping life stories, on the way to the crazy golf. She'd been an extra in *Coronation Street* and was the star in a commercial for cheese and everything. That was before TJ was born, before she moved to Portbay. And nowadays, his mum was involved in so many local acting groups and ran so many workshops that TJ ended up with Ellie skipping and singing after him a lot of the time.

"Yeah, but you get on with your mum, right?"

As I spoke, Bob rolled over sleepily and let me rub his tummy with my foot.

"She's OK," said TJ, looking faintly gloomy for a second. "It just bugs me that *one* minute she thinks I'm grown-up and responsible enough to look after Ellie, and the next minute she's babying me like I'm a cross between a six year old and a chihuahua!"

I nearly sniggered, but however much TJ *did* look like an adorable puppy, I could tell pretty well by now that his height was a real issue. I needed to say the right thing, to tell him he wasn't *that* short and didn't look anything like a cute little dog (both lies). But before I could work out the right words to say, a fat cat squished its way through the one empty square pane in the den window.

Uh-oh, I thought, glancing down at Bob.

"Uh-oh," said TJ out loud, thinking the same thing as me.

Unfortunately, clocking some different tone in his master's voice, Bob raised a hairy head, eyes inquisitive and tongue lolling.

Peaches – spotting Bob – stopped dead, his one yellow fang glinting ominously. I couldn't breathe, I couldn't move. Then the weirdest thing happened: Peaches inflated.

Ever seen one of those spiky blowfish, that fill up with air like a prickly balloon the minute trouble swims on to the horizon? There's one in the film *Finding Nemo* – if Jamie had been in here, he'd have been giggling and clapping his hands at Peaches' furry puffy efforts.

"Wow. . ." murmured TJ, well impressed by my cat's alarming and intimidating size. Bob, meanwhile, just looked cowed and confused, his ears flattened to his head like someone had Sellotaped them there.

Then, just as quickly as he'd inflated, Peaches let

all the air fizz out of his fur or wherever the heck it was hidden, and slipped down into his normal, scruffy fat cat proportions. Just as slowly, Bob's ears rose up to their usual position, only twitching very slightly. I don't know whether it was just a show of strength, or if Peaches had actually *hypnotized* Bob, but one thing was for certain; Bob wouldn't be leaping and barking at His Tubbiness any time soon. In fact, ever-faithful Bob didn't even *dare* make a fuss when Peaches casually waddled over to TJ via the desk and plopped himself comfily down on to his lap.

TJ and me, we stared at each other, eyebrows raised, not exactly sure what we'd just witnessed. We were so taken with Peaches' powers, that we both jumped when we heard Mum's voice.

"I see the sumo-wrestling poltergeists are at it again!" she said, standing in the doorway grinning, a basket of clean laundry on her hip, all ready to hang out. Behind her, in the jungle we laughingly called the garden, Ellie was spinning round in a circle with Jamie, singing "Ring-a-ring-o-roses", to the accompaniment of a distant CLANG!-*boiiinng*-CLANG!-*boiiinng*- CLANG!-*boiiinng*. . .

"Huh?" huh-ed TJ, glancing back and forth between me and Mum as he tried to figure out what she'd meant.

"The people in the holiday house over the lane," I began to explain. "They're making all these weird noises – we can't figure out what they're up to!"

A little light went on in TJ's eyes at the mention of that mystery; the same sort of light that flicks on when you tell a boy that you know where he can get free tickets for top seats to see his favourite football team play. When I spotted that, I felt a little thrill; maybe me and TJ could investigate the noises together? That could be a laugh. And after all, he *did* look a little bit like Shaggy out of *Scooby-Doo*, only half the size. . .

Then the moment was gone, with Jake whirling into the den like a chubby thigh-high whirlwind, coming to a crashing halt at TJ's knees.

"Oof!" TJ laughed. "Well, thank you! What's this?"

As soon as TJ picked up the thing Jake had dumped in his lap, half draping it over Peaches' head, I knew I wanted to die.

"Stella *pants*!" said Jake, smiling happily, as his new friend examined the lovely gift – freshly stolen from the laundry basket – that he'd been handed.

Great.

There's nothing like having your pink dotty knickers held in the air by your new – BOY – mate to make a girl deflate like a furry blowfish. . .

Chapter 9

Surviving the pants trauma

If anyone had been peeking in the bathroom right now, they'd . . .

a) be a bit pervy, and

b) probably assume that I was trying to drown myself out of sheer shame.

But I *wasn't* trying to drown myself, honest – even if the memory of TJ holding up my knickers to the world this afternoon still made me feel faintly sick. TJ seemed pretty mortified too, even though he tried to crack a joke about it at the time and put my knickers on Jake's head. The fact that he announced he had to go home about two seconds later was a pretty *big* clue that he was embarrassed, after all. . .

Anyway, another reason I definitely wasn't drowning myself was that there was too much distracting *noise* going on around here.

THUD-a-dud-a-dud-a-dud.

THUD-a-dud-a-dud-a-dud.

THUD-a-dud-a-dud-a-dud.

With my head tilted back, everything from my nose downwards was underwater. That included my ears, but somehow I could still make out those mysterious loud thuds (and duds) that had been radiating from the house at the bottom of the garden for the last half-hour.

THUD-a-dud-a-dud-a-dud.

Although Mum and Dad were pretending to mind their own business, I could tell all the unexplained racket was starting to get to them – when I'd left them downstairs earlier, they were tutting and turning up the volume on the *Channel Four News*.

"Ah . . . *whooof!*"

Now *that* was a new noise. A faraway, high-pitched, girlish barking sort of noise.

"Ah . . . *whooof!*"

And there it was again. I was quite comfy, submerged among the bubbles, but curiosity got the better of me. Slowly, I raised my head out of the water, and tilted it to one side to listen better, letting water dribble out of my ear at the same time.

"Ah . . . *whooof!*"

You know what? That *wasn't* a faraway, high-pitched, girlish bark – that was a nearby, high-pitched, cattish *sneeze*.

"Oh, hello!" I said to Peaches, who I spotted unexpectedly curled up on the closed toilet seat, delicately achoo-ing. "I thought you were doing an impersonation of Bob there!"

"Ah . . . *whooof!*" sneezed Peaches again.

It was the talc that was doing it, I think. A fine layer of powdery-ness covered most of the surfaces in the room, as a little reminder that it had been bath-time mayhem with the boys in here not so long ago.

But they were safely stashed in their cots now, and it was *my* turn to have the place to myself. I was making the most of it – mainly 'cause the bath wouldn't be here from tomorrow.

The old, worn, damp-smelly carpet, wall tiles and even the sink had already gone – turfed in the overflowing skip out in the driveway – and tomorrow, they'd be followed by the bath and the loo. Dad had promised that our shiny new bathroom suite (currently parked outside the front door, smothered in industrial-strength bubble wrap) would be all in place by the end of the day, but I wasn't going to bank on it.

So here I was, making like a prune, soaking in water that was so deep that if I wafted my little finger, a mini tidal wave would go slooshing over the edge. Does it sound like I was having a nice, relaxing time? Well, I *wasn't*, and it had nothing to do with the background thudding and sneezing, *or* today's pants trauma. . .

"I think I need to talk to someone," I mumbled, turning and staring at Peaches, and creating a major flood at the same time. "I should phone Frankie, shouldn't I?"

Despite the fact that in his feline wisdom, Peaches must have decided to come through and keep me company, he didn't respond at all to what I'd just said. Course, why should I have expected him to? He was only a cat. But then, in the short time I'd known Peaches, I'd begun to suspect that he wasn't your average Felix-eating, purr-rumbling moggy. For a start, he might have *looked* like a scruff, but I didn't know any other pet that wafted a trail of peaches and cream when they left a room. Then there was his habit of turning up where you least expected him; which was just *one* of Peaches' many psychic pussy traits. So the fact that he just started licking his bottom when I mentioned Frankie sort of threw me.

"Er . . . what about Eleni, then? She's always up for a chat."

[Lick, lick, lick. . .]

"Well, Parminder? She's pretty sensible."

[Lick, lick, lick. . .]

"Lauren? I mean, I know she's a bit *dippy*. . ."

[Lick, lick, lick. . .]

"Neisha?"

[Lick, lick, lick. . .]

This was *mad*: I was basing my decision on who to call and splurge out my troubles to on whether a cat would stop licking its bum or not. But whatever; I had one last name on my mind.

"Auntie V?"

Instantly, Peaches abandoned his bottom and stared straight at me.

"Prrrp!"

It was only a small noise, and just as instantly, Peaches turned back to continue his wash-and-brush-up, but it made up my mind for me.

(I tell you, my friends back in London would think I'd gone *mad*. . .)

"*One* minute," I explained, pressing my mobile against my ear, like that would make my call somehow more private, "they were all gaga about TJ: Dad was going on and *on* about how sorry he was to have missed meeting him, and Mum was totally *raving* about how nice he was. . ."

I was scrunched up on my bed, wrapped in a towel with a cat asleep on my feet, having a low-voiced moan to Auntie V about the conversation at teatime tonight. The one that began with Mum and Dad practically offering to start up the TJ Fan Club, and finished with them acting like they expected to see him popping up on *Crimewatch* later.

". . .but then I said to Mum, 'Oh, remember those boys that were sniggering at me in the Shingles café, that first time me and you and the twins went in there?', and Mum said yeah, and then *I* said, 'Well, TJ's been hanging out with them. They're a bit tough and I don't think he really likes them that much, but I think he's just doing it 'cause he's got this chip on his shoulder about being small, and a bit of him's chuffed that they're paying him attention.'"

"Let me guess. . ." Auntie V suggested drily. "Suddenly they're not smiling quite so brightly?"

"Too right," I said, nodding – not that Auntie V could see that. "They just sort of gave each other this *look*, and then Dad said to me, 'You mean he's in a *gang*?' And I just thought, uh-oh. They're not going to have a *downer* on him, are they?"

"And I take it they do?"

"Oh, yeah. It's like, I tried telling them the lads

weren't exactly a *gang*, and TJ wasn't *properly* hanging out with them, but they didn't look too chuffed. And they basically stopped talking about him."

"Hmm. . ." Auntie V sighed dramatically. I *bet* she was rolling her eyes. "The thing is, Stella my little star, I guess it's a parent's duty to be protective. I'm sure they get a rulebook the day their child is born and it says something like '*Rule 10: Be overprotective to the point where you drive your kids mad.*'"

That made me smile; that was exactly what I needed to hear. Peaches had been absolutely right about choosing Auntie V to blow off steam to. Honestly, I wouldn't have thought of her straight away, if I'd had to make up my mind on my own, without the help of a cat and its bum. I mean, I'd always got on pretty *well* with Auntie V, even if she did overwhelm me a bit by being a) gorgeous, b) sarcastic, c) dripping in confidence. But I'd never, *ever* had a heart-to-heart with her. Sure, when Mum and Dad were originally talking about moving to Portbay, I was more than happy to listen to Auntie V *snorting* at the very idea, while I nodded silently in the background. But tonight she was being totally brilliant, and hadn't sounded the *least* bit surprised when she'd picked up the phone and heard my moaning voice at the other end.

"And the thing is, Stella, one of the reasons your parents wanted to move to that dullsville little town you're stuck in was because they wanted to bring you and your brothers up somewhere they thought was safer."

Auntie V tended to refer to Portbay as "dullsville" because the idea of leaving London and its theatres and cinemas and shops and sushi bars was as nuts to Auntie V as volunteering to strap fish fingers to yourself and jump in a shark tank.

"But that's such a joke!" I blurted out, feeling defensive about my old home. "I never had any hassle in London!"

It was true; I wasn't sure exactly what my mum and dad were worried about, but back in Kentish Town, I didn't hang out with *anyone* in a gang; I'd *never* been mugged; nobody'd *ever* tried to offer me drugs. . . The closest I'd got to a real criminal was Eleni's cousin Georgiou, who got fined for being caught without a ticket on the tube once.

"*Tell* me about it, darling!" said Auntie V, laughing in that throaty voice of hers. "I mean, when I think about what your dad got up to in that so-called sleepy Norfolk village where we grew up, now *that's* the joke!"

What my dad got *up* to! What did she *mean* by that? I immediately thought of all the kiddie photos Granny and Grandad Stansfield showed us when we visited; millions of snaps of two gangly blonde kids waving at the camera, playing in paddling pools, mucking about on a tree-swing.

"Why? What was my dad like?"

"He hasn't told you? About the trouble he got in to when he was fifteen?" Auntie V asked incredulously.

"*No* . . . what happened?"

"Well, if he hasn't told you, I'm not really at liberty to say. . . But all I *will* say is, if he gives you any trouble about your little friend PJ, just you turn round and ask him to tell you about the paintballing incident."

I couldn't let her get away with that; she *had* to tell me more. I was about to launch into a full-on begging session (not even bothering to correct TJ's name), when she called a sudden halt to the conversation.

"Oh, Stella, there's a call waiting on the line – I've got to go. It's this awful actor client of mine; he'll be phoning to see if I've heard anything about the beans commercial he tried out for today. And how am I going to break it to him that the director said he didn't make a very convincing bean? Anyway, call me any time, Stella – I mean it! Bye!"

So my dad had a deep, dark secret to do with *paintballing*. What could he have done: splatted the side of a tractor, or a haystack or something? I might be dying of curiosity, but like Auntie V had suggested, I knew I should shelve that snippet of info and use it as ammunition if Dad or Mum got funny about TJ again. And even if they didn't, I could spring the paintballing question on him sometime, just for fun.

"Anyway, they're wrong about TJ, aren't they?" I whispered to Peaches, watching one ear flick in his sleep. "He's not some teen thug, is he?"

(Two flicks of the ear.)

"He could be a really good friend, eh, Peaches?"

(One flick.)

"Like me and you?"

(One flick.)

One flick for yes, two flicks for no.

There was one slightly mad, but completely true thing I'd learned since I'd been in Portbay: *always* trust a weird, scruffy, one-fanged fat cat that smells of peaches and cream.

Hey! I'd made up my first saying! Frankie's mum would be proud of me. . .

Chapter 10

Hark; a not-so-good noise

Frankie: mouthy, sassy, loyal as a loyal thing. Eleni: honest, upfront, brainy without showing off about it. Parminder: super-cool, super-cute, someone to look up to. Neisha: kooky, kind, kind of adorable. Lauren: ditzy, dreamer, total dipstick.

In a nutshell, that's what my old mates in my old neighbourhood were like. Not that you could tell any of that from the photos they'd just sent me: in the photo-booth strip I was gazing at, they looked like a bunch of hyperactive six year olds out to make the *Guinness Book of Records* for the Daftest Face Pulled In A Confined Space.

I was feeling much better this morning. The letter (and the photos) from the girls had really brightened my day, and last night's conversation with Auntie V had been pretty cool at reassuring me about TJ too. Peaches had been totally right to steer me in her direction (sort of); after all, *she* was the one who first came out with the phrase

316

"Stella etc.", putting the thought in my head that that an "etc." was *exactly* what I needed to help me feel at home in Portbay.

"What's that?" asked Dad, suddenly peering over my shoulder.

"Frankie and the girls," I explained, holding up the photo-booth strip for him to see, and pointing (pointlessly, as it turned out) at the envelope it had come in, which Jake had grabbed and was now using to stir the Ricicles around in his bowl.

"Yeah, but what's *that*?"

"Lauren's new belly-button piercing."

She'd got so close to the camera that her pink tummy was fuzzily out of focus. But you could still make out the silver hoop – and the fact that it wasn't what you might call dead-centre. . .

"Ah, what a laugh. Now *there's* the perfect friends for a girl to have, eh?" said Dad a little too brightly, squeezing my shoulders.

OK. So by that remark, Dad could mean one of three things. . .

1) Frankie, Eleni, Parminder, Neisha and Lauren were the perfect friends a girl could have.

2) Frankie, Eleni, Parminder, Neisha and Lauren were the perfect friends a girl could have, and I must miss them really badly.

3) Frankie, Eleni, Parminder, Neisha and Lauren were the perfect friends a girl could have, and a no-good boy who hung out with the local gang wasn't any kind of friend in comparison.

I had a funny feeling that in his own, not-very-subtle way, Dad was guilty of the third option, which made me bristle a bit and think about hitting him with the paintballing question. . .

"So, what's everyone's plans for the day, then?" Dad asked, pulling out a chair and sitting down at the kitchen table along with me, Mum and the boys. "Whatever they are, I hope they don't include going for a wee, because I'm just about to dismantle the loo!"

As he said that, Dad grinned around the table, but especially aimed his beaming smile at me. I think he was hoping for a beaming smile in return, but all I managed was a half-hearted twitch at the corners of my mouth.

"Well, I'm taking the boys to the Little Acorns Play Workshop this morning, so we'll be safely out of your way!" Mum answered Dad, while wiping margarine off Jamie's eyebrows with a piece of kitchen roll.

The Little Acorns thing: that was one of the notices me and Mum had seen in the window of the Portbay Nafferia on the prom a few days ago.

"And Stella? What're *you* up to today?" asked Dad, turning his cheery 100-watt beam of a grin my way again.

"Going to mug old ladies with TJ the Thug," I was tempted to say.

"Going drawing," I lied instead. We might not be planning on mugging old ladies, but before TJ had bolted yesterday afternoon, we'd vaguely arranged to text each other and maybe meet up today (and not mention the pants trauma, hopefully). Anyway, I didn't fancy telling my parents that, not after the way they'd cooled towards him.

But *urgh* . . . I had a funny feeling that my eyes were showing me up for the liar I was ("Big fat fibber!" they probably flashed). Luckily, Mum and Dad were temporarily distracted from my giveaway expression as they both rushed to stop Jake from eating the envelope from Frankie etc.

"Are you going drawing down at the beach?" Mum asked me, half-harassed, as Jamie tried to bite her outstretched arm.

"Mmmm," I mumbled, thinking that a vague "mmm" was less of a troublesome lie than a definite, truth-free "yes". . .

The ancient, brown, felt Victorian bonnet had lain unloved and undiscovered in the outhouse for a zillion years (OK, nearly eight decades, which was *practically* a zillion years, whichever way you looked at it).

Then I'd found it, dusted it off, and displayed it, as a memorial to the long-ago former owner of our house and this former studio.

But now, instead of hanging pride of place on the den wall, the flat, felt hat was perched on my head. I'd tied its faded ribbons under my chin, and was staring at myself in the old, rust-spotted, silver-framed mirror (another looky-likey archaeological find in my den), wondering if I looked anything like Elize Grainger. . . Er, when she was *thirteen*, not when she was a hundred, when the local paper came around here to photograph her in our/her garden. (That newspaper cutting was pinned on my noticeboard, waiting to be framed, same as Nana Jones and Grandad Eddie's photo. When I'd looked earlier in the week, the only frames Woolies had were pink and inflatable, which didn't seem too appropriate.)

"D'you think it suits me?" I turned and asked Peaches.

He'd followed me out here to the den after

breakfast, watched me text TJ (I hadn't had a reply yet), and kept a sleepy eye on me as I packed my pad and coloured chalk pencils into my rucksack so Mum and Dad believed my cover story.

"Well?" I quizzed him, seeing a whole lot of no response to my question.

And then I heard a rumble of a snore start up.

"Yeah, you're right. I look like a bit of a dork."

Maybe old-time floppy felt hats suited Elize Grainger (and they did – I'd seen her family portrait in Portbay Museum, dated 1840), but with *my* sproingy curls, I just looked like I was balancing a soggy, circular piece of cardboard on the top of my head. But I soon stopped wincing at my reflection when the sumo-wrestling poltergeists started up with today's bonkers noises. . .

"EEEEE-aaaaahhh-ooohhh-*yoooooooo*! EEEEE-aaaaahhh-ooohhh-*yoooooooo*!"

Hey, that was whole *new* noise coming from the house over the lane! Over the last few days, we'd had a "CLANK! CLANK! CLANK! *ScreeeeeeecchhhHHHH!*", then a "THUDDY-THUDDY-THUD-THUD,*boooooooinnnggg!*",then a "Take that! And THAT!", a "Rat-a-tat-TAT!", followed by "Thumpety-thumpety-*thump*. . .", and then the very similar "*Thumpetty-thumpetty-*

thumpetty-DOOF". And who could forget "*La, la, la, la, la-LA-LAHHHHHH*", and "CLANG!-*boiiinng*- CLANG!-*boiiinng*- CLANG!-*boiiinng*"? Not to mention last night's "*THUD-a-dud-a-dud-a-dud, THUD-a-dud-a-dud-a-dud, THUD-a-dud-a-dud-a-dud*".

That was it – I grabbed the chair by the desk and was determined to drag it to the bottom of the garden, clamber on it and get a good look at what was going on, binoculars or no binoculars. And then a completely different sort of noise made me stop in my tracks: a sudden crash, followed by a loud half-shout, half-groan.

"Andy?" I heard my mum call out from somewhere in the house.

Hearing the brittle edge of alarm in her voice, I dropped the chair with a clatter and went running through the garden and indoors.

"What's happened?" I panted, after taking the stairs two at a time.

Mum was crouched on the bathroom floor, next to my confused-looking dad, who was rubbing a hand through his tousled blond hair.

"He was taking the old cistern off the wall," Mum began to explain, pointing to an empty space up near the ceiling and then down to the cistern, which was lying sideways in the bath. "But it suddenly gave way when he was unscrewing it."

"Luckily, I managed to break its fall with my head!" said Dad, trying to be funny, even though his face was a strangely grey shade of white.

"Help me get him up, Stella," said Mum, putting one of Dad's arms around her shoulders. I was only too glad to help – maybe I'd been feeling a little bit resentful of Dad (and Mum) over the TJ thing, but now that he was hurt, I had a bad case of worried butterflies crashing about in my tummy.

"Is he going to be all right?" I asked Mum, as we began leading him down the stairs.

"Course I'm all right, Louise!" Dad interrupted brightly.

I'd have been more reassured if Dad hadn't a) been swaying, and b) called me by my mum's name. . .

"I think he might have a bit of concussion," said Mum (aka Louise), ignoring Dad altogether, "so I'm going to take him to the hospital – it'll be quicker if I just drive him straight there, rather than call an ambulance. Can you look after the twins?"

"Of course!"

As I spoke, I glanced down at the foot of the stairs and saw one skinny little boy and one pudgy one staring up at us with quivering lips.

One minute later, as I helped lower Dad into the passenger seat of the car, the twins were in full, megawatt wailing mode.

"WAAAAAAAAAAAAAAAAAAAAAAH!"

"DAAAAAADDDDDDDEEEEEEEEE!"

"Thanks, Stella," said Mum, smiling fleetingly, as she tried to disentangle Jake's arms from around her leg and get into the driver's side.

"No problem," I told her, holding on to Jamie, but leaning away from him so that his piercing howls stood less chance of puncturing my eardrum.

"Oh, and Stella. . ."

That was Dad, leaning over Mum in the driver's seat and grinning up at me.

"I know I'm supposed to be concussed, but are you *really* wearing a Victorian bonnet, or am I just seeing things?"

"You're seeing things," Mum told him, while throwing me a wink and starting up the engine.

As they drove off, I didn't know whether to laugh, cry or join in the wailing. . .

Chapter 11

A sudden case of deaf, dumb and blindness

"*RING-A-DING-A-DOSIES!*" the twins yelped happily in unison, with matching chocolatey smiles.

It had taken a whole hour, but my brothers had *finally* stopped wailing.

Even after Mum phoned to say that Dad was fine (there was just a bit of a dent in his head and he was probably going to have a headache the size of Finland), Jake and Jamie *still* wouldn't calm down. But then I guess when you're not quite two and a half, it's hard to be rational and grown-up. In fact, the only way I'd got the boys to cheer up was to put my hat back on and pull stupid faces. Once that got their attention, I told them we were going somewhere *really* special (Mum had asked me to take them round to the Little Acorns workshop thing, 'cause her and Dad wouldn't get back in time). I explained that in this really special place, they could play with *lots* of other children, and have the *best* fun. They'd both stared at me, not looking exactly convinced, till I added, "And we'll buy Chocolate Buttons from the shop on the way."

So, now, I was shoving the double buggy and sticky boys along the High Street, aiming for the community centre – down near the harbour – where my brothers could run riot and I could sit back, relax, read my magazine, and maybe try texting TJ again.

Or. . .

Or maybe I wouldn't have to *bother* texting him, 'cause (speak of the devil) there he was! Across the road, over the top of the jam of day-tripping cars headed for the beach, I could see a bunch of taller lads and one floppy-haired smaller one. So TJ was hanging out with Sam and that lot today; I s'pose maybe *that* was why he hadn't got back to my message.

"TJ!" I called out, waving my hand more madly than I meant to in my excitement.

Four (tall) heads turned towards me, while a (shorter) one dropped down to stare at the ground.

"Hey, TJ!" I tried again.

Er. . .

Hadn't TJ heard me above the growl of the traffic? Well, his mates certainly had, and were now grinning over like I was a penguin who'd just done a bellyflop in the zoo pool. Even Bob the blimmin' dog had heard me: through a momentary gap in the traffic, I could see him gazing across, recognizing the sound of my voice and giving me a friendly, answering "Wuff!" *Unlike* his master, Bob *hadn't* been struck down by a severe and unexpected case of deaf, dumb and blindness.

"STELLLAAAA! Don' stop!" Jake roared, wondering why we weren't going anywhere any more.

Ignoring my little brother's demand, I tried yelling again.

"TJ!"

Nothing. If anything, he dropped his head even lower to the ground.

I gripped tightly on to the buggy handle, stunned, as TJ and his mates (and Bob) turned into the alley where The Vault was. One of the lads – couldn't tell 'em apart yet – turned and gave me a sarky little wave before they disappeared.

I still didn't move, though I could feel my cheeks flooding pink. I had just been blanked, by my supposed friend. What in Bob's name was all *that* about?

And then it dawned on me . . . pants!

Had TJ told that bunch of boys about what had happened with Jake and my knickers?

Urgh, the *shame*. . .

For the first time in days, I suddenly felt like the old, stammering, *wincingly* shy Stella again – the part of me that I didn't so much love as loathe. And for the first time in days, I felt myself pining for Frankie. *Frankie* wouldn't have let those lads have the last laugh (or the last wave) over my stupid polka-dot pants. She'd have done or shouted something that would have burst their smug bubble, just like she had last Friday, when she stood up in the Shingles café and blew those boys a big, fat, fake kiss. They hadn't known where to look, mainly 'cause they probably hadn't come across a girl who was just as swaggering and full-on as *they* were.

That made my mind up; as soon as I got Jake and Jamie to playgroup, I was going to text Frankie. But first I'd have to get my legs to move . . . once they'd stopped being paralysed with mortification.

"Toffee?"

Candyfloss, apple pie, lemon cheesecake . . . just for a second, the faintest syrupy-sweet waft tickled under my nose, so that even before I turned to see who was offering me a sweet, I knew it was Mrs Sticky Toffee herself.

"Um, no. . ." I shook my head miserably at the rustly plastic bag being held out towards me.

The old lady, in her shimmery-green raincoat and ridiculous hat, tut-tutted at me kindly.

"Don't be silly – it's only a little bit of toffee!" Mrs S-T smiled at me from under her pink netting meringue. "Sugar gets a bad press and that's for sure, but it has its good points. Gives you a little energy boost, so they say, *and* it's good for shock."

Shock. . .

How could Mrs S-T have known I'd just had a shock?

But she doesn't, I told myself off. *She's just waffling, and you're making out it means something. . .*

"Thank you," I mumbled, giving in and taking a wrapped sweet out of the bag.

"Not seen you for a while, dear! Settling in to the town all right?" Mrs S-T asked, while stuffing the toffees back in her tiny, shiny cream handbag and rifling around for something else.

"Um, yes, thanks," I told her, realizing as I spoke

that not only hadn't I seen Mrs S-T for a while, but I hadn't wandered over to Sugar Bay – to Joseph's house – for ages either. Somewhere inside, I felt a ping of pining, a bit like I'd had when I thought of Frankie, my faraway best friend. . .

"Now for these little brothers of yours," muttered Mrs S-T, pulling out a puffy, pillow-sized bag of marshmallows, that seemed *way* too big to have come out of such a tiny handbag.

"Ta!" grinned Jake.

"'Ank yooo!" gurgled Jamie.

As the boys gently reached a hand each in to take a marshmallow, LOADS of muddled thoughts swirled through my befuddled brain:

1) I'd never seen Jake and Jamie so polite and well-behaved. Yeah, maybe when they were *asleep* they were totally good, but *never* when they were awake.

2) How did Mrs S-T *know* they were my brothers?

3) Well, it was a pretty straightforward guess, I suppose. I mean, who *else* would they have been? A couple of kids I'd stolen while their mum was choosing sausages at the butcher's shop we'd just passed?

4) Frankie . . . thinking about her all of a sudden

reminded me of that one weird moment in the den yesterday, when TJ had said, "Yeah, I know," when I pointed out her photo on the corkboard. Still didn't know what (if anything) to make of that. I should ask him. . .

5) . . . if I ever spoke to him again, of course. I mean, why had he acted like I was poo on his shoe just now, when yesterday, he'd really, *really* felt like someone who could be . . . well, *someone* to me? *Was* it because he'd told those lads about my knickers being on show, and was too shamed to look me in the eye 'cause of that?

6) Had my parents been right to be wary of him, 'cause of him hanging out with Sam's gang? Had I got it 99% wrong, and he was 1% an idiot after all?

7) Would my legs *ever* recover any feeling, or was I destined to be stranded here with the boys and the buggy, like some mad human statue on Portbay High Street? (Hey, maybe if enough tourists threw money at me, I could collect the train fare back to London for a visit. A *long* visit, preferably. . .)

"Friends of yours?" asked Mrs S-T, a marshmallow lodged in her cheek, as she nodded in the direction of the lane, The Vault and the now-disappeared lads.

"No," I said, unwrapping the toffee I was holding and hoping it would take away the bitter taste of disappointment in my mouth.

"Nice bunch of lads . . . to their mothers if no one else," Mrs S-T surprised me by saying bluntly. "Though you can't go tarring everyone with the same brush, can you, dear? There's always a chance of one good apple being hidden away in a barrel of rotten ones."

In the couple of conversations I'd had with Mrs S-T since I'd come to Portbay, she'd managed pretty successfully to confuse and bamboozle me, and today's little chat was going to be no different, it seemed. I'd grown up with Aunt Esme's weird and wonderful home-made proverbs, but Mrs S-T's muddle of sayings made no sense at all.

Unless. . .

Unless in her own freaky way she was trying to hint that TJ might not be as bad as the other lads?

OK – now I just remembered the *other* problem with talking to Mrs S-T . . . she was loopy, and made *me* feel loopy. (It was catching.)

"Uh, I'd better go," I said, while giving my legs a quick, nearly invisible shake just to check they would work. "Got to take my brothers to playgroup. Thanks for the sweets ... and, um, everything."

"Pleasure, dear!" Mrs Sticky Toffee called after me, as I hurried off as fast as humanly possible while pushing a heavy buggy laden with little boys. "And just remember, you can't judge a book by its cover!"

She might as well have said "you can't judge a fish by its bicycle" for all that meant to me.

"Lady NICE lady!" said Jake, tilting his head back and gazing at me with an upside-down grin.

"Lady MAD lady!" I muttered back to him.

Then I bit hard on my toffee, and imagined it was TJ's head. . .

Chapter 12

The end of the line. . . (Boo-hoo)

"'Nother 'mallow!" shouted Jake.

"'YESSS! 'Nother 'mallow, Stewwa!" Jamie chipped in.

Bleep!

Gee, *thanks*, fate. Thanks for arranging a text from my best friends to arrive *just* when I'm feeling particularly friendless. I mean, I *really* wanted to be reminded of all the fun they were having together in London, when the only company I had here at the back of beyond were two small boys who were demanding more *marshmallows*, for goodness' sake.

Start end-of-the-line project 2day! On northern line now! Will tell u more l8r. . . Par x

OK, here's what that was all about: you really *yearn* for school holidays, right? And then – kind of *tragically* – they can turn out to be mind-blowingly boring. Well, it was like that back at Easter, for me and my mates; we all overdosed on mooching around the shops and hanging out at Hampstead Heath (where we kept getting rained on).

So we got talking about what sort of stuff we could do in the summer holidays. Everyone came up with ideas, but not all of us were dead keen on putting together a hip-hop dance group (thanks, Neisha!), or working our way through every martial arts movie in the video shop ("You have *got* to be joking!" Frankie had sniggered at Lauren). Then Parminder came up with the end-of-the-line project. She pulled out the foldaway tube map of London in her Filofax and pointed at the coloured spaghetti of the criss-crossing tube lines. "See? They all end *some*where. But where? What do all these places *look* like?" Me and Frankie and the others bent over and began reading out random names, like Stanmore (sounded posh and sensible) and Morden (sounded depressing) and Cockfosters (sounded rude) and wondered what would be there when you got out of the tube and gawped around.

Anyway, the idea just seemed to wriggle its way into all our brains: this summer, we'd hop on a different tube every day, and see what there was to see at the end of the line.

But for me, the project had one small flaw;

my parents decided to move. So today, while my mates were trundling on a tube train to High Barnet, I was trying to ram a double buggy through the stubborn doors of a community centre in downtown Portbay. (How thrilling . . . *not*.)

Yep, you've probably spotted that I was feeling just a tiny – OK, *huge* – bit sorry for myself. But there was *one* good thing about that; caught up in self-pity, along with the burning anger and humiliation I felt when I thought about TJ blanking me, I'd managed to stomp my way boldly into a noisy room crammed with strangers (of the mum and children variety), and had sat down and freed my brothers from their buggy straps before I even *remembered* to be nervous.

In fact, it was only when I heard a familiar tippety-tappiting coming towards me that I snapped out of my thundercloud of a bad mood and properly took notice of what was going on around me.

"Hello, Jake! Hello, Jamie! Hurrah! You've come to play!"

"Ellie!" I said in surprise, taken aback at seeing this tap-dancing, smiley bundle of five-year-old blondeness right in front of me.

For a split second, my heart went squish, as

I panicked that TJ was here too. But then the little bit of common sense I had took over and told me that *couldn't* be right; he'd probably still be hanging out in The Vault right now, trying to impress his stupid mates or stupid Sigh or Si or whatever the boy in the shop was called. I could picture TJ now, trying to look cool, nodding his head in time to some track booming out of the speakers, even though none of his so-called friends would probably be able to *see* him over the top of the CD racks. . .

"Hello, Stella! Do you like my tap shoes?" Ellie asked blithely, holding up one foot right under my nose so I could get a really good look at her shiny, black, bar-strap shoes and the frilly white lace of her ankle socks. "I have to take them off in a minute, because Mummy says it's a drama workshop and you can't wear tap shoes in a drama workshop, but that's not fair, is it?"

"Er, no," I said, with a shake of my head, even though I wasn't very sure if I thought that or not, since I couldn't really figure out what kind of drama workshop you could *have* with such tiny kids like there were here today.

Which reminded me, I really should (urgh!) find the teacher and tell her that Jake and Jamie were here for the first time.

"Um, Ellie – which one is the teacher?" I asked her, feeling my mouth already going dry with nerves as I scanned the women in the room.

"My mummy, course!" Ellie giggled. "Mummy! Come and say hello to TJ's friend!"

A woman standing chatting only a little way away turned and came towards us. So *this* was TJ's mum, this person dressed head-to-toe in primary colours? She looked like she'd matched her red baggy trousers, blue trainers, green T-shirt and the yellow scarf (bundled in her wavy fair hair) to my brothers' Duplo bricks. How had I managed to miss her when I first came in? She was totally out of place in this big, drab, grey hall; she should have been on the set of a CBeebies show, singing about being a bee or something.

"Oh, how lovely! Stella, is it?" she beamed at me, her head of curls bouncing as she tilted her head enquiringly at me. "I'm Caroline O'Connell. And do these two little rascals belong to you?"

The twins were playing up as usual: Jamie had hold of Ellie's foot and was trying to wrestle her tap shoe off while Jake was pulling off his sandals and chucking them without looking to see who they might hit.

"Y-y-yes," I replied, steaming fast into the rest of the sentence, hoping that if I hurried, the stammer wouldn't get a chance to happen again. "They're my brothers. The chubby one's Jake and the skinny one's Jamie."

O'Connell . . . so it's TJ and Ellie O'Connell? I repeated in my head, processing the information. Not that I needed to know TJ's last name, not if we weren't going to be friends any more.

"Well, I'm sure the boys will have a *marvellous* time here, and my little sweet pea Electra will help settle them in, won't you darling?"

Electra!

"Yes, Mummy!" Ellie/Electra giggled, as she hopped around, trying to stop Jamie from making her lose her balance.

"Now if you'll excuse me, Stella, I'd better get the class started!" Mrs O'Connell smiled my way as she began to walk off. "And now that you and my little pumpkin Titus are friends, I'm sure we'll be seeing a lot more of each other!"

I didn't know which to be more horrified about: the fact that Mrs O'Connell had referred to TJ as her "little pumpkin", or the fact that she was to blame for naming him *Titus*. . .

It's just . . . *Electra* and *Titus*! Weren't they like

ancient Roman or Greek names or something? Why had TJ's mum (and Dad) thought ancient Roman names went with an Irish *last* name? And what on earth did the "J" stand for? "Jupiter"? "Jehovah"? "*Jam*"? No *wonder* TJ liked to be called TJ. And no wonder he got a bit funny that first day we hung out and I tried to fool around and guess his name.

I mean, imagine being short for your age, *teased* about it, lumbered with a terrible name *and* having a mum that dressed like the sort of kids' telly presenter who sings "The Wheels On The Bus Go Round And Round" while doing *all* the actions?

Y'know, for just a second there, I felt a sort of flurry of sympathy for TJ. And *then* I remembered that he'd made a total prat of me (and possibly my pants) in public and decided he deserved everything he *got*. . .

"OK, little ones!" Mrs O'Connell called out, clapping her hands. "We're going to have *such* fun today! And let's start by warming up our voices by shouting a big 'hello'!"

As thirtyish small children shrieked, shouted, roared and bellowed a deafening chorus of raggedy "HELLLLLLLOOOOOOO!"s in the hall, I winced, and wished I was far, far away – preferably on the Northern Line to High Barnet, North London. . .

Chapter 13

Revenge is sweet-ish

OK, stupid question, but can a house be your friend?

Let me put that another way; I had this sudden feeling that I really, *really* wanted to go over to Sugar Bay, to walk in the silent, deserted, echoing rooms of Joseph's house. It's just that I'd gone from resenting Dad, to stressing over him getting hit by a toilet; then there was the humiliation of being blanked by "Titus", and the sheer trauma of sitting through the Little Acorns shout-a-thon workshop. I was emotionally drained and it was only quarter to one this Friday lunchtime. And strangely, the only place that seemed calm and safe and *right* right now was the old broken-down derelict mansion that Elize Grainger had once called home. The only thing stopping me from rushing over there straight away was a matching pair of tired small boys who needed taking home for refuelling.

"Hey, Mum – it's Stella," I said into the mobile I'd tucked under my chin. (You can't push a double buggy with one hand; it'd be like trying to kick a fridge-freezer up a hill, believe me.)

"Hi, Stella! Where are you?"

"Just walking along the prom," I told her, watching seagulls swirl and white-edged waves tiptoe up the sands on the beach below. "So, how's Dad?"

"He's fine. When we got home, he was determined to get back in the bathroom to finish it off, but I've told him to lie on the sofa and relax, or I'm divorcing him."

"Oh, yeah? Well, that's OK, only what are we supposed to do if we need to use the loo, since half of it's lying broken in the bath?"

There was a couple of seconds of muffled silence, then Mum's whispered voice crackled on the line again.

"Sorry, had to get out of Dad's hearing range. He doesn't know it yet, but I called the emergency plumber to come round and fix it."

Poor Dad. Practically every DIY effort he had made so far had to be properly fixed or finished off by a professional someone-or-other. But when it came to our family's bladders versus Dad's feelings . . . well, there was no contest really.

"Anyway, how was the Little Acorns thing?" Mum asked, daring to raise her voice again.

"Awful," I moaned.

"Awful how?"

Where did I start? Awful as in awfully boring, awfully pointless, awfully embarrassing, or plain awfully *awful*.

"The teacher made all the kids pretend to be really corny stuff," I told Mum.

"Like?"

"Like . . . like they had to act out being little acorns."

"Which was what, exactly?" Mum asked, sounding like she was smiling.

"They had to curl up really small, and stay really still for ages."

"And Jake and Jamie managed to stay still for *how* long?"

"About five seconds."

I grinned to myself, remembering the frown on Mrs O'Connell's face when Jake reached his five-second patience threshold, uncurled himself and started singing "*HUMPTEEE-DUMPTEEEE SA' ON A WAAAAA'!*" at the top of his voice.

"Oh, dear. . ." Mum sighed, though I knew from

the hint of the giggle in her voice that she found it pretty funny. "But listen, tell me more when you get home – I think I hear your dad getting up and moving about. I'd better check he isn't trying to grab a power tool or something."

I'd no sooner said bye and ended the call when a familiar *bleep!* bleeped. Stopping the buggy for a second – right beside the ornate drinking fountain – I checked my incoming text.

High Barnet – boooorrrring. Dumping end-of-line project! Par x

Parminder couldn't have sent me a better message at a better time – at least I wasn't missing out on maximum fun with my old friends *after* all. OK, so now instead of feeling 100% lonely, I only felt about 75% lonely, which wasn't much difference, but as Frankie's mum used to say, "If you can't be glad for small things, then you're a very sad kind of person." And I was *determined* not to be a sad kind of person.

"Doggy drink!" Jake suddenly giggled.

I was just about to text Parminder a quick reply, but instead I glanced around to see what my brother was on about. He was pointing to the bottom of the water fountain, where – sure enough – some kindly Victorian architect had made a marble trough of water at doggy-drinking height. I hadn't noticed that before, when I stood here to meet TJ earlier in the week. I hadn't noticed the inscription on the water fountain either.

"'For the refreshment of the townspeople and animals of Portbay, presented by Miss Elize Grainger, 1880'," I mumbled in surprise.

I was also surprised to see a familiar hairy head appear as I read that out.

"Bob dog!" Jamie gurgled, as Bob (the dog), stopped lapping thirstily and smiled up at us.

Uh-oh; if Bob was here, that meant. . .

Before I'd even got to the end of that thought, four mean 'n' moody tall boys and one dumb 'n' dopey short one ambled up the steps from the beach, hands shoved in pockets, shoulders hunched up.

As four sets of eyes fixed sneerily on me, I fumbled my phone back into my pocket and got ready to push the buggy off at high speed the second I heard anyone shout *anything* to do with underwear. . .

And then something made me hesitate; a jumble of somethings about finding one good apple amongst the rotten ones, and not judging a book by its cover. My thoughts might not have made much sense (much like Mrs Sticky Toffee in general), but I knew I had to give TJ one more chance to make it right, to show that blanking me earlier had been just an accident, or maybe just a stupid mistake, and nothing to do with knickers.

And so I fixed my eyes on TJ . . . and got my answer immediately. This time, there was *no* excuse. I wasn't half hidden or drowned out by holidaymakers driving by in their Volvos. I was *right* here in front of him, with two small boys yelling his dog's name loudly, and his dog nuzzling my hand for a pat. But *still* TJ dropped his gaze to the paving stones and pretended that I was as invisible as a cold germ.

Bubbles of anger and humiliation began rumbling through my chest again, when – out of the corner of my eye – I noticed a huge seagull flap itself down on to the top of the fountain, and stare ominously down at the group of lads; or, more likely, at one person in *particular* in that group of lads. And that suddenly put an idea in my head, an idea about getting my *own* back. . . Oh, yeah, the old, shy Stella just wanted to run away fast, and ignore the fact that TJ was doing a very good job of ignoring *me*. But the new, improved, *braver* Stella had something *else* in mind. . .

"Hi, Titus!" I said very loudly, very brightly, staring *very* hard at TJ.

And with that, I held my head high, gave Bob a quick farewell scratch on the head, and strode off with the twins and the buggy, feeling almost giddy with surprise at my own courage.

"*Titus*? TJ, your name's *Titus*?"

Just like I'd known they would, Sam's gang immediately began hooting and roaring with laughter. Yep, with those two little words, I'd got my revenge. I felt *well* happy.

Until I glanced over my shoulder and saw the sad, crumpled face gazing at me from the midst of the hooting, horrible lads. . .

Chapter 14

Sorry, with strawberries on top

"What a *prat*! Don't you *dare* go feeling sorry for him, Stella!"

It was Saturday morning and Mum had gone to the beach with my brothers, and taken Dad with them, since he was still banned from doing DIY or anything else that required a brain for a few days. Downstairs, the proper plumber (who was getting very familiar with our house, since he'd already had to fix pipes Dad had broken) was clattering about, finishing the job he'd started yesterday, when Mum had called him out.

And me? Well, I'd told my parents that I wanted to stay home and have a yak with Frankie, which is exactly what I was doing now, spilling all about TJ, since there was no point in keeping it to myself any more – not now I'd found out that my instincts were 99% wrong and he was truly a 1% idiot.

"Well, it wasn't so much that I felt *sorry* for him exactly," I tried to backtrack. "It was just that when those lads started teasing him about his name, this look came over his face that just made me feel a bit, I dunno, sort of. . ."

". . .sorry for him!" Frankie finished my sentence for me. "Look, he's mates with a bunch of mutt-heads, so you're better off without him!"

Frankie was right, which is why I was glad I'd phoned her and poured out all of yesterday afternoon's humiliation, but she still didn't seem to *get* the fact that I was kind of disappointed to see my first potential friend in Portbay slip-slide away. . .

"Uh-oh . . . listen, Stell – I didn't realize the time. I promised my gran I'd be round to hers at ten to take her out shopping, and it's nearly ten now. Can I call you back later?"

"Yeah, course," I told her, as I scratched Peaches' purrily vibrating head.

As we said our hurried goodbyes, a sudden loud *loudness* from outside threatened to drown us both out.

Bedooooiiiinnnnnggg-TWANG!
Bedooooiiiinnnnnggg-TWANG!
Bedooooiiiinnnnnggg-TWANG!
"HuzaaaahhhHHH!"
"What are they *doing* over there?" I wondered

out loud for the trillionth time, as I clicked the end-call button and chucked the phone on the bed.

"Prrrp!" said Peaches in reply (ish), as he stretched himself into a luxurious arch on the bed, and casually clawed the phone closer to him, as if it were a catnip mouse.

"I *might* be able to see something if they hadn't got their curtains closed," I muttered, peering out into the sunshiney brightness and seeing the darkened windows of the house opposite.

Peaches yawned and began to do the reverse of his big stretch (i.e. he more or less ignored me).

"Hey, *I've* got an idea!" I said, turning around and clocking Peaches now tucking his legs up underneath himself like a furry picnic table. "Maybe I could attach a tiny camera to your collar, and you could sneak your way into that house to see what's going on?"

There were times when I convinced myself that Peaches was psychic, but it didn't seem like he had much of a sense of humour. Or maybe he just thought *my* sense of humour was a bit lame. Whatever, he went right on purrily blanking me and began staring purrily at my phone, two millimetres from his neat little nose, his green eyes practically *crossing* it was so close.

Meanwhile, I went back to staring out the window, straining my ears for more weird, inexplicable noises, and tried *not* to think that only two days ago, I thought that maybe me and TJ could have fun trying to suss out the source of the noises together. . .

When my mobile suddenly started trilling, I jumped, but Peaches didn't seem to. When I whipped my head round and hurried over to the bed, I saw that his once-crossed eyes were nearly closed and his whiskered snout was almost mimicking a Cheshire Cat grin. For some reason, it reminded me of my mate Eleni, when she'd go guessing the end of movies when we were only halfway through watching, and then give us all this *told*-you-so smug smile when the lights went up.

"Hello?" I answered, frowning a little since I hadn't recognized the number flashing up on the phone panel.

"Stella?"

Now *there* was a voice I hadn't expected to hear, even if *Peaches* had. . .

Her name was Amber; it said so on a rectangular badge pinned to her dress. I'd seen her a couple of times before when I'd been here in the Shingles café, but I'd never known what she was called.

"You want something?"

The grumpy, red-haired teenage girl was hovering over me, a pad in her hand. Not just her cheeks but her whole *face* was flushed red, like she was really angry with me for daring to be here and bother her with my order. Or maybe it was just that she realized that it was one of *my* little brothers who'd tripped her up while she was carrying a full tray of dirty dishes last time we were in here.

Still, annoying as that must have been for Amber, it was hardly as embarrassing as what happened to *me* last time I sat at this very same table with my family and Frankie. I mean, it was *my* head that Amber spilt a plate of cold pasta over, after all. . .

"Er, strawberry milkshake," I croaked out, trying to keep my eyes from wandering over the terrible black cotton dress and white apron the tall, skinny girl was wearing. She was obviously job-sharing that old-fashioned get-up with another waitress; one who was a lot *shorter* and *squatter*, by the looks of it.

I wished TJ would hurry up . . . even though the café was packed, I felt kind of awkward and conspicuous sitting here in the window seat, like a bug-eyed goldfish in a pet shop window. It didn't help that I felt I was being stared at from a table at the back by Rachel and Brooke and whatever the rest of the café crew were called. (Help. . .)

But never mind them; the other reason I wished TJ would hurry up was that I was *dying* to hear what he had to say . . . I mean, *apart* from the garbled snatch of conversation we'd had on the phone half an hour ago, when he'd said stuff like "sorry about yesterday" and "can we meet in the café?" and "I just want to explain and everything".

So what *was* TJ's explanation "and everything" for ignoring me (twice)? Well, I was still waiting to find out but then I *had* got here a few minutes early, I realized, checking the time on my mobile on the table in front of me.

Desperate for something to do so that I didn't look to the *entire* clientele of the café (especially Rachel and co) like I'd been stood up, I thought about texting Frankie – but felt too stupidly fidgety to think of a message and ditched that idea for now. Tapping my nails on the pink plastic coating of my phone, I gazed around, letting my eyes settle on the front page of an open newspaper some old man was holding up and flicking through at a nearby table.

Vandals Strike Again! screamed the inky black headlines of the *Portbay Journal*. *Teen gang thought to be responsible for—*

"Hi!" said TJ, sliding into the seat opposite. "Didn't know if you'd come!"

He was hunched down low in the chair, wearing his "I'm With Stupid!" T-shirt, a nervous smile on his face. He suddenly reminded me of Dexter, Lauren's kid sister's hamster, who looked cute but concerned at all times.

"I didn't know if *you'd* come!" I told TJ, realizing too late that I was smiling. Drat – I'd planned to act all aloof till he explained himself properly. "Er . . . who're you waving at?"

TJ was looking somewhere over my shoulder, wiggling his fingers half-heartedly at someone-or-other.

"Just Rachel and that lot," said TJ, sounding pretty unenthusiastic.

"Thought you said you didn't think much of them?" I said, remembering a snatch of conversation we'd had that first, excellent day we'd spent together, crazy golfing and talking rubbish.

"Yep, I think they're a bunch of stuck-up moos, but they're waving at me, and I'm not up for falling out with people unless I really have to."

"Oh," I mumbled uselessly, guessing that he included me in that, or we wouldn't be here.

"Anyway," said TJ, stopping with the finger-wiggling and flashing me a nervous-ish smile, "this is the same seat you were sitting in the very first time I saw you!" he blurted out.

"The first time. . .?" I frowned. "But the first time we met was on Monday, down on the beach!"

"Um, *yeah* . . . that was when we *met*," TJ shrugged. "But it wasn't the first time I *saw* you. The first time I saw you was last Friday night, when you were in here with your mum and dad and brothers and stuff. When your mate Frankie blew that kiss over to us, when we were sitting up at the back of the caff. . ."

Blam.

Cue surprise, shock, horror, etc.

"Um . . . you mean you were with Sam and those lads that time?" I gasped in surprise.

But then (doh!) it sort of made sense; that's why TJ had recognized Frankie's picture when I showed it to him in the den, wasn't it? And another thing; that evening, same as now, there was a big gormless Alsatian tied up outside Shingles. 'Cause last Friday, hadn't Dad taken Jake out to pat the dog, while Mum had gone to the loo with Jamie? That's when me and Frankie were left alone, and Frankie had cheekily blown the kiss to the gawping boys. . .

Seeing me glance his way just now, Bob put a hopeful paw up on the glass at the other side of the plate-glass window.

"But why didn't you tell me before?" I turned to ask TJ, while reaching my hand out to "touch" Bob's paw from *my* side of the glass.

"Well, you'd already talked about the lads, when we were walking to the crazy golf on Wednesday, and you said how they'd laughed at you and taken the mick out of you the first weekend you'd moved here," TJ shrugged. "So I didn't think you'd exactly be too *chuffed* if you knew *I* was there with them last week. Specially not 'cause of what happened, when Amber spilt all that stuff all over you. . ."

As I quietly cringed, I guess I understood why TJ had stayed schtum about that, even when we were getting on well.

OK, so that was fair enough . . . but then *why* didn't he seem to care about my feelings *yesterday*, when he completely blanked me?

"When you phoned this morning you said

sorry. . ." I mumbled, dragging the conversation around to the *real* reason we were here.

"Yeah . . . yeah, I mean sorry for not talking to you when I saw you yesterday. It's just that Sam and them are kind of *funny* about girls. I mean, they *fancy* some of them – like Rachel and *her* lot," TJ explained, nodding his head in the direction of the cliquey girls posing at a table at the back of the café. "But they don't think it's cool to be *mates* with a girl."

"So, *that's* why you ignored me?"

"Uh-huh," said TJ, wincing and looking pretty ashamed of himself, I was glad to see. "I know it's dumb, but they've only just sort of accepted me, and I didn't want to, y'know, go and mess things up."

Oh, yes, yes, *yes* . . . none of this had ANYTHING to do with my knickers, by the sound of it. (Phewwwww. . .)

But I still needed to ask TJ a straight-out question.

"So does that mean we're friends – or not?"

"Course we are!" said TJ, looking sheepish again, and starting to agitatedly spin a stray teaspoon around on the table with his finger.

I was about to ask him how it was going to work exactly; if that meant he was going to act like he knew

I *existed* next time we bumped into each other when he was with Sam and the others. But a strawberry milkshake and a sour face interrupted us.

"There you go," Amber announced flatly, thudding the tall glass down so hard in front of me that my phone rattled on the formica table. "What *d'you* want?"

"Nah, nothing," said TJ, glancing up at her and shaking his head.

Amber seemed to flush redder, furious at TJ taking up valuable bum space without buying anything, and stomped off with a clatter of her chunky black shoes.

"Can't stay," he suddenly told me, ignoring Amber's glaring huff. "Mum's got a class to teach this afternoon, so I've got to get back to look after Ellie."

At the mention of Ellie's name, a little ripple of guilt wibbled its way up my spine. Maybe *I* should take a turn apologizing.

"Er, I'm sorry I called you Titus in front of Sam and everyone. I just wanted to embarrass you, 'cause you'd embarrassed *me*. . ."

"That's OK. I guess it makes us sort of even," TJ shrugged across the table. "So Mum told you, huh? She said she met you at that kid thing she runs."

"Yeah," I nodded. "Pretty fancy names she landed on you and your sister!"

"They were names from plays she was in at drama school," TJ explained, wrinkling his nose in what looked like disgust.

"Um . . . can I ask you something?" I ventured, wondering if I was about to be *way* too cheeky. "If Titus is the 'T', what's the 'J' stand for?"

"'J'," he repeated, idly spinning the teaspoon around on the table.

"Yeah, the 'J'," I nodded.

"No – the 'J' is just for 'J'. That was my dad's idea. He said that if me and Ellie didn't like our first names, then we should get to choose our second names ourselves, but he thought it would be fun to give us just an initial to start us off."

Wow, that was the first time TJ had ever mentioned his dad.

"So," I said slowly, *"you're* Titus J O'Connell. . ."

". . .and Ellie's Electra Z O'Connell," TJ finished my question off for me. And then disaster struck.

"Oh– oh, no! *Sorry*, Stell. . .!"

Y'know, when it came to the Shingles café, I think I was *jinxed*. After all, *last* weekend, I'd ended up with carbonara dribbling down my neck;

today, TJ had made a grab for his spinning spoon and managed to spill the whole of my strawberry milkshake on to my lap.

"Oh, God . . . *here*! Take this!" TJ muttered, looking as red-faced as grumpy Amber the waitress, while he yanked handful after handful of paper towels out of the serviette dispenser and chucked them at me.

"It's OK, TJ," I tried to tell him, even if it didn't really feel OK to have sticky pink milk seeping through my T-shirt and denim miniskirt.

"Look, you better go to the loo and wash some of that stuff off," TJ bumbled. "Maybe they've got one of those blow-dryer things. . ."

"Yeah, I will," I nodded, getting to my feet and clutching bundles of serviettes over the worst of the stains. "Back in a sec. . .!"

No surprises, but it took more than a sec. And no surprises, but I heard a couple of bitchy, witchy comments from a certain table at the back when I was on my way to the loos ("What a *state*!" "Yeah, *again*! Ha, ha, ha!")

Whatever . . . a few minutes later, as I stood holding my soaking (but cleanish) T-shirt under the hand-dryer in the ladies' loos, I vowed a couple of things. First, never to speak to Rachel and her stupid, snippy girlfriends, whether they were in my year at school or not; and second, *never* to moan again about my name. It's just that I *used* to feel self-conscious about being called after something showy like a star when I was so shy, but compared to the real, full names poor TJ and Ellie had been lumbered with, Stella was plain and simple and just about *perfect*.

Checking in the toilet mirror that I was still dampish, but at least not *pink* any more, I headed back out to the café (blanking my eyes and ears to the table closest to the loos) . . . only to find a totally strange family sitting at the window seat, and no Bob outside the window staring in either.

"Thought you'd sneaked out without paying," said the waitress called Amber, gruffly shoving a bill in my hand.

"Um . . . do you know where my friend went to?" I asked her.

"Dunno. His mates came. He left with them," she said bluntly, obviously desperate just to get me to pay and go, so she could get on with her job of being rude to other customers.

Titus J O'Connell, I thought to myself as I stepped out of the bustling café and into the blazing sunshine, *what ARE you playing at. . .?*

Chapter 15

The secret of the sweet-talking trick. . .

I'd tried to get hold of Frankie first, to tell her what had happened, but she must've still been at her gran's or something. Whatever, her mobile was switched off and there was just the answering machine on at her house.

"So there was no sign of PJ when you came out of the café?"

Auntie V had always been rotten at remembering the names of my London friends, and it looked like she was going to be exactly the same with any *new* friends I made here in Portbay. Not that I was entirely sure at the moment about whether I could count on TJ as a friend or *not*. . .

"No. I mean, TJ *did* say he couldn't stay long 'cause he had to babysit Ellie. But it's just the fact that he didn't wait to say bye, and just went off when Sam and the others turned up."

"Stella, darling, you've already told me the poor boy has a chip on his shoulder about his height. If his mother mollycoddles him and his parents give him a name that's too impossibly over the top to live up to, no *wonder* he's rebelling a bit and hanging out with the bad boys!"

"But it's not fair, Auntie V!" I protested. "He's supposed to be my friend too!"

"I didn't say it was *fair*, Stella my little star, I'm just saying it's totally understandable!"

When I'd got back home, the plumber had finished clanking about for the day, and my mum and dad *still* weren't back from the beach with the boys. As I had the place to myself, I'd plonked down on the sofa with the house phone and called the *one* person I thought might understand what I was going through. But since Frankie wasn't around, I was now wondering if the *other* person I thought might understand really understood at *all*; I mean, it almost sounded as if Auntie V had decided that TJ was better off hanging out with Sam and the other lads instead of *me*.

Hadn't she?

"Listen, I could be wrong, but PJ sounds like a bit of a sweetie."

OK, so maybe I'd got that wrong. And at those very words of Auntie V's, Peaches – presently curled up fatly on my lap – began purring so hard

I practically felt myself vibrating.

"Well, sometimes I think he *is*, and sometimes I think he *isn't*," I replied.

Just like sometimes I felt sorry for TJ and sometimes I didn't.

"You know, Stella; I somehow think he'll come to realize that those boys aren't *true* friends – they're only using him for their own entertainment; having a laugh at his expense, by the sound of it. You'd be a *much* better friend to him."

"I know – but what can I do?"

"Enough of *my* gut feeling, Stella, darling – what's yours? Do *you* think PJ's worth one, last chance?"

It was like the volume and vibrate buttons had been turned up to "10" somewhere on Peaches' furry body – his manic purring was getting more insistent by the second.

"Um, yes . . . I guess," I told her.

Peaches blinked loving eyes at me. The big, fat, catty weirdo.

"Well, in *that* case, you're going to have to sweet-talk him, darling."

"I have to *what*-y?" I double-checked.

"Sweet-talk him! I just mean, be your usual funny, lovely self, try to think of great things to do together, and whatever you do, *don't* slag off his friends, or that'll make him defensive about them. It's *then* that he'll realize that you're *much* more gorgeous a person to hang around with than those horrible, sarky boys."

"Are you *sure* that'll work?" I asked dubiously.

"It's a trick that's worked for me *many* a time. And it certainly worked with your dad, when we were teenagers."

"What – that time you were telling me about, when he got into trouble, with – with the paintballing thing?"

"Oh, yes. Have you talked to him about that yet?"

"No. . ."

"Well, I'm not going to spoil that story for you – I'll let him tell you himself. God, I'd *love* to see the reaction on his face when you ask him!"

"Auntie V!" I groaned. "You can't *not* tell me now!"

"Yes I can!" she replied breezily. "But I *will* tell you that he was hanging out with a few *morons* at the time, and I told him, actually I *yelled* at him that he was being the biggest moron of the lot for being friends with them. Course that got me nowhere, so I decided to change my plan."

"What did you do?" I asked, moving slightly to adjust the weight of Peaches, since the feeling was starting to go in my legs.

"Well, like I say, I tried the sweet-talking technique. I decided to be *extra* nice to your dad, with sugar on top. It confused him – for a while – but sure enough he came round, and started moaning to me about his mates and their exploits. I just tried to be sympathetic, and eventually it dawned on him that they truly were idiots and I was *completely* brilliant!"

The way Auntie V came out with that, I was giggling so much that I didn't clock the sound of the front door opening.

"Hey, is that laughing I can hear? What a nice sound to come home to!" said Dad, his beaming face appearing in the living-room doorway. "It must be that mad Frankie you're talking to!"

"Is that your DIY-disaster, former teen terror of a father?" Auntie V whispered in my ear.

"Yes, it's Dad, and no, Dad, it's not Frankie, it's Auntie V!" I replied, answering both their questions at the same time.

"Great! Let me have a word with my favourite sister then!"

Dad strode across the room enthusiastically,

holding out his hand towards the phone, leaving Mum out in the hall to deal with the twins.

"S'pose I'd better have a word with that doughball of a brother of mine!" Auntie V muttered in my ear, making me giggle again. "Anyway, bye for now, Stella, darling – and good luck with the sweet-talking!"

As I handed the phone over to Dad and gently poured Peaches on to the sofa, I found myself excited, i.e. kind of quiveringly hopeful that her advice would work.

"Hey, I think these two brought half the beach home with them!" Mum laughed, as I went through to the hall and found her unstrapping the damp, happy, sandy twins from the buggy.

I smiled; half at the blissfully messy boys, and half at the knowledge that later, after lunch, I'd go out to the den and text TJ. I wouldn't mention the fact that he ran out on me at the café – I'd just suggest that we meet up tomorrow or sometime to do something fun, like hang out at Sugar Bay. . .

"Ooh, that's *lovely*!" Mum suddenly announced, pausing with a *Finding Nemo* bucket and spade set and a nappy-bag in her hand. "What *is* that smell? It's like peaches and cream, almost!"

I glanced down as Peaches curled his way

around my bare ankles, gazing up at me with his adoring green almond eyes, and knew instantly that he *totally* approved of my plan. . .

Chapter 16

The amazing, disappearing mobile

I was feeling sick.

I was feeling *so* sick that I hadn't been able to face the full-on Sunday morning mega fry-up breakfast that Dad had put in front of me this Sunday morning.

"Not hungry, Stella?" Mum said, frowning at me across the table, noticing that I was doing a great job of swirling beans in an interesting pattern around my sausages and not much else.

"*Ish*," I answered her, forcing myself to nibble the end of a sausage so Mum didn't think I was going anorexic on her or something.

"Are you *sure* you're OK, Stell?" Mum frowned some more, studying my face for signs of impending illness.

"I'm fine!" I lied, feeling really, horribly *sick*.

"Don't fuss, Louise!" Dad said good-naturedly, as he reached over for another newspaper from the bundle he'd brought back from the shop this morning. "If Stella isn't hungry, then she's just not hungry. And it means *all* the more for me!"

Flicking a newspaper upright with one hand, he expertly nicked the other *un*nibbled sausage that was on my plate with the other.

After that, thankfully, Mum *did* get off my back, giving up her line of questioning with a roll of her eyes at Dad.

"So . . . what're the local headlines then?" she asked him instead, getting back to eating her own breakfast, while keeping a wary eye on the boys in their high chairs. (They were eating nicely and quietly now, but knowing them, a food fight could break out at *any* minute, with lumps of soggy Weetabix and eggy toast being chucked at anything that did or didn't move.)

"The local headlines . . . well, let's see," said Dad jovially, while scanning the paper.

"Let me guess. . ." said Mum, as she put a hand out to stop Jake spooning bits of breakfast on to the floor. "*Man Grows Giant Turnip*? Or how about *Nothing Happened In Portbay This Week Shocker*!"

"Hmm, not quite!" Dad replied, all of a sudden furrowing his eyebrows together. "Listen to this;

Vandals Strike Again! Teen gang thought to be responsible for spate of smashed phone boxes and bus shelters around town."

"Oh!" Mum gasped, looking a bit flustered.

I didn't really listen while Dad read out the whole story to Mum; I was too busy feeling sick. Sick because my mobile was gone. Gone, as in missing . . . lost . . . stolen. . .? I didn't know which. I'd only realized that I didn't *have* it any more when I went to text TJ after I'd spoken to Auntie V yesterday afternoon on the house phone.

I'd checked in my room, in the den, around the house, in case I'd put it down somewhere without thinking. Then I checked under cushions on the sofa, *under* the sofa, and down the *sides* of the sofa, in case it had slipped out of my back pocket when I was chatting to Auntie V on the regular phone. I noseyed in trainers, in the washing machine and even down the new loo, in case one of the boys had been playing hide-the-mobile when no one was looking.

When I'd searched everywhere and couldn't find it, I'd pretended to Mum and Dad that I wanted to go down to the High Street to see if any other shops sold frames for Nana Jones and Grandad Eddie's photo – and instead, hurried straight to the Shingles café to ask if I'd left my mobile there and if anyone had handed it in. "No," red-faced Amber had said bluntly, as she carried a teetering tray of ice-cream sundaes to a table of OAPs. That was the end of that – it must have dropped out of my pocket when I'd been walking home at lunchtime, maybe.

And so the rest of yesterday, and all this morning, I'd felt sick. The thing was, it wasn't just *losing* my phone that was making me feel sick, it was the whole keeping-secrets thing that was making me feel yucksville too. Y'see, I hadn't got round to telling Mum and Dad about losing my phone yet – not 'cause they'd flip *out* at me or anything – but because the first thing they'd say would be "When do you last remember seeing it?". And the answer to that was at the table in the window of the Shingles café – with TJ. Spot the secret? I hadn't told them I'd seen him, just 'cause I thought they had that silly downer on him. If I went and told them now, they'd probably blame TJ for making me turn all secretive on them. God, they might even go putting two and two together and come up with some totally mad idea that TJ had something to do with my phone going missing. . .!

Stella – this is stupid! I suddenly thought frantically to myself. *Mum and Dad wouldn't necessarily think bad stuff like that! And maybe they don't have that much of a downer on TJ at all – maybe you just overreacted the other day when they were talking about him. . .*

I was just about to offload and spill the news about my mobile when Mum got in there first by gazing up from the *Portbay Journal* and asking me something.

"Stella – that gang that you said your friend TJ was hanging about with. . . Um, you don't think maybe *they're*—"

"Mum!" I gasped, a sudden rage coming over me before she'd even finished her sentence. "You're *always* telling me not to jump to conclusions about people! And those boys that TJ knows aren't exactly going to be the *only* teenage boys in the whole of Portbay!"

"You're right, Stella," said Dad, looking a bit shamefaced. "We shouldn't jump to conclusions, it's just that your mum and I thought that when we left London we'd be moving away from any potential trouble like this. . ."

"I'm not hungry – I'm going to go and e-mail my friends," I muttered, getting up from the table and not responding directly to Dad's semi-apology.

It felt kind of mad that I'd just stood up for four boys that I didn't even know properly but knew enough not to *like*, but I hated hearing my parents act all bigoted in that way. Not to mention hypocritical. . .

If I could bear to go back in the kitchen right now, I'd ask Dad about what he got up to as a teenager – that whole paintballing thing that happened – see how guilty he feels then! I thought darkly (even though I didn't have a clue what I was on about), as I sat down in front of the computer and waited for it to boot up.

"*Hi Stella!*" I read, as Frankie's message pinged on-screen. "*Sorry I had to dash off to Gran's yesterday, but you know what a state she gets in if me or Mum are ever late round to hers (thinks we've been run over by a double-decker bus or something). So what's new with you?*"

I stared at the screen and wondered where to start. I *wanted* to tell Frankie about meeting up in the café with TJ after I spoke to her, but since she already thought he was a loser, I had a feeling she'd freak out at me if I told her a) that I'd seen him at *all*, and b) that he did a disappearing act on me. And if I told her *that* stuff, then I should also tell her that I was thinking of giving him (yet) another chance – and somehow I didn't think that Frankie would be too wild about Auntie V's sweet-talking trick. ("*Sweet*-talk him? Tell him where to get off, more like!")

I stared at the screen some more and tried to figure out how I could put it across without Frankie telling me I was insane. But I didn't get very far, mainly 'cause the doorbell rang and – out of habit – I started running to answer it, till I remembered we *weren't* in Kentish Town, where my mates popped round all the time, and so whoever was at the door probably wasn't calling for *me*.

Wrong.

"Stella! Visitors for you!" Dad's voice drifted through to the tiny office I was hunched up in.

I think it was the scrabble of claws on bare floorboards that gave it away before I got through to the hall and saw my dad standing chatting brightly and towering over TJ.

"Hi, Stella!" said Ellie brightly, before her brother got a word in edgeways. "Can I go see Jake and Jamie, please?"

"Um, sure – they're in the kitchen with Mum."

And in a blur of pastels she was off.

"Hey, really, *really* great dog, this – eh, Stella?" Dad grinned at me, as he ruffled a grateful Bob's head. "And I was just saying to TJ that it's *excellent* to meet him at last!"

TJ was smiling at me too, but there was a slight panic in his eyes – I could tell he was totally confused by how over-the-top my dad's welcome was. But *I* knew what Dad was up to; making up to me *big*-time, to prove he *wasn't* making presumptions about TJ and his other mates. I kind of appreciated the effort, but it was pretty cringeworthy to witness. . .

"And hey –" Dad suddenly added, pointing at the "I'm With Stupid!" logo across TJ's skinny chest – "cool T-shirt, dude!"

"Dude"? My dad just said "Dude"? *Omigod*. . .

And it didn't stop there; Mum and Dad both flurried embarrassingly around TJ for so long – offering him sausages, bacon sarnies, orange juice, carrot cake, spare keys to the *house* practically – that it took about ten minutes for the both of us to get away from them and escape out into the garden (with Bob).

"They're all right, your mum and dad," said TJ as we ambled towards the den.

(*You wouldn't be saying that if you'd heard what they were talking about five minutes ago*, I thought.)

"Yeah, they're OK," I shrugged, as I tugged at the stiff hook that kept the door safely shut against inquisitive toddlers.

"Is it all right to leave Ellie with them? She's not going to bug them, is she?" he asked, chucking a thumb over his shoulder in the direction of the kitchen, where we could hear Ellie belting out some old Kylie song, pausing for intermittent tapping breaks.

"Hey, if she's keeping the twins occupied, my parents will love her for *ever*."

Out of the corner of my eye, I spotted TJ grinning at that remark of mine, and suddenly realized how pleased I was to see him.

"Glad you came round!" I told him, pushing the door open.

(Notice something? I could have opened with "What happened to you yesterday?", but I didn't – Operation Sweet-Talking TJ started *here*, whatever Frankie might have thought of it. . .)

"Yeah, well, I just . . . *whatever*," he said vaguely, looking momentarily shy or something as he followed me into the den.

377

"Hey, check this out!" I smiled, pulling my latest photo-strip of the girls off the corkboard.

As I pointed out Eleni and Parminder and Neisha and Lauren to him, my brain was working overtime, wondering what sort of sweet-talking I could do to win him round. I should have asked Auntie V for some examples. . .

"Hey, *she's* pretty cute!" said TJ, his index finger right next to Neisha's face.

"Well, she'd think *you* were pretty cute too! She likes indie boys!"

"Yeah?" said TJ, shuffling awkwardly, but looking kind of chuffed, all the same.

Brilliant – that was a successful bit of sweet-talking I'd done there, even if it wasn't exactly true. I mean, Neisha liked her boys hip-hop flavoured. Dunno *what* I'd do if she came to visit sometime and they met up, but I'd have to worry about that later (or get TJ to swap his grunge T-shirts for some serious street style).

Be-*doinnnnnnggggg*, be-*doinnnnnnnnggggg*, be-*doinnnnnnggggg* – "WHEEEEEEEEEEEEE!" – *thud*.

"What was that?" asked TJ, his eyes wide.

"Our spooky neighbours, up to their spooky stuff again," I explained.

"Wanna take a look?"

"Sure!" I said, grabbing the chair by the desk.

TJ beat me to the bottom of the garden, of course, mainly 'cause I was humfing the chair with me. And Bob beat me too, since he bounced fearlessly through the thigh-high weeds, wild flowers and nettles, instead of taking wary baby steps like me.

"Wait!" I called out, as TJ started scrambling up the bricks. "You can stand on the chair!"

"S'OK! I'm good at climbing!" he said, already pulling himself up on to the top of the wall.

"What can you see?" I asked him, trying to take a step up on to the wooden chair but realizing my denim mini was too tight for such a big step up.

"Not much. . ."

TJ had one jeaned leg dangling on our side of the wall, and the other dangling on the lane side.

". . .they've got their curtains closed."

"That's the same as last time!" I sighed, giving up on wriggling my skirt up a bit and clambering on the chair if there was nothing to see.

"But hold on," said TJ, suddenly darting his head around like an inquisitive chicken as he peered towards the house over the lane. "The curtains aren't *totally* closed. I think I can just see something moving. . . *Urgh!*"

Something moved all right – TJ scrambling at hyper-speed off the wall, and tumbling into a sniggering heap on a clump of dandelions and dusty earth.

"What happened? What did you see?" I urged him, kneeling down beside him.

It was almost infuriating; he was laughing so much he could hardly get his breath, let alone speak. It wasn't just me who was getting wound up; Bob was frantically pacing backwards and forwards around his master, snuffling at him like he was worried he'd broken something or gone mad. The only one who was calm was Peaches, who'd appeared out of nowhere (no surprise there) and jumped up on the den chair. He was staring coolly at TJ, like the headteacher waiting for the hyperactive kid to calm down before giving him a telling-off.

"Someone – someone –" TJ started to hiccup out, sounding a bit like me at my stammering worst.

"Someone *what*?" I demanded.

"Someone started opening the curtains – they nearly caught me!"

I was shocked, absolutely shocked.

"Stella?" said TJ, concern in his slightly breathless voice. "Did you hear what I said?"

Yes, of *course* I'd heard what he'd said, but I was too shocked to care about stupid, weird neighbours and their stupid mystery noises when I'd seen what I'd just seen.

TJ hadn't registered Bob rummaging his snout in his master's jeans' pocket just now. But as he followed my stare, he soon saw what was wrong.

"Oh, God. No, it's OK, Stella – I can explain!"

But exactly *how* TJ was going to explain away what Bob had innocently grabbed out of his pocket, I had *no* idea.

"Good dog," I said to Bob, gently taking my mobile phone from between his teeth. . .

Chapter 17

The dare, and big, old, dumb me. . .

Outside in the sunlight, butterflies hovered prettily, bees buzzed busily, and dragonflies soared and dived over our tangled garden like it was a prickly kind of paradise.

Inside, I sat hunched over my desk in the den, trailing my finger over the carving I'd done in the windowsill last weekend: *Stella + Frankie, M8s 4eva, 2004*.

Frankie and me, mates for ever . . . and there was me and TJ, whose friendship had lasted for a whole four *days*.

Hey, who'd have guessed that sweet-talking TJ would stop before it even started? But then, who'd have guessed I had such lousy judgement when it came to people? Or that I'd end up picking a lying, cheating thief for a potential new friend?

Still, TJ had certainly tried his best to sweet-talk *me*.

"I was going to give it back to you! That's why

I came today! I didn't *want* to nick it!" he'd tried to explain, stumbling up out of the dandelions and dust, as I'd stared blindly at the dog-drool-covered mobile in my hands. "It's just . . . well, I *knew* it was all wrong, but then when your mobile rang and it was one of your mates, it felt *really* wrong."

Now it made sense – the end of Frankie's e-mail, I mean. TJ was the mystery boy who'd answered her call yesterday.

"They said I had to do it!" TJ blundered on with his excuses, while I was too dumbstruck to say anything out loud about anything. "They said that they'd tell *everyone* at school what my name really was, unless I did a dare!"

Bob – picking up on the fact that something was wrong, even if he couldn't figure out what that might be – dropped his hairy head on to my lap and gazed up at me with soulful brown eyes.

"And I said, fine, I'd do the dare – but then Aiden said the dare was to nick something off *you*!"

I didn't care about the dare; I just cared that I'd stuck up for TJ in front of my parents and Auntie V, and been so dumb as to give him a big, fat, sweet-talking second chance.

"Ben said it didn't matter what it was I

nicked off you, but then Sam said it couldn't be something lame like a hairslide or whatever, it *had* to be something important. And then when I met up with you in the Shingle, I thought, I just can't *do* it. But after I spilt your milkshake and you went to the loo, the lads all turned up at the window, and Marcus was tapping on the glass and pointing at your mobile. You'd just left it sitting there on the table. And – and –"

Er, was TJ making out that it was almost my *own* fault that he'd stolen my phone? No way – he'd stolen it because his other "friends" egged him on. His other "friends", who mattered more to him than *me*. . .

"Hey, guys!" Dad had suddenly called out from the open kitchen doorway. "We're just going to have some ice-cream. You want some?"

I said nothing, mainly because my vocal chords were temporarily paralysed with shock. TJ stared beseechingly at me for a second, but seeing that I wasn't too likely to say anything any time soon, he did the talking for me.

"No thanks, Mr Stansfield!" TJ'd called back, brushing the dust off his jeans. "Me and Ellie have to get home now!"

And with that – and a whispered "Sorry,

Stella!" – TJ clambered across the garden towards the house, calling Bob after him.

And that's when I'd come in here to the den, to lick my wounds and straighten my head out.

"What am I going to do, Peaches?" I softly asked the purring furball sprawled out across half the desk. "I know *you're* my friend, but who else have I got here?"

Slowly, Peaches elegantly clambered to his feet, and after a wide catty yawn, he shook himself, like a dog caught out in the rain. Only, instead of sprinkles of water, Peaches sent a fine shower of glinting, golden sand shimmering out of his scruffy ginger fur.

And then I knew.

"You all right in here?" Mum asked, peeking around the door of the den.

"Yeah," I nodded, even managing a smile. "I was just thinking about going out for a walk."

It was quite possibly bordering on the insane, but my best friends in this town so far were a fat cat, an old lady, a house and a couple of ghosts I hadn't even *seen*. And I'd been neglecting one of them in particular lately; I hadn't been to Sugar Bay and the old mansion there in *way* too long. . .

Chapter 18

The frazzle marble

My Granny Stansfield (my alive-and-cuddly-and-living-in-Norfolk grandmother), has these blue-as-the-sea beads that she brought back from Portugal once as a souvenir. "They're worry beads!" she explained to me when I was little, and loved to hold the cool, smooth string of stones in my pudgy little hands. "If you're worried, you're meant to run the beads through your fingers – and doing that over and over again will calm you down and help you think more clearly."

Well, right now I wasn't so much worried as frazzled. And I might not have had a set of worry beads, but I *did* have a marble. Did that count?

Walking down the windy lane from my house, I'd come across the green marble tucked in the pocket of my shorts. It was the one I'd caught Peaches playing with on my bedroom floor a few days ago. I'd meant to stick it in the den, in the bowl that held shells and stuff, but I'd forgotten

386

all about it.

Anyway, as I was stomping in the direction of Sugar Bay, my feet took an unexpected detour – and I blame the marble for that. I'd been rolling it around in my fingers, trying to defrazzle my brain from tangled thoughts of TJ, when I found myself . . . lost.

I hadn't come across this little street of higgledy-piggledy houses before, but my pink flowery flip-flops seemed to think that this was a perfect short cut to the path that would take me up over the headland to the Seaview caravan park, and the shiny, sandy bay just beyond it.

It wasn't till I caught a glimpse of the street name that it dawned on me exactly where I was.

"Pottery Lane. . ." I murmured, staring at the street sign on the corner of the old building, and hoisting the slippery nylon rucksack further up on to my back.

Pottery Lane, I repeated in the privacy of my head. *This is where he told me he lived. I even remember the number; "Thirteen, same as my age, this year anyway!" he'd joked. . .*

All that random stuff that TJ had spoken about last Wednesday, on the way to the crazy golf; whether I wanted it to or not, some of it had seeped into a filing tray in my head.

At the thought of suddenly running into him, I got a bad case of the frazzles again and started spinning the marble madly in my fingers.

TJ wouldn't have had to do the dare, if you hadn't told those lads his name in the first place. . . I thought bleakly, feeling a twinge of guilt.

Flippety-flop, flippety-flop, flippety-flop. . .

My flowery flip-flops were at it again, leading the way till I found myself in front of a big shiny red door, with a less-than-shiny brass number "13" screwed dead centre on it. To the side, three plastic bells were stacked one on top of the other on the doorframe, with scribbled or printed names underneath each one.

"'Holman'," I murmured reading the first one. "'Brown', 'O'Connell'."

Before I could chicken out, I pressed on the third option.

"Ah-woo-ooo-ooo, oh yeahhh!"

Er . . . I was pretty sure that was Mariah Carey warbling away. Since I hadn't expected an American singing diva to answer TJ's intercom, I was just about to let go of the buzzer and run away as fast as my flip-flops would let me, when I heard *another* voice.

"Hello?" said someone who didn't sound very old.

"Ellie?" I asked, hearing an insistent barking in the background – as well as Mariah – and knowing that I had definitely got the right flat.

"Who's that?"

"It's . . . it's Stella," I spoke into the impersonal plastic box.

"Stella!" the little girl's gleeful voice warbled down. "Come up!"

And so half a minute later – just slightly out of breath – I found myself on the third floor of the building, being let into a flat that smelled of flowers and sherbet, perfume and incense, shower gel and *dog*.

"Hello, Stella!" said Ellie, looking extra small and dainty as she held open the heavy, old-fashioned door.

"Wuff!" barked Bob, tappity-tapping his claws with excitement on the varnished floorboards, as if he was doing an impression of Ellie at her tap-dancing best.

"Ah, hello . . . Stella, isn't it?" smiled Mrs O'Connell, coming out of another room in a rush of steam, wearing a piled-up white towel on her head and a deep orange kaftan-type thing. "I *thought* I heard the doorbell when I was getting out of the shower just now and wondered who on *earth* Electra was letting in. So how are you? And how are those adorable brothers of yours?"

Maybe Mrs O'Connell wasn't a very good actress, because when she smiled and called Jake and Jamie "adorable" you could tell she didn't mean it. At all.

"They're fine," I mumbled, finding myself following her into the living room, while Ellie slipped a tiny hand into mine.

Thankfully, Mrs O'Connell went to turn the CD player down. I know some people adore Mariah Carey, but I always think her voice is like someone just *shouting* in tune.

"So what brings you around, Stella? Got a message from Titus, that little rascal of mine?" asked Mrs O'Connell, talking to me via her reflection in an ornate mirror above the mantelpiece, as she loosened the towel and freed her damp wavy hair over her shoulders. Right beside her was a huge glass vase of giant tiger lilies. I could just imagine Mrs O'Connell casually tearing one off to tuck behind her ear.

"Er . . . no. I . . . I sort of hoped he'd be here," I tried to explain, glancing around the huge room, which seemed awash with yet more vases of flowers, competing with vivid flowering potted plants for exposure. And every corner of the room seemed to radiate colour, with jewel-coloured satiny throws and cushions draped over two fat sofas and several saggy armchairs. I'd never seen such a hippie, girlie room and I'd never seen so much stuff crammed on someone's walls. I mean, back in London Eleni's living-room walls were decorated with the most amazing gold icons of the Virgin Mary and all sorts, but Mrs O'Connell's room was totally different. You could hardly see the fuchsia-pink walls for bookshelves and CD racks and Indian wall hangings and Victorian-ish posters advertising old-fashioned potions and pills. And any spare bits of wall seemed to be made up of a patchwork of blown-up photos of Mrs O'Connell when she was younger. They were "stills"; the sort of publicity photos from plays and musicals that Auntie V had up on *her* office walls. And then there was this one shot of a huge, tall, tanned guy with a chest the size of Ireland and a tiny kid on his shoulders.

"That's my daddy!" Ellie explained, spotting what had caught my eye. "That's TJ up there! I wasn't even not nearly born!"

How weird . . . now I looked at it, it was like someone had superimposed TJ's face on to Arnold Schwarzenegger's body.

"Oh, that," said Mrs O'Connell flatly. "Yes, that's my ex-husband. That was taken in America, when he got his first break over there."

"He's an actor too?" I asked warily, sensing that Mrs O'Connell was about as fond of TJ and Ellie's dad as an attack of killer bees.

"Was. He's now a stuntman in Hollywood," she said with a sneer. "Doing fantastically well, apparently, though he doesn't bother to get in touch with us that often to tell us himself. I'd take that photo down, only Titus won't let me."

Squish. . .

That was the sound of my heart softening for poor TJ. Apart from everything *else* that could give him a chip on his shoulder, how could TJ a) live up to an Action Man dad who paid him no attention, and b) feel comfy living in Hippie Barbie's house? Him and Bob must stick out here like a pair of old socks in a basket of kittens. . .

"Oh, dear – what *is* Titus like!" sighed Mrs O'Connell, turning away from the subject of TJ's dad and checking the time on the clock on the wall. "He is *such* a naughty little pumpkin. He *knows*

I've this rehearsal for the Portbay Gala show this afternoon, and that I need him to look after Ellie. And what does he do? Comes home and leaves this smelly dog of his, then goes out again without a *word* of explanation, slamming the door behind him! *And* he's not answering his mobile. Where on earth can he be?"

I knew *exactly* where he'd be . . . hanging out somewhere with a bunch of lads he didn't even *like*, all because he thought he'd driven me away as a friend.

I *wished* I could tell him he hadn't. . .

Chapter 19

A crashing tinkle or a tinkling crash?

After I escaped from the Hippie Barbie flat, I tried to phone TJ – but like his mum said, his mobile was switched off. Walking along I scanned the skies, hoping to spot a lurking seagull that might lead me to him, but with no luck.

And so I'd decided to go back to Plan A, and head over to Sugar Bay, at the same time letting the sea breezes blow thoughts of TJ out of my still-frazzled head (I hoped).

Now here I was, little me on a huge chunk of headland.

Stretched out endlessly in front of the headland was a vast expanse of sea, out over the horizon towards infinity. (Er . . . though I guess *technically*, over the horizon was *France*, but that's a bit less poetic than "infinity", isn't it?)

Behind me lay a bunch of ugly old caravans. (And there wasn't *anything* very poetic to say about Seaview Holiday Homes, especially since they spoiled a very picturesque spot.)

I was doing my best to ignore the caravans – and getting my breath back after the climb up the path to get here – by stopping and soaking up the sea view through the viewfinder of Mum's camera, which I'd shoved in my rucksack when I left the house earlier. Sweeping to the left, I could make out the packed beach at Portbay. Sweeping to the right, the deserted golden sands of Sugar Bay curled around in a perfect, unspoiled crescent. And if I turned right just a teeny bit more, I'd be able to see –

EEK! A *face*! A huge, distorted face *leering* right into the lens!

"Hello, dear!"

As soon as I heard that – and sniffed the scent of something sweet – I dropped the camera down, and found my view of Joseph's house blocked by a small, smiley, ordinary (ish) old lady.

"Uh, hello!" I nodded, wondering if Mrs Sticky Toffee had any other clothes apart from her apple-green raincoat and her pink netting nest of a hat.

"I've only seen you doodling with your pencils before," she smiled, her cheeks dusty with a layer of face powder that old ladies seem to have to wear by law. "Didn't know you were a bit of a snapper too!"

I wasn't *really* a snapper too. It was running my fingers along the "*Stella + Frankie, m8s 4eva*" carving in the windowsill of the den that had put the idea in my mind. I'd decided that I *had* to get myself to that upstairs room in Joseph's house and take a photo of the original carving that'd inspired me: "*Elize and Joseph, friends for eternity*"...

Then something suddenly fluttered into my mind; I still hadn't been able to point out Mrs Sticky Toffee to my parents ... maybe I could show them a photo of her instead? At the same time, I could get Dad to scan it into the computer for me, and zap it off to Frankie etc. And (of course) I should take a photo of Peaches, and my den, and the view out of my window and stuff too... Frankie had seen all that, but my other mates hadn't.

"Can I take your picture?" I asked Mrs S-T, holding the camera up.

"Oh, no, dear!" she shook her hand, making the small cream handbag dance around in the crook of her elbow. "I'm far too old and ugly. I'd just crack the lens!"

I was sort of disappointed by her answer, but it seemed rude to insist. And I was too shy to tell her that she wasn't ugly at all – she was lovely, like ... like an icing-sugar-coated meringue or something.

"Toffee?" offered Mrs S-T, like a consolation prize for refusing my request.

As we unwrapped our sweets and let the strangely sweet, salty, buttery tastes tingle over our tongues, me and Mrs S-T stood in silence, staring out at the view.

"Kissed and made up with your friend yet?"

I nearly choked on my toffee.

"S'cuse me?"

"The boy on the other side of the High Street when I met you. That nice one. Not very tall, but a big heart."

"Um . . . not really," I mumbled, hoping she wouldn't ask me any more, since the whole TJ situation was way too complicated to start explaining to a stranger. Even a friendly, toffee-sharing stranger.

Luckily, what I said seemed to be enough for her, and we went back to staring out at the dancing white-tipped waves again.

"You know something?" Mrs S-T started up again, after a whole few moments' silence. "She'd have *hated* to see the tin cans here. She had *totally* different plans, you know. . ."

I *didn't* know, but that was because, just like always, I wasn't really sure what Mrs S-T was on about.

"Sorry?" I squeaked.

"The caravans – they wouldn't be here if Miss Grainger had had her way. Oh, no," Mrs S-T shook her head, as if what she just said was as plain as day, instead of as clear as mud.

"But . . . but they must have set up this caravan park *long* after she died," I frowned, doing some maths in my head. The newspaper cutting I had of her was celebrating her 100th birthday in 1930 – and the caravan park might have looked a bit tatty, but it must only have been here since the 1960s or 70s.

"Oh, yes . . . but Miss Grainger *loved* the view from this spot, when there was nothing much up here apart from grass and rocks," Mrs S-T smiled. "She always hoped to one day build holiday homes and an arts centre here, specially for underprivileged children – children from the slums of London. She needed to find a buyer for the old house down in Sugar Bay to afford to do that, but – of course – it never *did* sell."

I blinked and looked out at the view again, and thought about the fact that there were no actual *proper* slums in London any more, but there were still plenty of families struggling for money, and kids who never got to see the seaside, never mind go on holiday. It would have been brilliant to think of a place here that they could come to over the years. . .

"So, you're off down to Joseph's house now, are you, dear?" Mrs S-T burst into my thoughts. "Lovely day for a picnic there."

"I wasn't *planning* on having a picnic," I frowned at her, trying frantically to remember if I'd actually *mentioned* that Joseph's house was where I was heading.

"Oh, well you must take *these*, then, dear!" Mrs S-T insisted, pulling a clear, plastic bag of mini fairy cakes out of her mini-sized handbag.

"But, I – I couldn't," I bumbled, staring down at the grass in total shyness. "I mean, it's really *nice* of you . . . but I couldn't just take them. I mean. . ."

I fluttered my eyes upwards, hoping Mrs S-T could understand my nervous attempts at politeness, but. . .

But there was no one – apart from a lone, swirling gull in the sky – *anywhere* on the headland with me.

So what could I do except pick the bag of fairy cakes up off the grass and carry on down towards Sugar Bay. . .?

*

It was a crashing tinkle.

Then again, maybe it was more of a tinkling crash.

Whichever, it made my heart take a downward, bellyflopping *dive*...

A few minutes ago, I'd been walking down the hill towards Joseph's house, feeling strangely light-headed. Part of it was to do with Mrs S-T trundling off at surprisingly high speed for someone so old, and then there was also the fact that I'd been passing the time on the downhill path by gawping at the sun through my frazzle-marble. The warped rainbow of shades refracted through it was prettier than any of the colours of chalks in my art box in the den. I'd still been silently "wow!"ing about that when I stopped dead outside the railings to the garden of Joseph's house, halted by the newly erected sign that Portbay council had thoughtfully placed there.

"*Condemned Building*," it reminded me bluntly, "*. . . demolition due 30 August . . . proposed new development by Seaview Holiday Homes. . .*"

I mean, yeah – what this bay needs is fewer historic mansions and more stupid caravans, I'd thought to myself, right before I heard the crashing tinkle/ tinkling crash, and the roar of raucous laughter that followed it.

Hurriedly shoving the marble back in my pocket, I dipped through the space in the metal railing where a post had rusted to dust and crouched my way through the undergrowth of the former garden, towards the nearest open window.

"Hey, nice shot, Aiden!" someone was bellowing. "Your turn, Ben!"

"No problem!" a voice called out, followed by another shattering smash of glass and a growl of approval.

As I crept closer to the open window of the ballroom, I stretched one hand behind me and held on to my rucksack – it was probably just me being paranoid, but the rustle of the packet of fairy cakes I'd stuffed inside seemed deafening.

"Sam! Sam! Sam! Sam!" came a rhythmic clapping of hands and a call of voices next.

At the sound of another smash, a bellow of voices shouted, "*Yessss!*"

"C'mon, *Titus*! Your turn!"

"Yeah, *Titus*! *Do* it!"

As I stared upwards at the brick windowsill, my heart was doing a tap-dance in clogs across my chest, but I *had* to find out what was going on.

"No *way*!" I heard TJ's voice yell, as I willed myself to do a Peaches and leapt up to grab on to the sill, my flip-flops softly and silently scrabbling for a hold on the wall.

"You've *got* to do it. He's *got* to do it, right, Sam?" I heard a mean, whiny voice say, just as I managed to lever my elbows to take my weight and get a look inside.

And then the swaying, dancing twinkles of light made me realize what was happening: the only grand thing left in Joseph's house – the great, ornate, crystal chandelier hanging from the ceiling – was being used as target practice by Sam's gang. . .

"Forget it! I already *said* I didn't want to do it!" TJ barked, chucking aside the stone or pebble being held out to him.

"Look, just chuck the stupid rock, *right*?" a menacing voice ordered.

I saw TJ stare out the lad who was speaking. And in that split second, I finally got my first proper look at the four tall boys. The one who'd just talked *had* to be Sam; he had the arrogant look of a ringleader, chin up, shark-eyed. The others were three nearly identical grinning hyenas, loving the wind-up, loving having someone to be mean to.

"Forget it," muttered TJ, stomping off towards the nearest window . . . and *me*!

"Hey, is that your *girl*friend, *Titus*?" snickered one of the hyenas, as my feet started scrabbling at the brickwork to keep my balance.

TJ stared my way, shocked to see my furl of curls and mess of freckles peering over the windowsill.

"*Aww*, going to dump us for your little *girl*friend, *Titus*?"

That was Sam's voice, his words drenched in sarcasm. Only I didn't get to *see* him say them, since flip-flops – as I found out at that precise second – aren't exactly reliable climbing equipment.

As I flumped into an ungainly pile on the ground, hunting around for the flip-flop that had pinged off, all I could hear was TJ saying one word: "Yes!" But in the couple of breathless seconds before he got the chance to scramble out of the window and bound down beside me, I noticed something odd. . .

It was yet *more* twinkling of light, coming from straight up above on the headland. At first I thought it was just the sun reflecting off one of the caravan windows, but then I realized it was a) moving, b) blue, and c) *flashing*. It wasn't until the police car came to a halt at the top of the path that I guessed what might be about to happen.

"Look, I'm sorry about that," TJ started twittering

in explanation the millisecond his baseball boots hit the ground beside me. "I mean, I know you're not *really* my girlfriend, Stella, but I just *had* to get away from those dorks and—"

"Shhhhh! Stay *down*!" I ordered TJ, hauling on the edge of his T-shirt to get him to come down to my crouched level (which wasn't much of a drop for him, let's face it). "We've got to stay out of sight – follow me!"

"What are we doing?" asked TJ, copying my crawling routine through the matted undergrowth of wild rose bushes and foxgloves. Somewhere above us, Sam's gang were still cracking up at TJ's expense before one of them realized they needed to get back to business and get on with destroying the chandelier.

Kerr-ASHHHH!

"*Yessssss*!"

"Look, the police are coming!" I looked back and told TJ urgently. "We've got to get away, so they don't think we've got anything to do with this!"

TJ's face went white, then red, then white again – but thankfully the shock made him speed up more than anything. And so a couple of swift-crawling minutes later, we were lying nearly flat in a dip in the sands not that far from the water's edge, sneaking a glance back the way we came, only to see three policeman cautiously creeping up to the house.

"How did they find out?" panted TJ.

"Dunno – someone up in the caravans must have spotted what was going on, or heard the noise, and called the police," I whispered.

"Listen, Stella . . . honest, I didn't know that's what Sam and them were coming here to do!" TJ looked at me earnestly. "I just thought we were going to hang out. *Then* they started boasting on about all the bus shelters they've done in, and started chucking rocks at that old, fancy light thing, and I thought, this is *bad* – I've got to get out of here!"

Ninety-nine per cent of me took one look at that pale, drawn face and knew he was telling the truth.

"They haven't sussed about the police being here yet," I said, shuffling around on to my side in the sand for a better look. "They're making too much noise!"

TJ nudged up on his elbow.

"Uh-oh. . ." he muttered, shrinking right back down just as quick.

"What is it?" I hissed.

"One of the policemen – I think he *saw* me.

What if he comes over? What if he checks us out? He could think we were with Sam and them, and trying to sneak away! What're we going to do?"

I couldn't believe what I came out with next. I could've believed *Frankie* saying it, maybe, but not *me*; not shy Stella Stansfield. I would have *sworn* on Peaches' life that I wouldn't have said something like that in a million, trillion years.

But I did.

"Kiss me."

"Huh?" TJ squawked, as loudly as the seagull that was now starting to swirl above our heads.

"Kiss me!" I repeated. "If the policeman looks over and sees a boyfriend and girlfriend snogging on the sand, he's not exactly going to suspect us of vandalism, is he?"

It only took TJ a panicked second to see sense, and another second to reach over and do what he was told.

I guess it's a strange way to have your first on-the-lips kiss – smooching a boy who's only a mate (and a much smaller mate; not that you could tell that lying side by side in the sand), with a seagull circling ominously above your head.

But as I had already started to suss out, I'd moved to a pretty strange kind of town. . .

Chapter 20

The shameful shame of the you-know-what

I'd never been so glad to see a bird before.

Even if it was a big, bad-tempered one.

At least it meant that me and TJ had something to think – OK, make that *panic* – about, instead of . . . of you-know-what.

I mean, I couldn't speak for TJ, but personally, I was so totally embarrassed by the whole you-know-what, I felt pink all over. I could've sworn that even my *hair* follicles were blushing. . .

And on that fast, furious sprint away from Sugar Bay, I didn't dare glance at TJ to see how *he* was doing in the blush department. I just took the fact that he was saying nothing to mean that his brain was so weighed down with sheer mortification that it was squeezing any other thoughts right out of his head.

I mean, yes, so the you-know-what might have got us out of a whole lot of trouble, but that didn't mean either of us could handle it happening.

Especially *me*; I couldn't believe I'd actually told a boy to *ki*—

But before I relived the sheer, shameful shame of it all again, there was that first, menacing swoop.

"Oh, God!" TJ groaned, crouching lower to the ground. "Not that stupid bird again!"

"Just be glad he didn't come after you when the police were around. We'd *definitely* have been spotted then!" I said, bending warily too, though I didn't really think the seagull was remotely interested in me. "Hey, look – isn't this your street?"

Great. In a few seconds, TJ would be safely away from flapping wings and pointy beaks, and I would be safely away from him, and could get on with pretending that the you-know-what had never happened. (Ha! Like it would be *that* easy. . .)

"Er, I'm not really up for going home right now," said TJ, pushing his floppy hair off his face and gazing in the direction of his flat. "I just managed to avoid getting grilled by the police. I don't really want a grilling from my mum about where I've been. . ."

Having met TJ's mum again at the flat a little while ago, I kind of understood what he meant.

We'd both been shaken up by what had happened (watching Sam and his gang getting arrested, I mean, not the you-know-what), and the thought of Mrs O'Connell twittering and scolding was exhausting just to *think* about, never mind hear.

"Well . . . you could come back to mine for a bit, if you want!"

I felt like I *had* to suggest that . . . you-know-what or *no* you-know-what, me and TJ'd been through so much together in the last little while that I couldn't just leave him on his own, aimlessly wandering the town.

And so nine dive-bombing attempts and a steep, winding road later and we were nearly at my house.

"He *hates* me," moaned TJ, straightening up after dive-bomb number ten. "How long do those things live for? It's going to follow me around till *one* of us dies!"

"Hey, you chucked a stone at it, remember? No *wonder* it hates you!"

We were just about level with the little alleyway that ran at the back of my garden, I was vaguely aware.

"It was an *accident*!" said TJ, raising his shoulders in a show of innocence. "I'm not a rock-chucking kind of person, if you hadn't noticed!"

I'd noticed all right. Actually, *everyone* who'd passed us on the way here had noticed that, even if they didn't understand what they were seeing. Both knees of his jeans being green was a bit of a clue. *That's* what you get when you're crawling away from trouble at high speed through a garden. By comparison, my bare knees were pink – not 'cause of blushing, but because I scrubbed the grass stains off them in the sea with a handful of sand after the coast was clear and the police and Sam's gang had gone. Whatever, green and pink knees were a proud badge of innocence as far as me and TJ were concerned.

"OK, OK, so it wasn't deliberate. So you've got to show the gull you're sorry. Get him to be your friend!" I said, relaxing now that we both seemed to be ignoring the you-know-what.

"And how do I do that?" asked TJ, completely perplexed.

The faintest sugary scent of peaches 'n' cream put the idea in my head.

"Sweet-talk him," I told TJ, catching sight of a bundle of ginger fur on a wall down the alley.

"Sweet-talk him? What's *that* supposed to mean?"

Confusion brought TJ and his baseball boots grinding to a halt on the crunchy gravel.

"For a start, look up at him," I said, stopping too.

With a guarded glare at me, TJ did what he was told and stared up.

"Urgh . . . he's staring back at me."

"No – that's *good*. Now you've got to smile."

Poor TJ; he was so desperate for the gull to get over the grudge that he seemed to be willing to do anything (stupid) that I told him to do.

"Stella . . . I'm smiling, but I think it's just making him angry!" said TJ through a wide, forced, teeth-gritted grin.

"Hold on. . ." I said, rummaging in my rucksack for the magic ingredient that I thought would make all the difference.

"Stella! He's coming straight down! He's going to dive-bomb me again!"

Sure enough, the gull had tucked in his wings and was hurtling down at high speed in our – OK, just *TJ*'s – direction.

"Here! Hold this straight out!" I ordered him, shoving a mini fairy cake in his hand.

I don't know if birds have brakes, but the seagull seemed to put *his* on. One glimpse of the outstretched fairy cake and he swooped *out* of his death-defying beak-first dive and tilted backwards into an elegant flap of wings, hovering just close enough to TJ's hand to gently grab the cake from between his quivering fingers.

"Prrrp!" prrrped Peaches approvingly, ambling along the wall – of the house opposite ours – to get a better look at what was going on.

"What just happened?" TJ asked warily, as the seagull settled itself on the top of the nearest street-lamp to gulp its snack down.

"I think you just made a friend. . ." I grinned at TJ, hoping he understood that I didn't just mean the bird. "And if you ever fancy joining the circus, you've got a great act – 'TJ and his Amazing, Guzzling Gull!'"

Thud-a-thud-a-THUD-a-THUD-a-THUD . . . *TWANGGGGG! DOOF.*

I looked at TJ; TJ looked at me. Peaches looked slant-eyed down at *both* of us, as if he was daring us to finally find out what all the noises were about in the sumo-wrestling poltergeists' holiday home.

"Look – down the alleyway! The door in the wall is open! We could sneak into the garden and check it out!"

I *meant* to say, "Absolutely no *way* – do you

want us to get arrested for trespassing and end up in the cell next door to Sam's lot?", but instead I said, "OK." (After what had gone on at Sugar Bay I think I must still have had excess adrenaline shooting around in my system. Well, that's the only excuse *I* can think of.)

So me and TJ were back to crouching – if not quite crawling – through shrubbery for the second time today.

Thud-a-thud-a-THUD-a-THUD-a-THUD . . . *TWANGGGGG! DOOF.*

"It's coming from that room!" I hissed to TJ, as I pointed to the ground-floor window with the curtains drawn shut – the same one he'd tried to peek in from the wall this morning, before we fell out over my mobile.

Above us on the wall, Peaches mimicked our tiptoeing, stealthily padding his fat, furry way along the top of the brickwork.

"If we get up close, we'll probably be able to see through the gap in the curtains," TJ turned and whispered to me.

Slowly, slowly, hearts pounding somewhere in our throats, me and TJ lifted our heads above the windowsill and. . .

"EEEEEEEKKKKK!"

413

That was me, getting the fright of my thirteen-year-old life as a sweet-toothed seagull landed on my backpack with a thunk, and started pecking at the buckle to release the other fairy cakes it somehow knew were in there.

"AAAAAAARGHHHH!"

That was TJ, as the curtains were pulled open and a *terrifying* face glared out at us. . .

Chapter 21

And for my next trick. . . (Oof!)

Omigod. We were in the lair of the sumo-wrestling poltergeists.

Rumble-rumble-rumble-rumble-rumble-rumble-THUNK!

"Want a try?"

Er, to be honest, close up, the friendly, sporty-looking woman holding the unicycle out to TJ didn't look much like a sumo-wrestler *or* a poltergeist.

"Er, OK, Mrs Mystic . . . er, Mrs Marzipan. . ." said TJ warily, sneaking a quick worried glance at me before he clambered up on the one-wheeled bike she was holding steady for him.

"I told you, just call me Bev," said Bev, now giving him a gentle push off.

TJ only made it to *rumble-THUNK!* No – he didn't even make it to *THUNK!*, 'cause *THUNK!* had been the noise Mrs Mystic Marzipan (Bev) had made when she hopped elegantly off the unicycle as she demonstrated it to us just now. With TJ, it was more of a *rumble*-"Oooof! Owwww...".

"What about you, Stella? Fancy a go on the trampette?" asked Mr Mystic Marzipan (otherwise known as John, otherwise known as the person with the terrifying face). "Maybe you could try a double somersault! You look like you're pretty agile, the way you scramble out of your bedroom window all the time, like that cat of yours!"

Urgh ... so I thought *I* was the one doing the spying on *them*, but the people in this house had done a much better job of spotting what everyone in *our* house was up to. And speaking of that cat of mine, it turned out that Peaches was already on purring terms with the Marzipans – he'd been in and out all week, they said. He was sitting at their open window now, catching a few rays on his ginger fur while he idly watched TJ make a fool of himself.

"Um, I don't think so," I said, shaking my head shyly, as I stared at the trampette and the banner behind it that read *"Meet the Marvellous, Magical, Mystic Marzipans!!!"*

"Well, I don't think we'll be asking these two to join our act, darling!" Bev joked with her husband, while smiling down at TJ, who was trying to disentangle himself from the unicycle.

"No, I don't think so," said Mr Mystic Marzipan, his smile scarily wide. "And they're a bit too noisy to make good private detectives!"

Nabbed by clowns – can you believe it?

It was the seagull's fault of course, and no faked kisses could get me and TJ out of trouble when the window flew open and Mr Mystic Marzipan and his white clown face loomed out at us.

"What's this?" he'd boomed cheerfully. "Trying to get a sneak preview of the show or something? Better come in then!"

We'd looked at each other, then at the loud and gaudy props and Punch & Judy stall inside.

"Tell you what," Bev had said, appearing at the window. "You live across the lane with your family, don't you? Why don't you pop across and invite your parents and those cute little boys over?"

And that's what we did. And that's why Dad was practising juggling in the corner just now, while Mum was attempting to stop Jake and Jamie from clobbering each other with the Punch & Judy puppets. And that's how we'd come to find out that Mr and Mrs Mystic Marzipan had been rehearsing their circus skills in the house they'd rented on the other side of the back lane. They'd been booked to appear in all sorts of shows and events during the Portbay Gala in a week or two's time, and had been just in the middle of perfecting their latest balancing act when me and TJ and a very greedy seagull had nearly put a sudden end to their careers.

"Think my entire *bum* might be bruised. . ." said TJ, finally untangling himself from the unicycle with a bit of help from Bev.

"Probably serves you right!" grinned Dad, still keeping his eyes fixed to the clubs he was juggling. "It's kind of dangerous to give people surprises, specially when their wife's trying to do a backflip on to their shoulders!"

Dad was right of course, but how were we meant to have known? It's not *every* day you find yourself with a backflipping, fire-eating acrobatic clown act living in the house at the bottom of the garden.

"Ah, now don't be too hard on them," said Mr Mystic Marzipan, giving me and TJ a wink as he took off his red nose and gave his real nose a scratch. "I'm sure we all got up to some mischief or other when we were young!"

And then it hit me – it was *exactly* the right time to ask Dad the question.

"Dad . . . what happened with you and the paintballing thing? When you were fifteen?"

There was a deafening clatter as the clubs fell out of sync, out of Dad's hands and on to the floor.

Dad looked horrified. Mum looked like she might burst out laughing. Mr and Mrs Mystic Marzipan and TJ looked confused. Jake and Jamie carried on hitting each other with puppets.

"Before you ask, Andy, *I* didn't tell Stella!" said Mum, as she wrestled Punch off Jake's hand.

(Jamie had just spotted Peaches and was running over to him, brandishing Judy. With an elegant "floop!", Peaches did an impressive disappearing trick that the Mystic Marzipans would be proud of.)

"Auntie V said I should ask you," I told Dad, solving the mystery for him.

I held my breath, waiting for him to speak. Back in London, Dad was a smart, sussed, suited lawyer who never got flummoxed, but right here right now I'd never seen him look so sheepish. (Well, apart from when he sledgehammered through a pipe and flooded the house last week, or when he used his head to dismantle the toilet, of course.)

"I. . ." he began, rolling his eyes upwards so he

was talking to the ceiling. "I . . . I mean, me and my friends at the time . . . we thought it would be a laugh to go out with these paintballing guns and . . . and splat a flock of sheep."

"*Sheep*?" The word came out of TJ's mouth with a squeak and a giggle (a squiggle?).

"And before you ask, Stella, none of them were hurt – your dad and his friends weren't close enough to do any real damage, thankfully," Mum explained, while Dad shuffled and blushed.

"They were just a bit scared. And multi-coloured, by the time we'd finished," Dad mumbled, acting as shamefaced and shifty as a schoolkid who's been caught writing rude words on the loo door. "The farmer went mad at us – never mind your gran and grandad. . ."

As sorry as I felt for those poor, bemused sheep, I couldn't stop the giggle that was vibrating its way up my chest. Not that anyone could hear it, not above the booming laughs of Mr Mystic Marzipan and his missus, which of course got everyone else started (no surprise, since it's in clowns' job descriptions to laugh a lot, isn't it?).

Anyway, Auntie V was right – it *had* been worth waiting for. I'd never be able to take my dad seriously again, and I think he pretty much knew it.

"Wait till I get hold of that sister of mine. . ." said Dad suddenly, laughing too, his cheeks still telltale pink. "Your Auntie V's got a lot to answer for!"

TJ was leaning on the bucking unicycle and grinning, without having a clue who we were on about. Course, how could he know that without Auntie V – and all her advice – me and him might not be friends? I mean, thanks to her, I was Stella, and TJ was my etc.

But you know something?

If TJ *was* going to be my friend, there was one thing he was going to have to do for sure; same as me.

He'd *better* keep pretending that emergency kiss *never* happened. . .

From: Frankie
To: *stella*
Subject: **The great mobile mystery SOLVED!!**

Hi Stella!

So it was just TJ I was talking to? Boo . . . there I was thinking it was some secret boyfriend you hadn't told me about, and all the time it was Portbay's biggest teen gangsta (OK, make that teen *hamster*).

Still can't believe TJ had the cheek to nick your mobile off you though. If I'd known I was speaking to a thief I'd have said more than "Hi, is Stella there?" before he hung up on me! But I guess after reading all that stuff in the attachment, I kind of think I might *possibly* reckon TJ's all right now . . . sorry, but I can't help being protective!

Better go – Mum's due back soon and I promised to take a turn cleaning Peetie's cage out. I haven't started yet, but you know how it is – cleaning out parakeet poop or watching MTV with a packet of Munchies . . . not much contest, is there?

Miss you ☹, but M8s 4eva ☺!

Frankie

PS Tell Peaches I found one of his hairs in my toothbrush the other night(?!).

PPS Parminder says she phoned you yesterday, and you told her that some girl called Rachel and her mates are giving you hassle. Want me to come down and sort them out? You know me – wouldn't let anyone take the mick out of you. Why isn't TJ standing up for you? Oh, that's right – you said he's kind of on the short side. Couldn't he just go and bite their ankles, then? Ha!

Want to know more. . .?

Check out Karen's super-cool website!

karenmccombie.com

For behind-the-scenes gossip on Karen's very own blog,
fab competitions and photo-galleries,
join her website of loveliness now!